THE REED

A novel set in Ea

THE REED FLUTE

TESSA WEST

FOX BOOKS

Tessa West
The Reed Flute

Published by Fox Books,
16 Broad Street, Harleston, Norfolk, IP20 9AZ

British Library Cataloguing in Publication Data
A catalogue record for this book is available from the British Library.

ISBN 0-9543627-1-3

Cover design by Roland West
Printed in Great Britain by Biddles Ltd, King's Lynn

Tessa West lives on the border of Norfolk and Suffolk. Her first novel, *The Estuary*, was published in 2002.

ACKNOWLEDGEMENTS

I wish to thank Sara Maitland for her encouragement and her constructive observations on the manuscript as it approached completion. I am also indebted to Peter Clark, an expert on Arab affairs. In a more personal capacity, I have valued greatly the constant support from my brother, Roger Williamson.

There are many other people to whom I owe thanks: Marwan Abouraban, Sue Butcher, Clare Barkley, Nick Clark of the Britten-Pears Library, William Khan, Jennifer Monaghan, David Nettleship, Helen Rowles and Cathy Terry of Norfolk County Council, John Saunders, Jackie Somani, Tim Strudwick of the RSPB, the late Sir Wilfred Thesiger and Ann and Peter Wiggins. My particular thanks go to Stephen du Sautoy who has been an invaluable source of advice.

My four children and their partners have also been loyal supporters who have listened with patience and interest to my ideas and progress reports, and my special thanks go to Roland for the care and work he put into producing the cover, maps and illustrations.

In addition, there are three books which have been of core importance to me in writing *The Reed Flute*: Wilfred Thesiger's *The Marsh Arabs* (1964), Gavin Young's *Return to the Marshes* (1977) and Gavin Maxwell's *A Reed Shaken by the Wind* (1957). I am grateful to the Random House Group for allowing me to use two of Gavin Young's drawings.

For William and James

THE REED FLUTE

Listen to the tale of the reed flute
Jalal al-Din Rumi

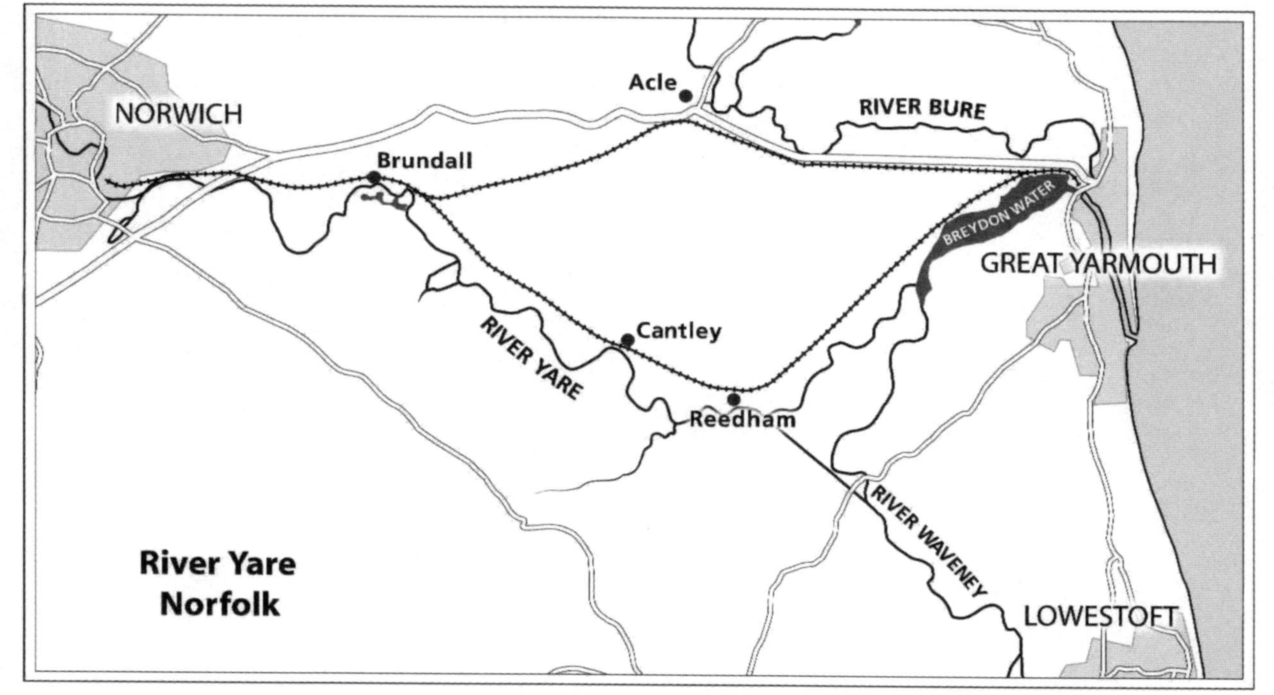
Acle
NORWICH
RIVER BURE
Brundall
BREYDON WATER
GREAT YARMOUTH
Cantley
RIVER YARE
Reedham
RIVER WAVENEY
River Yare
Norfolk
LOWESTOFT

I was thankful the train was coming into the station. I knew it was the end of the line.

I had been watching a young family opposite me. The woman had eaten throughout the forty minute journey, opening packets, taking some of the contents herself and passing some to the small girl beside her but not to the man with them. I did not know why they ate this food - which was not bread, nor fruit, nor fish nor meat - for they were fat, and they did not seem to enjoy it or even want it.

I had had a cup of tea early that morning but my stomach was hurting from the previous day's meal. That had been my first real meal here, apart from the one at the Police station. I should not have eaten so much after so many months of eating little but the food was there in front of me, and the Moroccan I had met in London was encouraging me to eat: "Abbas, you don't know when you'll get your next meal," he said, "so give thanks to Allah and make the most of this one." It was hard to refuse when he was so concerned for my welfare, especially as he had bought me these shoes. I looked at the bright white trainers with their blue and yellow lines. Although they were not really wide enough for my feet they were better then my last pair, but that morning my fingers had found it hard to tie the long laces.

I stretched my hand out, examined the back of it. The skin was like rough brown earth, with knuckle ridges, bones running under the surface, veins crossing, nails like corrugated stones, grey hairs like thin, sparse grass. I turned my hand over and cupped it. Little pads of flesh rose up from the bowl of my palm.

Straight lines scored each finger. When I stretched my hand open and pushed out the thumb, it flattened, leaving only a slight dip in the centre. There was no pain in my hand as it rested on my knee in the train, but I knew that things like buttoning my shirt or even cutting food were becoming increasingly difficult. And worse, since starting on the journey I sometimes woke with a strange feeling in the tips of my fingers, as if they were full of fleas. This did not hurt, but it was new, and it was another sign that I was old. And something else was wrong with me too, but I pushed the thought of that away.

I badly wanted a cigarette but they had told me I must not smoke on the train. We were slowing down now. I was not there yet, and things could still go wrong.

The man opposite had spent the whole journey in silence, taking no notice of his woman or his child, just staring into space and from time to time adjusting the small machine on his lap. Wires led from this to little pads in his ears and a grating sound had been coming from them.

Now that the train was stopping he took out the pads, put the machine into a case and followed the other passengers towards the doors with his family. As everyone moved out I had room to pull myself up by the back of the seat next to me. My belly felt sore as I picked up my suitcase and stepped down from the train.

What if I did not recognise Sarwat, or if he did not come? I did not know how to ask for things I wanted, and I did not know if the notes and the coins in my pocket were enough to buy what I needed. I did not know anything.

It was dark. I put the suitcase down and watched people walk away along the platform. It looked a long way to go, and since losing my glasses anything more than seventy or eighty metres away was a blur. I took my cigarettes from my pocket, pulled one out, bent my head towards the match and inhaled my first sweet breath of nicotine for well over an hour. I looked down at my bag, ashamed that I found even this small case too much to carry, and then up to the signs which must have said the name of this place, but I could not read English. I could not even read Arabic.

Two large grey and white birds flew down to pick up food that had spilt from a paper bag. They came close and had no fear of me. They pecked quickly at the bits on the ground, jerking their heads, and then flapped back up to the roof.

Suddenly I was covered in sweat, just as I had been in the back of the last lorry. I had to sit down. I turned round looking for a seat.

A man came running up and grabbed my arm, "Uncle Abbas, Uncle! Here I am!" Immediately, I heard my elder brother's sharp tone – something I had not heard for a decade – in my nephew's voice.

I was taken along the platform, out of the station and into a car. When Sarwat leaned across me to fix the seat belt, I smelled his new black leather jacket and the scent in his hair. He turned to me and smiled. "We're going to my flat. You will be very welcome." He switched on the engine, pressed one button, then another. There was a blast of loud music.

"Iraqi music! This will make you feel better!"

I had not been in Iraq for nearly ten years, but I knew Sarwat might not have known that. I resolved to tell him about it one day. He drove faster and I saw signs, cars, buildings lit up – all quite unlike the places I had just travelled through on the train. Then, almost every time I had looked out of the window I had seen only blackness, so I thought we must be going through an empty land.

But this town was like the one where we first arrived in England – not that we ever knew where we were going or that we would end up in England.

I suddenly felt bad again and told Sarwat I was going to be sick.

He pulled over, undid the seat belts and hurried round to my side to open the door. I crouched, coughing, by the front wheel. The pavement was cold and wet, bright with the orange reflections of street lights. I eased myself to a squatting position and Sarwat said in his sharp voice, "Come on, we can't stay here." I let him pull me up and on to my feet and help me into the car again. He got back into the driving seat and said more gently, "Uncle Abbas, this isn't a good place to be ill."

I replied, "There is no good place to be ill. Never in my life have I been anywhere where it is good to be ill."

"You are right, but now you are old it will be very bad. And it is even worse if you are a foreigner."

I closed my eyes, let myself be driven as I had done for weeks, for months. May this, I prayed, be the end of the journey. May there be no more travelling. Over the last twenty months there had been times when I longed to be back in the refugee camp in Iran, despite the lack of purpose and the frozen winters. Our journey by boat, by truck, on foot had seemed endless. No, not twenty months of travel, for we spent at least three months in Turkey, waiting in a cellar for a contact who would move us on, and then six weeks in a grey, concrete house in Greece where, if it had not been for a tree outside the window and the small brown birds which gathered in it each evening, I might have given up. And then things moved suddenly and within a week we were in England.

I wanted to go to Holland because three members of my family live there, but though I begged the agent he said he could not arrange it unless I paid him more. All my money was gone so I had to get into yet another van to cross yet more land and sea. At last, when we were finally pushed out of the dark interior of that van into a corner of a car park, Abdul Aziz, a student with us who knew some English, immediately understood where we were when two men spoke to us.

We passed the word "England!" round in excitement. We were relieved and elated because we all knew that England, even if it had invaded Iraq with America, would be fair and honourable. We would be safe.

And then, the very next day, we learned Saddam had been captured. We had spent all that time getting away from him and now, on the day after our arrival, he was found, and there were pictures of him on the front of all the newspapers. We felt such a mixture of feelings. While we were joyful and excited to know of his capture, it also reminded us of what we had lost – our families and our tribes and our land.

"Here we are," said Sarwat. "This is where I live and where you will live." I struggled with the buckle and let Sarwat undo it. He opened the door for me and waited while I got out slowly. Then he took my bag and led the way, turning into an opening between two buildings.

Suddenly there was an explosion, then another. Instinctively I squatted down, waiting for the shouting, the shots. Sarwat stayed standing. "Down! Get down!" I yelled. "For the sake of Allah, get down." There were more retorts, and the whining of something through the air. I knelt in a puddle, waiting for the boom. I prayed, bowing my head to the tarmac, covering my face with my hands. Had I come so far only to find myself yet again in danger?

Sarwat was making a strange noise. I did not know what it was, but at least it meant he was alive. I slowly lifted my head, unbowed my back. Sarwat's legs were in front of me. I looked up to his face and saw he was laughing. How could he be laughing? How?

He helped me to my feet. I did not understand. And then there was another boom, and this time there were slow blue and red lights in the sky. I wanted to shelter again, but he held onto my sleeve and kept me upright. I shoved my head into his collar, into his scented hair. I could feel my heart beating. When it was quiet again, I opened my eyes and looked over his shoulder. Lights in the sky were spitting into lines that dropped gold stars quietly onto the buildings.

"It's all right. Don't worry. They're celebrating New Year." He moved away from me but kept his hand on my arm. The stars floated down but the buildings did not catch fire. "Come on," he said, "come inside."

He led the way through a doorway and up a staircase and I followed him slowly, willing myself on. There was a smell of dampness, smoke and food, and when he pushed open another door, the sound of a television blared out. Two young men turned to look at me. A third was talking on his mobile phone. They greeted me and I tried to respond. Then they turned back to the television, to the conversation. I stood there getting my breath back from the shock in the street, from climbing the stairs. I could hardly stay upright and I urgently needed to relieve my bowels.

Sarwat showed me where the toilet was and I just managed to undo my clothes in time and sit on one of those western seats that I was having to get used to. I shut my eyes and let the fear pour out of me. After a few moments I heard more whining missiles and my stomach contracted again. I felt myself go hot and then cold. I sat there shivering with my elbows on my knees, my head in my hands, my trousers soaked from when I was on the ground.

At last I stood up. I stopped myself from looking to see if blood had come from inside me, for that night I did not want to know. I wished I could wash myself properly, but there was hardly room in there to move so I just rinsed my hands and face and dabbed at them with a damp towel.

I returned to the room and sank onto the settee. My back hurt. My legs hurt. My stomach was no longer so taut but it felt better if I drew my knees towards my chest. Then someone put a cushion under my head and helped me to lie down. I felt my laces being undone, my shoes being pulled off. Sarwat asked me to uncurl myself so he could undo my belt. A cover was put over me and the television and the lights were switched off.

I was safe, and I prayed that Allah would watch over Khadija.

Today was the day for the bird books. Richard had resolved to list them before phoning a couple of secondhand bookshops, starting with the one in North Walsham. There was no point in Estelle's collection just sitting there unread. There must be someone who would want the books.

He picked out a CD from the shelf: Scheherazade. He stood still listening to the first notes before taking his reading glasses over to the table where he had spread the books out. There were about twenty of them, and on the floor were two piles of old copies of the RSPB magazine. Some of the books were modern and still in their glossy paper jackets, while others were shabby with pages almost furry from use and from being wet. Seeing them lying there made him think that many would be rejected immediately by any secondhand bookshop.

But the first was a new, solid paperback – *Birds of Norfolk.* Inside, there was a handwritten inscription:

To Estelle, with all our thanks for your work.
Best wishes for many bird-watching years ahead
Julie, Tina, Helen.

It was dated less than three years ago. He remembered Helen, a colleague with whom Estelle had not always seen eye to eye, and Julie, whose husband worked for whatever Eastern Electricity had become.

In turn he picked up *The Birdwatchers' Guide to the Wetlands of Britain; Collins Wild Guide – Birds; Field Guide to Birds of Britain and Europe; A Season of Birds: A Norfolk Diary 1911.*

He leafed through some of them, looking carefully at the illustrations. There were photographs, delicate colour plates and sketches. Many showed birds as they would never be seen – a male and a female (sometimes showing the different winter and summer plumage) and a juvenile, all facing the same way, or as if in flight with their wings extended identically to show shapes and colours. There were pages devoted to beaks, to feet, to feathers, to footprints.

And there were pictures of eggs, almost all in soft, subtle shades. Some were spread out evenly, in order of size, supported on the page by invisible means. Others sat in a bundle of grass attached to a bullrush, or in a proper nest in the fork of a tree, or camouflaged amongst stones in a field.

There were maps too, to show distribution. On one page pale green spread over the Highlands, on another there was a wash of blue over a swathe of Wales and Cornwall. Some maps had only a speck of colour, while others were almost covered.

He skipped most of the text, but noted the various ways birdsong was depicted, and found himself enjoying phrases like "an insistent but slow cheeek, cheeek" or "harsh owk, also uk-uk-uk."

A number of pages had Estelle's notes in the margin – Minsmere (Canopy Hide) 12.8.98; Ranworth 4.12.96; Holkham Bay Dec 10th 1999.

He picked up, in turn, each of the three small, fat volumes of *The Birds of the British Isles and Their Eggs*. He liked the rounded corners to their pages and the way they fitted his hand comfortably. As he took up the third he wondered how he had even considered giving away or selling these books.

Next he chose an old one. It was *Birds Beasts and Fishes of the Norfolk Broadland*, by Emerson, published in 1895. He looked at the elegant frontispiece and read the titles of Emerson's other books: *A Son of the Fens, Wild Life on a Tidal Water, On English Lagoons*. He opened it at random and began to read.

Eels will eat anything fresh – they do not eat carrion. They are fond of baits, such as birds, beasts, frogs, and worms, as the babbers know well. But the water must be thick. If the water is thick, and the weather propitious (S. wind), you may catch as many eels by day as by night. Eels, as is well known, will travel over river-walls, from the dikes to the rivers, or vice versâ, *choosing dewy grass to travel upon.*

The broad-nosed eel bores into the dike-shores, and has been dug out buried two and a half feet into the shore, coiled up like a snake. I know of one dug out four feet from a dike, in the solid marsh.

The methods of capturing eels in the Broadland are numerous, and some of them are wonderful.

1. *Netting.*
2. *Darting, or pricking, or pitching – 7lbs. being the biggest one got by darting.*
3. *Skimming.*
4. *Babbing.*
5. *Hooks – night lines and liggers for big eels that lie in pea-soupy beds of rivers.*
6. *Eel-baskets.*
7. *Bow-nets.*

Emerson's entry for The Barn Owl read:

When the silvery mists are rising and lurking in marsh and mere like phantoms, you may hear the shrill screech of the barn-owl as he beats

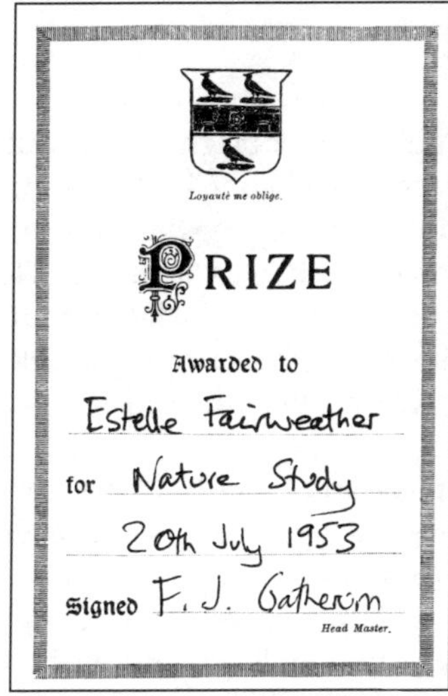

Loyauté me oblige.

PRIZE

Awarded to

Estelle Fairweather

for Nature Study

20th July 1953

Signed F. J. Gatherum

Head Master.

with heavy flight round the stacks of some lone marsh-farm in search of mice or young rats.

Reading these extracts clinched Richard's decision to keep them. All he would part with were the RSPB magazines – they could go to the dentist's.

He picked up another book from the edge of the table. It was unusual in that it had a linear measure printed in gold on the back in inches and centimetres. The title was *The Popular Handbook of British Birds.* A small book-plate had been pasted inside the front cover and he read this twice before closing the book. Then he turned to the back again and ran his finger along the indented gold lines. He imagined Estelle's ten year old fingers doing the same thing nearly half a century ago.

The CD ended and he realised he had completely missed the oboe part he had intended to listen to. Never mind. There was plenty of time before the concert.

When he turned on the television to catch the News he was blasted with fanfares, shouting, a sea of arms waving wildly. It was hideous. For the last hour he had completely forgotten New Year's Eve. He was glad he had decided to stay at home. The year before last, just before he and Estelle moved, they had invited Mary and Eric to a final New Year's Eve celebration in their Aylsham house. Last year he had told everyone he wanted to hibernate alone at New Year, and so this year – now that he was coming to terms with things – it should have been his turn to go to Mary and Eric's. But he had again decided to be on his own, especially as he had just spent Christmas with them and their son and daughter-in-law and month-old grandson.

He turned the television off, not wanting to face its frenetic run-up to midnight.

The light which stayed on all night was not bright, but I could see the seven other beds in my room. Each one had a woman asleep in it. In the bed on my left I could only see the curve of a back, but the woman in the bed on the right was facing me. Her face was half hidden and I could not see the scar by her mouth. I would not have wanted a scar like that, right across my cheek. I wondered if she had had that scar all her life and if it had stopped her finding a husband.

It was my second day in that place and I was thinking about my Grandfather and my aunt Laila and my sisters, as I did every day. I wanted them. Any one of them would have done. I even wanted Fatima. I did not know if they were alive or not, and they did not know if I was alive or not. I wished and wished I had never left Iran. I wished I was not in this place. They had told me I would not be there for long, but that was what they had said when we reached Germany, and we were there for months.

I listened to the breathings in and out of the woman facing me, and I peeped out again to see her scar. At that very moment her blanket moved, uncovering her hand and arm. I suddenly saw that her little finger was missing. How terrible. How terrible to have a scar on your face *and* a finger missing. I wondered what had happened. Had she been in an accident? Had both things happened at the same time?

Now the woman in the far corner was getting up. I did not know what country she came from, but it could have been Africa because she was very black. I knew she spent a long time doing her hair and putting on makeup. The day before I had looked at her in the mirror as she was putting cream on her face. She smiled, turned round, and put a dab of it onto my nose. It smelled like some kind of fruit. I spread it over my cheeks and hoped they would become soft.

Other people were beginning to move. The big light was turned on. I pulled back the curtain behind my bed and looked out. It was still night, but there were lights everywhere shining on the wire fences. The woman with the scar got up and walked towards the showers in her night clothes. I went to the washroom too but I dared not go into the shower and be naked. I washed at a basin and cleaned my teeth with my new toothbrush. Then I brushed my hair with the brush they had given me. I looked at myself in the mirror. Sometimes the face I saw looked like me, but sometimes the girl in the mirror seemed like someone else. Sometimes, when things were bad, I moved out of myself and looked at me from somewhere else. It was different from looking in a mirror. If I moved out of my body to the ceiling, I could look down on my head, watch myself move across a room. If I moved out of myself to in front of me, I could see my expressions. I liked doing this. I did it when things hurt too much.

I lined up in a queue in the dining room but was not sure what most of the food was, or if it tasted good. I took some bread and some tea, but stood holding my tray until two women from my room beckoned me to join them. They were white, the same colour as most of the guards. When I was in Iran I did not know anyone who was not Iraqi, because everyone in our camp was Iraqi. I was very young then and had no idea there were other people in the world who had had to leave their countries. On the journey I heard there were refugees from many, many countries – and some of them were rich, and some were Christians.

I drank my tea and ate my bread slowly, because I did not know what to do next.

After some time, I followed the women I had been sitting with back to our room. Then I looked inside my bag. I had more things by then than at the start of my journey. I had set off with only what I was told to take: a bottle of water, an empty bottle, a few spare clothes and a small blanket. I did not know what the empty bottle was for until I was in the lorry. Luckily, I was not the first who needed one, but we soon got used to that.

When I came to this place I was given some new clothes and a pair of shoes. Well, they were not really new, but I liked them, especially the trousers and the blue shirt. I had been needing shoes for months and these ones fitted well. And I liked my jacket. I stroked its furry hood.

Then I went out to the entrance area where there were notices in many languages, and I read the ones in Arabic. There was other writing that looked a bit like Arabic, and some like Farsi, but all the others were very strange. The letters were quite different to ours and I could not imagine how you could even begin to read them.

Then I went into the long room where the television was. About ten people were watching a programme where fat toys were running, falling over and speaking in voices that did not sound like any language I had ever heard. I wanted to leave the room but I did not know where to go or what to do. I knew I was going to cry. I wanted Grandfather and my aunt and my sisters. I wanted to go back to the camp.

I screwed up my eyes, froze, and moved out of myself to the windowsill. I looked at myself nearly crying and curled up and rocking like an old person. A woman I didn't know came over to me and took my hand. The moment she did this I was back into myself and I let her lead me out of the room. She talked to me and asked me things and pushed the hair back from my face. I could not understand a word, but I knew she was trying to help.

She went up to one of the people in uniform and spoke to them. They gave her some paper and a pen. Then she took me back to the television room, and we sat down at a table in the corner. She pointed at herself and said a word. I knew it must be her name. Then she pointed at me so I said, "Khadija." She repeated it, and I repeated her name: "Grace." Then she took the paper and drew a man and wrote something underneath it, while saying another word. Of course I could not read it but I knew she had said and written the English word for man. Then I took the pen and drew a car next to it, and wrote and said the Arabic word for car. And so we went on, taking turns to draw and to say the name of what we had drawn. It felt so good to write again, because I had not written since I was in the school at the camp.

Suddenly everyone was getting up and going because it was roll call, and Grace and I were laughing. We had covered the paper with pictures. There was a baby, a house, a hand, a foot, a head, a car, a tree, a boat, a bicycle, a lorry, a new moon, a sun, stars, a shoe, a book, a dog, a bird, a mountain, a river.

Sometimes we had not been able to guess what one of the pictures was. When I drew a boat Grace thought it was a banana, and when she drew a river I thought it was a road, so she put a fish in it.

When we had been counted and checked we went to the dining room and I sat next to Grace. She told me - with signs - that she was going to make a phone call. I understood this, so after the meal I went back to the television room where there was a film of aeroplanes dropping bombs on a town. I did not want to watch this so I went out and looked for Grace but she was not where the phones were. I thought she might be in the bedroom, but she was not there either. I went to the entrance area, and as I got near I heard a lot of noise. Grace was shouting at a man in uniform, but I could see that although he was listening there was nothing he could do and she knew that. I saw all that in just a few seconds. She saw me but went on shouting, and then her shouting changed to crying. I went up beside her and she pulled me hard against her so the silver cross she was wearing round her neck dug into my cheek, but I didn't mind. I could feel each sob shake her body and I began to cry with her.

We went back to the bedroom and she lay down on her bed. I did not want to rest, but I lay down on my bed too. I thought about how we had been laughing that morning. What had happened to make Grace cry? The worst thing, I thought, must be never to go back. Everyone had told me that I would never go back, but I couldn't not want to. I kept on having the same nightmare. In it I was travelling home on another long journey, but when I reached where I used to live, nothing was there - my house, my whole camp was not there. All that was left was the bare hillside.

Fatima and the other grown-ups who travelled with me in the lorries used to talk in the morning about being desperate to leave the camp, but at night they used to weep for the families they left behind. I thought that was how it must be for Grace. She was in this place like everyone else, waiting until she was allowed to stay in England. That day she must have been thinking of her homeland, but I do not know which country she came from. I know she was speaking English, but she was black and I was sure English people were white. And if she was in this place she could not be English. This was one of the things I did not understand. But, if she was thinking of her home, why was she so angry? I did not understand that either, but I wanted her to get up so we could do more words together and laugh again.

But she did not get up again that day except for the roll calls, and then she went straight back to her bed. At first I went to see her often and I called her name quietly, but when I saw she was still lying with her face hidden I went away again and looked out of the window. I moved out of my body and went outside the window and looked in at myself standing there. I was very still, not moving at all. I did not look happy or unhappy. I did not look anything. Just a girl, staring out of a window and seeing nothing.

In the 1990s my son-in-law died. Things were very bad in Iraq so I took my closest daughter and my favourite little grand-daughter Khadija to Iran with the two younger girls. We lived in a camp for seven years. Then, when my daughter also died I decided to bring Khadija to the west. I could have stayed in the camp until the time of my death but she was my most precious grandchild and I wanted to give her a better future. She reminded me so much of my best daughter. I had some money sent from my family in Canada, and they told me to try to reach them. I knew other Iraqis who had gone to the west, and so I decided to pay all I had to an agent who was trusted by some of my friends. My relations listened to what I said and asked me to take the younger daughters too, but I did not have enough money and so I left them. May Allah keep and protect them.

Khadija cried when I told her what we were going to do. She did not want to leave her aunts, her sisters or her friends. I told her that there was a better life in the west and that her parents would want her to obey me and have a good education and future. I worried about her a lot. What would become of her if she stayed in the camp? Although it was not their fault, most of the young men there seemed to have no purpose and no energy and I wanted her to find a better husband than one of them.

I found a man who wrote down for me, in Arabic and English, the three names and addresses of the members of our family in Canada, Holland and England. He copied it out for Khadija, and she promised she would keep her paper as safe as I would keep mine.

Because the women were to travel separately I searched for a woman to look after Khadija and I found one who was already taking her own daughter. Her name was Fatima. The agent told me the women would never be far from us, but I soon saw it was not possible for anyone to know whether they were near and it was very likely they were not. I was sad when I realised these things, and angry that I had not been told the truth. Because I was not near Khadija it felt as if she was in more danger.

I could not have known then how difficult or how long the journey would be. As time went on I saw how every stage had to be planned and re-planned according to the information the agents received. We did not know where we were going. Our route to the west took us in all directions, and there were times when we had to spend days travelling to the north and south and even to the east.

Sometimes we were told to wait for a signal, and we sat in darkness with the few things we carried, but the signal did not always come. Once we were told we were going to be driven over a pass in a truck, but we ended up walking for two days and two nights behind shepherds and their mules.

I heard nothing certain about the women until we reached Greece, and then someone told me they were in Germany. This was a miracle, for anything could have happened to my little Khadija. When I heard news of her my spirits rose and I prayed she would be returned to me if Allah willed it.

I looked carefully at the place my journey had brought me to in England. Sarwat's main room was quite big, but it was too full when he and his friends and I were all there at the same time. These friends often ate with us and I think they had sometimes stayed there too until I came.

Soon after I arrived Sarwat took me to an office where I had to sign papers and answer questions which he translated into Arabic for me. He was very polite. He was happy when we finished and told me I would now receive some money each week and that it was a good thing I had come to live with him. He said he would need my money for the rent and food, but there would be a small amount left over which he would look after for me until I spoke some English.

"But take this," he said. "That will be enough for you for now." He gave me two bank notes. It did not feel right that he should keep my money, but it was true that I spoke no English.

I could not understand why he and his friends did not work. He had told me he had been refused permission to stay in England and was appealing against this. Even so, I thought he should have been working. He got paid for driving other men to work and then collecting them at the end of the day. This meant he often spent hours sitting in front of the television watching English programmes. From time to time he would watch the news in Arabic. I watched too for there was nothing else to do, but the English programmes did not interest me and the news reminded me of what I had escaped from. This made me fall into despair.

Why was he not doing a real job? And why weren't his friends working? I wanted to work too, but Sarwat told me none of us were allowed to. I did not understand this. Even though I was old and not feeling well and so perhaps could not have worked hard at that time, he and his friends were young and strong. Hassan, a Kurd, had told me how frustrated he was, because he was a qualified mechanic and used to manage a garage.

They all said they were prepared to do anything: dig, load, carry, clean, paint, build, wash, cook, drive, repair. But they had no papers, or the wrong papers. Why did they need papers to work when – they told me – there was work that needed doing and employers who wanted them?

They all spoke Arabic but they came from different places – Iraq, Afghanistan, Iran, Morocco – and so they had different accents and different words. Sarwat had the same words as I had, but he used English ones too, so I sometimes had to ask him what he meant.

One of the Iraqis laughed aloud when he first heard my accent. He turned to Sarwat and I overheard him say, "You didn't tell us your uncle was a yokel!" Sarwat did not look at me and the man went on laughing.

At least his friends made me tea. I drank tea all day, and there was plenty of sugar. This was one good thing. Sarwat made me tea too, but he sometimes complained he wanted a woman in the house to cook. When I heard him do so one morning I told him he should look for a wife. He turned on me.

"How can I find a wife? How? How can I do it?"

He gave me no time to answer, and shouted again, "Do you think I don't want a wife? You are too old to want a woman, but I'm not! Of course I want a wife just as you did when you were young, but how can I get one?"

The others watched him as he yelled above the sound of the television.

"How can I marry? I have no money, no job. I am not English, I am a foreigner. I am a Muslim. I am not wanted here - not to work, not to live. I have been told I cannot stay here, and although I will appeal I may fail. And anyway, who would I marry? Would an English girl want me if I cannot stay here? And who else is there to marry? We are only men here. Our girls and women are not here, are they? So, old man, don't tell me to find a wife."

He stormed out of the room slamming the door. Nobody spoke.

I was stunned with shock as I turned to the screen again. An empty car was driving itself along a wet road while music played softly. I took a cigarette from the packet. My hands were shaking as I lit it. How could he treat me like this?

I prayed to the Lord of the Two Worlds and recited:

With every hardship there is ease. With every hardship there is ease.

An hour later I was still sitting there fingering my beads and still smarting from his rudeness. He had insulted me, his father's brother. How my brother would have been ashamed of him. I had seen already how Sarwat could be depressed, but this was much worse.

When Amir brought me some tea I stirred in the sugar and let its warmth and sweetness comfort me, but I knew I would never be able to forget how Sarwat had offended me. I was his elder and his uncle, and he should have respected me.

Amir brought his cup of tea over to where I was sitting. He was very embarrassed for he said, "Sarwat was wrong to speak to you like that. I am sorry he said those things, and I am sorry I heard him say them." Then he said that some of what Sarwat said was right, and that for all of them finding a wife would be difficult.

I thought about this. Although Sarwat had been here for nearly two years and had somewhere to live, and a television and a car and a leather jacket, I could see it must be hard for him – for all these men – to get on with their lives if they could not work and were not sure they could remain here. I had heard them talk about the authorities here, and the rules. Sarwat said it was hard to know what the rules were, and there were constant rumours about them changing – about who could stay in England, who could work and where they could live. A recent rule, he said, was that asylum seekers would not be able to get advice from a lawyer without paying for it, and who, he asked me, could pay a lawyer's fees when they had just paid all they had to an agent to get here?

He said, "All we want to do is to work and earn a living and live ordinary lives. Some English people try their best to help us do that, but it all takes so long. We have to be very careful. If only they would give us half a chance."

I thought of Khadija. What would life in England be like for her? I thought she would be safe, but would she find a husband? Allah willing, she *had* to find a husband, otherwise who would look after her when she grew up? Did I want her to marry someone who had no job? Suddenly, I was filled with new anxiety. For two years I had been worried about my plans for travelling, and paying for travelling and then the journey itself. I thought life would get better once I was in the west, but now I was here there were different things to worry about.

I tried to imagine Khadija as she had looked on the last day I saw her. She was small for her age. Eleven? Already twelve perhaps? Even if she was taller now, she would be thin from the journey, as I was.

I got up and went to the window. Outside it was already dark but orange lights lit up the street. Several of those fat birds were hurrying along the pavement looking for scraps. They never seemed to sleep.

Sarwat was so wrong. I saw that at times he did not follow the right way, and that made me sad. And I was sad too because they told me there was no mosque in this town. My stomach was hurting again, and I was not at peace, so I went back to the settee, drew my knees up and tried to sleep against the sound of a television show where coarse women were talking and laughing too loudly.

♪

Richard put away the dishes. It did not seem worth using the washing-up machine for only a couple of plates and a few pieces of cutlery. He was completely familiar now with changing sheets, washing and hoovering. Estelle had always done most of the housework because the pair of them had been, he had come to realise, quite traditional, and although she had worked for most of their long married life, she had usually only had part-time jobs.

He carried a glass of whisky through to the lounge, put on some Elgar and settled himself down on the pale sofa they had chosen together in John Lewis. Increasingly he found himself doing this on most evenings, unless he went to a rehearsal. He would sit for an hour or so with a drink and have another look at The Guardian, then watch the News, then pour another whisky or make a cup of tea. Then, in the company of a composer he liked, he would just sit and think until it was time to go to bed.

He wondered if he was depressed, and, if he was, whether he should go to the doctor. But which doctor, anyway? When they moved to Norwich from Aylsham they had not got round to registering with a new practice. Estelle's collapse had taken them straight to A & E at the Norfolk and Norwich, and there – except for one month at home – she had stayed. Four months of tests and treatment, and then she died.

He told himself again it was not depression he was experiencing, but bereavement, and it was quite normal and to be expected. He balked at the thought of spending yet more time with doctors. He reached for the remote, and tuned in on the stroke of ten. Another two American soldiers killed. Beagle Two up and away. Men searching through the rubble caused by the earthquake in Iran.

He poured his second drink. Perhaps he should get a cat. Or even a dog. He had always rather wanted a pet, but, once it became clear they were not going to have any children, he had left that decision to Estelle. He thought she might have been hurt if it looked as if he had settled for a pet instead of a child. He would not have done this, of course, and although Estelle had said several times that she 'would not mind' having a cat, neither of them had made the move to get one.

He could honestly say that when he was younger, after those years which led towards accepting they would not have children, he had not minded when he heard friends talking about their sons and daughters learning their first words or winning races or arguing about what they should wear. It was only when he retired that he began to feel it. No children's university applications to discuss, no requests for loans, no grandchildren. He had not shared his feelings with Estelle, but a few days before she died she had said, completely out of the blue, "It's a pity we didn't have children." He had just squeezed her hand, not knowing what to reply.

They had taken early retirement less than three years ago within a few weeks of each other, and they celebrated with a tour of Canada. Then it was Christmas and by the end of February they had moved out of the house they had been in for more than fifteen years and into their new Norwich home. They were sure town life was what they wanted at this stage: no more driving to exhibitions or the theatre or restaurants, and an elegant trouble-free house.

But things had not turned out like that. They had only just begun to enjoy the advantages of being right in Norwich when

Estelle was admitted to hospital. Tickets for the Theatre Royal and the Maddermarket had sat in their envelopes on the shelf in the hall for many months until Richard threw them out.

And now, strangely, he was missing the children they had never had as much as he was missing Estelle. He found himself wanting the phone to go. He did not want Mary or Eric to ring again, or Dan whom he used to work with, or Ian, his brother they had visited in Canada with whom he did not have much in common. No, he specifically wanted Estelle or a son or a daughter to phone. Or even his parents, both of whom died a decade ago. Someone who mattered to him a lot. Someone who mattered a lot even if they were dead or had never been born.

Surely thinking all this, thinking like this, proved he was depressed?

No, he decided there and then, he would not get a dog or a cat. It would make no difference. This desire was for human contact, for connected, close human contact. And it was specifically for people who were not and would never be available to him.

He got up to change the CD, and ran his finger along the cases until he came to Debussy. No, on second thoughts, Delibes might be better.

He had noticed others wondering if he would find a new partner. Eric had told him tentatively that Mary thought he should find himself "a nice lady friend". Ian, in his Christmas card, clearly assumed he was actively looking. He wrote: "The internet's the place to look. I've heard amazing success stories."

The last thing he wanted was another woman. God, life was complicated enough as it was.

And so was death. Even now there were still things to do. At least the will was sorted out at last, but there were more of Estelle's possessions to deal with and he was still getting letters from government departments asking for information he had already provided.

There were things to be done in the house too. Back in Aylsham they always knew exactly who to go to if they wanted a job doing such as getting the mower sharpened, or an exterior light fitted. Here in Norwich, they had had to start from scratch.

Moving, he had concluded, certainly earned its high position in the stress league table, even if it wasn't preceded by retiring or followed by your wife dying.

So, it was easy to dismiss other people's plans for him. There was plenty going on already. Except on winter evenings and nights. This, he recognised, was loneliness. Not depression, nor bereavement, but loneliness. He could not decide if Delibes was causing these feelings or accompanying them.

And it still seemed too soon. Even though Estelle died nearly eighteen months ago, it felt too soon to think of another relationship. His loneliness was centred on Estelle. Even though he knew his feelings might change over time he could take no interest in someone he did not know, had not met.

He resisted the desire to pour himself a third drink but knew he was not ready to go to bed. Going to bed when he felt like this would mean he would lie there churning over everything. He decided on a cup of tea, even though that guaranteed he would have to get up in the night.

He sat down at the kitchen table, determined to be more positive. Doing things. That was what helped. In that first summer, within two months of Estelle's death, he had spent hours in the garden. And this summer just gone it was more gardening – specifically digging – that had kept him going, had kept him in one piece. He enjoyed giving his neighbours lettuces and carrots. And every time he went to orchestra practice he had taken a bag of whatever surplus he had – tomatoes, or the most gorgeous plums. He was already impatient for the spring.

In September he had made masses of plum jam, and he was working his way through it. Now, on getting up to look in the cupboard, he saw there were only three jars left. Suddenly he remembered how he and Estelle used to make marmalade. It used to take up a whole day and the whole kitchen. They had loved doing it, and they had loved the jars of shining orange marmalade they made, and used to leave them out on the side for a week because it seemed a shame to put them away. Yes, he would make it again, soon, for the Seville oranges would be on the market in a week or so. He went to Estelle's shelf of recipe books and found one of her favourites. He prised apart pages stuck together with what must, he judged from the texture, be dried chutney. As well as oranges he would need sugar, lemons, small circles of waxed paper, bigger circles of cellophane paper, a dozen or so jars. From a box by the back door he retrieved a pickle jar and a peanut butter jar destined for the bottle bank. Tomorrow he would ask his neighbours for more. And it was orchestra tomorrow too, so he could phone a few people and ask them.

Grace went away on my fifth day in that place. Without words I understood she was leaving and so I asked her where she was going, but she could not explain that without words, and although I had by then found some women who spoke Arabic, their Arabic was not like mine, and anyway they did not speak English and so Grace could not tell me. All I understood was that it was far away.

She gave me her gloves. I had never worn gloves before, and I put them on my hands at once. They were red and too big for me and I loved them.

And then she went. She walked out carrying one bag over her shoulder and a bulging black plastic bag in front of her. I went outside in the cold with several other women and watched her walk away with a guard. She was not crying and nor was I, but some of the women were. When she got to the gate she turned and waved. The women called out to her, but I didn't. I moved out of myself and went to the top of the gate, by the jagged wire. I looked back and saw myself standing in my black trousers and blue shirt and my new red gloves. My hands seemed too big for my body. Then I saw myself lift one of my hands and wave it. Then I saw my body turn and go back inside again with the other women. I did not know what to do next.

I walked along some corridors and looked in through a window to a room for children. I had not seen it before. A girl had her back to me and for a second I thought it was Zaineb, my youngest sister, but of course it couldn't have been. When she turned round I saw she was nothing like Zaineb.

I tried to open the door but it was locked. Although I was becoming grown-up I wanted to go in and sit on the floor with the children. Mothers were there too, and a woman was reading from a book to two boys sitting on cushions.

Then it was time for another roll call and another meal. I was not hungry but I went to the dining room and ate some chicken. And, for the first time, we had oranges. I sat with the women who pronounced words in a strange way, and I saved the orange until the end. When I picked it up I seemed to notice the colour properly for the first time. It was *so* orange. I ate it slowly and it tasted good.

After lunch I went back to the children's room, but the door was still locked. Inside, a group of women and children were sitting in a circle, singing and clapping. One woman sat a little apart from them, rocking her baby. I very much wanted to go in so I knocked on the door. One of the staff unlocked it and asked to see my name badge. At first she was not sure whether to let me in or not but then she held the door open for me. I was years older than any other child in there, but I was in.

Everyone made room for me at the circle and I liked being there with the women and children. I tried to join in the song although it was not in Arabic. After a while one girl wandered off to play somewhere else, and then another did. But the women kept on singing and when the song ended they all laughed and held their hands out to each other and to me and to the young woman with the tiny baby. But she was crying, not laughing, and she kept on rocking her baby to and fro, to and fro.

I got up and looked round the room. There were toys, a place for drawing and painting, a bookcase full of books in writing I couldn't read. There were children's paintings on the walls, and English letters and numbers, and pictures of animals, and on a desk there was a ball of the world. Once I'd seen a map of the world in the camp, but this was quite different. The countries were different colours and they spread round the ball so you had to turn it to see everywhere. The sea was all the same bright blue, and it was hard to tell if there was more sea or land in the world.

I knew the sea was not blue, but brown. After I had become separated from Fatima and we were on the last bit of our journey to Denmark, we were in a lorry that drove onto a ship to go across the sea. I was very, very ill. I don't know if it was the movement of the ship, or the sea, or the smell of petrol, but I remember leaning my head against the metal side of the lorry and thinking that both my body and my brain were sick of travelling. I was longing for everything to stop.

At last we did stop. And that was when we were found. The lorry back was opened up and we breathed in the bright fresh air and the rain. We were stinking and scabby, and the policemen put on yellow rubber gloves before they helped us down. They were kind, which is what some women expected them to be, but others thought they would be angry. Some women were saying that very few of the Police carried guns, and that was a good thing and meant we would be safe here in Denmark. Then I saw the sea and it was pale brown. And then we found out we were not in Denmark, but England.

In the children's room I turned the ball slowly, but I did not know where England was, or Denmark, or even Iran or Iraq, or anywhere.

The woman who had let me in came and stood next to me. She said, "England" and pointed to a place on the ball. Her finger almost covered it. I said "Iran?" and she pushed the world round, looking for it. She didn't know exactly where it was but she found it. It was not near England, and it was much bigger than England, but it was not as far away as I thought it would be. Then I said, "Iraq?" and she looked carefully again and pointed to a place next to Iran. Iraq was much bigger than England too.

Another woman whom I had seen before came over to us. She said something to me but I did not know what she meant. She said it again, and then I realised she had said "Grace." She turned the world a little bit the other way, pointed to an island in the middle of the blue sea and said another word I thought must be the name of the island. So Grace had gone to this island. It was nowhere near Iraq or Iran, or even England. I looked at the distance from Iran to England. If our journey had taken about eighteen months I wondered how long it would take Grace to reach that island. The world was so big. Then the woman held her arms out and swayed her body. A plane – Grace must have gone on a plane.

Then we all had to go out of the children's room so I started to walk back to my bedroom, but one of the guards called me. She asked me if my name was Khadija, and I said it was. She told me to follow her into a little side room. Two women I had never seen before came in and sat down at the table and one told me in good Arabic to come and sit there too. She was angry. She explained they had been waiting to see me for two hours for an interview but no one knew where I was. She asked me crossly why I did not stay where I could be found, so I told her no one had told me anything about an interview. Then she told me they were going to ask me some questions, because they wanted me to leave this place as soon as possible so I could live with a family. That made me feel scared and excited at the same time.

She checked my name and age. I was not certain how old I was, but I thought I was thirteen, so I said, "Thirteen." She asked my date of birth and I said I was born in 1989. She said that could not be right, for if I was born in 1989 I must already be fourteen. Was I sure it was 1989? I was not sure, but I said yes. She asked which month and which day I was born, so I told her my aunt Laila said I was born in winter. Then she wanted to know which country I had come from, so I said, "Iran, but I am an Iraqi." Who had I travelled with? What countries had I come through? Did I have any family here? The other woman was writing down everything I said. She wrote fast even though she was writing the wrong way round, from left to right, but of course she must have been used to it.

I told them about Grandfather and Sarwat, and showed them my piece of paper with the three names and addresses on. I told them I had kept this all through my journey and showed it to the Police when I first arrived here, even though it had become more like soft cloth than paper. The English woman copied down what was written on it and talked to the interpreter for a few minutes, and then they asked me if I wanted to live with my family or someone else's.

What a strange question. Of course I wanted to live with my family. Why would I have wanted to live with anyone else's? The interpreter said they would try to contact Sarwat and see if they could find out where Grandfather was. I did not say I did not think they would find him. I had not heard of him for more than a year, and now that I had seen that ball in the children's room I knew there was all that world to get lost in.

Then both of them said goodbye to me. The interpreter was not cross any more and she told me I would hear from them soon. We went out of the room and they went over to the staff desk. One of the guards held out her hand towards me with her thumb sticking up. I knew this was a good sign.

The next Friday was special because an English woman from the authorities had come to the house to tell us Khadija had been found safe and well and was going to come and live with us. I gave thanks at once to Allah, and Sarwat promised to take me that evening to the house of some Moslems who met together for Friday prayers.

The woman who came about Khadija had talked with Sarwat for a while, asking him questions and writing down what he said. At one point he showed her his bedroom, so when she had gone I asked him where he was going to sleep if Khadija was to have his room.

"I'm staying in my room. Khadija can sleep in here. I will find a mattress for her."

I told him that she should have his room, a proper room, for she was a female.

"Uncle Abbas, Khadija is only a young girl. It is best that she sleeps in here with you. She does not need a room."

I did not argue with him because I was not sure what was best. In the camp all the women helped each other, but here it was different. And so, although I was very happy she had been found, I was already worrying about her again.

As soon as the woman went, Sarwat went too and I was left

on my own in the flat, but I did not like being there alone. Amir, who was one of Sarwat's closest friends, had told me that many people in England lived alone and there were many houses with only one person. This seemed to us to be a strange way to live. I have never been alone in my life for more than a few hours since I was very young and out in my small boat on the water, and in Sarwat's flat I found that if I watched the white birds above the sea I did not feel so alone. But today I could not see any birds.

I had already prayed twice that day. At least it was easy to know where Mecca was, because the window looked straight out to the rising sun so I knew where the south-east was. On the journey, when we were inside for weeks at a time and often had to be silent, we had to imagine where Mecca was, imagine kneeling and pray under our breath.

Sarwat and most of his friends did not pray, not even on Fridays. I had not asked them about Ramadan, because I feared they had not kept a fast and would dismiss me again as an old fool. Some of the meat they ate was not halal, and they showed me little respect. Amir was the only one who had held to the right way, and Sarwat was amongst the worst.

All these things made me angry and hurt, and I fell asleep on the settee until Sarwat came back. He had had his hair cut and was carrying a new plastic bag with a box in. I asked him again to take me to the house where they held prayers.

"Later, later. I'll take you in an hour or two."

I was angry again that he dismissed me in that way, so I put on my coat and went out. For the first time he did not tell me to be careful as I let myself out of the door.

I was not feeling strong but I walked along where the wind coming in off the sea blew sand into my face. Although it stung it somehow felt good. I kept away from the buildings full of the loud, flashing machines that Sarwat had told me were games where people won and lost money. Further down the street things merged into a blur and I wished again that I had a pair of glasses.

I did not want to go back to Sarwat's flat. His house was not my house although it should have been. I felt trapped. After all that travelling I had reached a place where I did not want to be. I pushed away the thought of another journey. I was too old and weak.

Then I saw something so unexpected I did not believe I was seeing it. But there it was in front of me. A palm tree. It was not tall and it did not have any dates and it was in the wrong place, but it was a palm tree and I gave thanks. I prayed it was a sign that things would be better. I longed to touch it but it was in an enclosed area, so I walked onto the sand. Dozens of sea birds flew up and away and I was sorry that they were frightened of me.

A couple came out of a café and as the door opened I smelled coffee and decided to go inside. Apart from a man behind the counter, it was empty. When I sat down and lit a cigarette the man called over to me but I did not understand what he was saying. Then he pointed to a sign above the counter with a picture of a black cigarette with a red line across it. He was telling me I could not smoke, so I walked to the door and threw my cigarette into the street after one final draw. When I went back in he handed me a menu. I pretended to read it and then said, "Coffee." He gestured for me to take a seat.

I sat down, took out my beads and waited for the coffee. How strange it was not to be allowed to smoke. My cigarette had fizzed as it hit a puddle and I thought about going outside to have another while I was waiting. Instead, I counted my beads and rested my head against my hand. I thought of all the coffee houses I knew in Majar al Kabir, in Najaf, in Qurna, in all the villages and towns and cities all over Iraq. How full they were of men talking, laughing, playing dominoes, smoking! How full of life!

But Allah had brought me to this place.

The man brought me a big, white cup and a brown pot of coffee and held out a plate of small red packets which I thought must contain cakes. I took one and put it in my pocket. I took a sip of the coffee. It should have been bitter and strong, but it hardly had any taste, so I picked up one of the little paper tubes of sugar and tore the top off. My fingers found it awkward and most of it spilt. I tore another more carefully and tipped the sugar in. The coffee was still not sweet enough, so I poured in a third and fourth tube and stirred it well.

Then it tasted better and I sat there drinking it slowly, looking out of the window on to the street and watching the man come and go between the café and the kitchen. I felt myself calming down.

I poured more coffee and thought about Khadija again. If Fatima was no longer with her – and I somehow felt she was not – how could she live with me and Sarwat but without other girls or women? What sort of a life would this be for her? I tried to think back to my reasons for coming to the west, and all I could remember was wanting her to be safe and have a good education and find a good husband. Because of this I made her leave everything and everyone she knew.

I wondered what her aunt Laila and the rest of the family would say if they knew I had nearly lost her. They were so sure she would be safe with me, but I had made her go through danger to come to this place where I now knew I did not want to be and where I did not want her to be.

And I was not sure if we could stay here or not because Sarwat and the others talked about the immigration rules using English words. I wanted to know if I would be allowed to stay for ever, and everyone had said that was what they all wanted, and then they all said the same few English words together. For a moment, it sounded as if they were praying.

I asked what the words meant and they each translated them in different ways, but Hassan explained that one of them meant "go away" and one meant "stay." I did not understand, because these words have opposite meanings. How could anyone go away *and* stay? And then Sarwat's Iranian friend said that another of the words meant "uncertain," but he did not want something *uncertain* – he wanted to be certain about staying, and so did I. But Amir seemed to understand it all and he told me that at present I was allowed to stay here, and that was as much as I could hope for.

The previous night I had heard Sarwat talking about his appeal against the decision not to allow him to remain. He had seen a lawyer, but now he was worried about whether he would have to pay her. And they were saying things could become worse, because they had heard there was going to be another new rule. Soon, if an asylum seeker was turned back to their own country but refused to leave, any children they had would be taken away. What did that mean for Khadija? Could she be taken away? Would she be put in another camp again, an English camp? It was all so complicated. I was so confused about everything that it was tempting to leave it all to Allah.

I did not want to go back to the flat but I had to, even though I was still low in spirits and that morning there had been blood on my clothes. I would ask Sarwat a third time about seeing a doctor. I pulled myself to my feet and went to the counter. Next to the sign on the wall with the crossed-out cigarette there were postcards and a map. The man spoke to me and when he saw I did not understand he wrote something down, but the marks on the paper meant nothing to me. So I reached into my pocket, took out a small handful of coins and held them out across the counter on my open palm. He laughed and picked out a few of them, then pushed my hand away. Then he walked round the counter to the door. With one hand he opened it and with the other he saluted me like a soldier. We were both smiling and I thanked him in Arabic.

I sheltered in a doorway and lit a cigarette. One of those big fat grey and white birds was pecking in a puddle, so I took out the cake from my pocket, unwrapped it and broke off a piece. Within seconds five birds were at my feet so I spread the crumbs over the pavement. I noticed that two of them had a silky greenish shine to their feathers, while one which was a softer pink colour was very timid. I waved my arm at the bolder ones and then the timid one pecked fast, tipping its head and looking at me with its bright eye between each peck.

I walked back to the flat with the wind behind me. The sky was darker now above the sea, but the streets were full of artificial light. The days were so short here in England that I did not know how people found time to live in them. I walked slowly up the stairs.

Sarwat said, "There you are! I can take you to prayers now."

I felt tired and cold by then but I wanted to go to prayers, so I agreed. I fetched my mat and followed him downstairs. He turned on the radio in the car and tapped his finger on the steering wheel to western music. He was wearing new shoes and his leather jacket, and I could smell a different scent on his hair. He seemed happy and I wondered if he was going to see a girl, despite what he had said about women. I decided not to ask him about this or about seeing a doctor, but as we passed a church lit up with coloured lights, I raised my voice above the music to ask if English people were believers.

"No," he replied. "I've been told their churches are empty. They do not believe in a God. They are not like us. Perhaps they are not bad, but they are not so good either. How can they live without a God?"

I thought about some of the people I had met in England – the policeman who took me to a doctor and gave me a good meal, the woman who helped me find the right train, the man I had just met in the café. And I thought of the agents who took all my money, and Saddam, and the evil that had been done by some of the Muslims in Iraq. But I was pleased to hear Sarwat suggest that everyone needs a God, and I too did not know how anyone could live without one, for I could not.

Sarwat stopped the car and led me to a door. He knocked and waited with me until a man answered it and invited me inside.

♪

Richard was disappointed. He could not make the marmalade when he planned to because the Seville oranges were not yet available. Still, there were other things to do on a beautiful Sunday afternoon.

He had not had a proper look at the garden for weeks, so he put on his jacket and wellingtons and went outside. Despite the weak sunshine, it was pretty bleak. The modern brick wall at the end looked stark now that everything in the bed underneath was dead. Perhaps he should plant something with berries there. Berberis, or viburnum. He walked down to the wall and looked back at the house.

It was the French windows that had struck them the first time they came. The garden received plenty of sun, but these windows faced east and they had imagined themselves sitting there on sunny mornings with a pot of coffee and the Sunday papers, or with a bottle of wine on a warm evening, looking out on the den of colour he was going to create. But by the time Estelle came home from hospital for that month after she had finished the treatment, their view had been of piles of topsoil, crates of stone slabs, and minor earthworks marked off with orange twine. The saving grace for Richard was a blossoming plum tree in the middle until Estelle had pointed out that recently her life had been marking time with the life of the blossom. As it faded, she lost strength. And when he realised – when they realised – she was going to die very soon, they would have given anything to be back in their old house in Aylsham with its thick, protective hedge of copper beech and the swifts zizzing overhead.

He came across a pile of scattered bricks and decided to tidy them up there and then. As he dislodged them several insects scuttled out from their place of safety, and he discovered a line of snails securely sealed to a fence post. A robin appeared from nowhere.

He glanced up to the bedroom window Estelle had loved looking out of each morning. She was always the first up, and if it was light enough the first thing she did was to report to him on the activity around the bird table.

The bird table. Where was it? He had not seen it for months. He went back towards the house and it was in its usual place, of course. The two feeders hanging from it were empty, and he decided immediately to replenish them and another one he found on a nearby branch.

He pulled off his boots by the back door and took the feeders inside. Where had she kept the birdfood? He tried two drawers, and then, in the cupboard next to the freezer, found a polythene bag of seeds. It was getting towards dusk by the time the feeders were filled and back in their places. It felt like a small job well done, and one that Estelle would want him to do. When they first came here she had started to keep a list of the birds she saw in the garden – blue tits, chaffinches, blackbirds, thrushes, long tailed tits, sparrows, starlings, rooks, one green woodpecker, magpies, jays, some sort of warbler, robins, a pair of pied wagtails. She had hoped to see a bullfinch, but none had yet appeared.

Later on, as Richard crossed the hall with a cup of tea he noticed the answerphone light flashing. It could wait. He drew the curtains and watched the rest of the sport, though since England's victory against the Australians everything else felt like an anticlimax. He leafed through the TV supplement and checked what was on that evening. Not a lot.

On the dining table was a pile of post waiting to be dealt with. There was a newsletter from the RSPB and he told himself for the nth time that he must cancel Estelle's subscription which was still being debited from his account. He had bought her this subscription for Christmas in 1992? 1993? There was something too from RIBA, and a leaflet about lectures on Norwich and Norfolk that he had requested. He took this back to the settee. There were a couple of things there which sounded OK. Yes. They might be interesting.

However, nothing was interesting this evening. He stood up, annoyed with himself for feeling unsettled. He took his cup back to the kitchen, stopping en route to play the answerphone message.

"Hallo Richard, it's Harriet here. Thanks for giving me a lift to orchestra last week. I've got my car back now, thank God. I'd forgotten what life's like without one. Anyway, I was wondering if you could help me. Well, help Polly, I mean. She's practising like mad for her Trinity exam, and I wondered if you could listen to her play a couple of pieces, and comment on them. As a violinist, I don't think I'm much help. She needs an oboist."

He could hear Harriet's voice slowing down, and her taking another breath. "Could you phone me back, please? It's about four on Sunday and I'll be in all evening. Bye for now."

Richard looked at his watch. It was just after half past six, which meant there were at least five hours to get through. He had planned to do an hour's practice before getting a meal together, but as he was practising more now than he had done for years there was no need to do it. He poured himself a beer, took it through to the sitting room, and drank it slowly.

He did not know Harriet well. She had joined the orchestra about two years ago, and they had played in a few concerts together, but during Estelle's illness he had missed at least two, including one of the best ones – the one they held in Salle church each summer. He had missed all the rehearsals for it but Estelle had insisted that he attended the concert even though she was in hospital.

He had gone in past the tall and ornate font cover to the pale, gorgeous, familiar space they had so often visited together. He had taken a seat at the back, closed his eyes and tried to forget that Estelle was in hospital dying, that she would soon be dead. He had leaned forward and wept inside himself. And now, recalling these feelings, he found himself near to tears again. He cried less these days, and for less time than he used to, but it still happened. He looked at his watch again. Quarter to seven. Only thirteen minutes had passed.

He went to the shower room, rinsed his face and looked at himself in the mirror. Then he went back to the hall and took out the orchestra list from the drawer in the hall table. Harriet Watts. He dialled her number.

"Hallo, 453890."

"Hallo, is that Harriet? It's Richard."

"No, it's Polly. I'll get Mum."

He heard Polly calling Harriet, and the sound of someone approaching the phone.

"Richard, thanks so much for phoning back."

"That's fine. How are you? Got the car back, I hear?"

"Yes, I have. It cost me nearly two hundred pounds. I was horrified. But at least I've got it."

"Tell me about Polly – I presume she's your daughter – and this exam."

"Yes, she is my daughter! Sorry, I didn't think. She's fifteen. Well, they have something now called a First Concert Certificate. It's supposed to be like giving a concert, so she has to perform – not just play the music, if you see what I mean."

"Yes. OK. Of course I'll listen to her. I'm not sure how helpful I'll be, but I'll try."

"It'll be so good for her to play for a real oboist. She's got her teacher, and he's excellent, but it was his suggestion that she play in front of someone else. Could you come over this evening?"

He hesitated.

"It would be nice if you could. Not if you don't want to, of course, or if you're going out or something. We're just having a family snack – cheese on toast, or soup. And I think we could find you a glass of wine."

By twenty-past-seven he was on his way. He had never been to Harriet's before, and as far as he could remember he had not met her husband. It was the percussion player whose house the orchestra usually went to if there was a party, although one summer they had all come out to Aylsham and Estelle had prepared a barbecue.

He turned left at the traffic lights then right at the little supermarket. There was her blue Honda, taking up the whole of the narrow driveway. The smart VW parked outside must belong to her husband.

As he stood outside the door he could hear an oboe. Harriet answered the door.

"Hallo! Do come in."

He was shown into the front room where Polly was waiting, oboe in hand. She was smiley and looked very much like her mother, and he felt her light, young handshake. She was a little embarrassed.

"Well, I've come for my concert. Where would you like me to sit?"

Polly laughed and gestured to the settee. She showed him the list of what she had to play while Harriet went out of the room to fetch a glass of wine.

Polly announced: "I'm going to play the 3rd and 4th movements from the Sonata in A Minor by Telemann. I'm meant to sort of introduce it but I haven't worked out what I'm going to say yet."

"That doesn't matter now," said Richard.

He could tell she had practised this piece well, and there was little to comment on. "Well done. That's good, and it's not easy."

"That's my best one. The others aren't so good."

"Go on then, play me the next."

"I'll try to do this one without the music."

She started on an Adagio by Bach, then stopped and apologised and started again. It was not bad at all, and she did not get stuck once. She was a little breathless towards the end so Richard borrowed her oboe and showed her another place where she could breathe.

She had another go, but stumbled.

"Never mind. Take your time. Try again."

And she did, and it worked.

"Shall I play you the one I'm worst at? It's The Islamite Dance, by Goossens."

She struggled through it and ended up embarrassed again, "It's hopeless. I'll never manage it."

"Yes you will." He got up to look at the music, and pointed to a particular place. "There, from there. Have another go at that part."

Harriet came in and stood by the door to listen.

Richard watched Polly, and the more he watched her the more she looked like Harriet. He saw her arms and shoulders lifting and falling. She was much too tense.

"It's hard work," she said.

"Then you must remember it's a *dance*. Try to relax. Try to imagine yourself dancing - perhaps dancing when someone you like is watching you - and you want them to watch you and be attracted by you. Imagine yourself in a special dress and dancing to this music."

Polly looked at Harriet and they both burst out laughing. Richard had no idea what the joke was.

"Sorry," said Harriet, "we're laughing because you should see Polly when she goes out with her friends. And you can imagine the sort of music they like to dance to!"

Richard said that even so, this was a dance - an Islamite dance. Perhaps not her sort of dance, obviously, but she would play it better if she thought of it like that.

She played it a third time and then Harriet beckoned her and Richard into the kitchen.

"Come and have some food. Adam's famished."

At the kitchen table, eating crisps, was a boy of about ten wearing a green and yellow football strip. Richard suddenly realised that Adam was Harriet's son and not her husband, and also, in the same second, that perhaps Harriet and her husband were separated.

"Richard, this is Adam."

"Hallo. Is Polly any good?"

"Yes, she is. She plays very well."

"Help yourself to some bread. I've made onion soup."

"Who do you support?" asked Adam.

"Chelsea, I suppose, but it's really the rugby I follow."

"I think football's best. You know who I support, don't you?"

"How could anyone possibly know?" said Polly in an ironic tone.

"Norwich City! On the ball City! City!"

Richard smiled. "I'm glad you told me, I would never have guessed, never in a hundred years."

He drove home at ten. It had been an unexpected and enjoyable evening. He liked helping Polly and having supper with them and even letting himself be taken upstairs to admire a poster of the whole Canaries squad. He also found himself listening to a short biography of each player and meeting Adam's two real canaries – Delia and Darren – whom Adam was hoping would produce babies.

"The man in the pet shop said they might have some next year."

"Adam," said Polly from the doorway, "they're not even trying."

Richard had liked being with a family, even though he was not used to it. He had found himself thinking about what sort of children his and Estelle's might have been and what it must be like to have a child who looked like you.

No husband had been mentioned until Adam, when told it was time for bed, complained that when he was at his dad's he did not have to go to bed until much later.

Richard let himself into the house. It was always good to come home. He was just in time for the News. There was Blair, making a surprise visit to the troops. But still no sign of Beagle Two.

Later, he lay awake for a while, his mind moving amongst music, canaries and the image of a lost space probe sitting alone on Mars and unable to communicate.

Within a few days of my interview the interpreter and the social worker came back and told me I was going to leave this place and go to my family! They had found my cousin Sarwat *and* Grandfather! Although I had told myself that Grandfather and I would never find each other again, I only did that so it would not hurt so much if I really did lose him for ever. So when I found out he was alive and I could live with him, I cried. I was to go some distance away from where I was being kept now, to the town they were in. I would be driven there in a taxi, and when I got to Sarwat's home another Authority person would come to meet me.

They showed me a paper they said was a map of England but at first I did not understand it, because it was not at all like the map of the world I'd seen or the ball of the world. They explained it was a sort of picture of a place seen from above and made flat. They showed me where we were now, somewhere near the middle of the picture, and the town I would be going to which was over on the right, next to blue sea. They asked if I knew about north, south, east and west, and of course I did, and then I could see how it worked. I would be going to the eastern part of England, and the interpreter wrote down for me in that backward writing the name of the place I was going to. And then she told me her husband was born in a city near where I was going and pointed to it on the map. That city had quite a short name but my town had a long name. She told me to repeat the names of these places after her, because I ought to learn them. She made me do it three times and then she smiled and nodded because I was doing it well.

The news about going to Grandfather and Sarwat was the best thing that had happened to me in my whole life, the very best thing.

The staff must have told people about me because everyone was happy for me except the Chinese lady who had moved into the corner bed a few days ago. She just sat and stared at the wall, and took no notice when anyone spoke to her.

I hardly slept that night and when I got up early the next morning the very black woman who spends so long making herself beautiful was coming out of the shower without any clothes on. I ran out of the washroom quickly but she called me so I went back slowly. She had wrapped a towel round herself and was laughing, and she indicated that I should have a shower. I shook my head and said, in Arabic, that I did not want to. It would be so shameful to be seen naked now that I was becoming a woman.

Then she set out on the bench her jars and bottles. In turn, she took each one and undid the top, and let me smell what was inside. She showed me a special soap for washing with, a different liquid to rub into hair, and then another cream for hair, then some pink cream for rubbing into the skin of the body and another for the face. So many things just for getting clean! Then she fetched another towel, bigger than mine, and mimed how I could undress behind the shower door and have a shower using any of the bottles and jars that I wanted to.

I was not sure about this, but they smelled like ... I did not know what they smelled like, but *she* smelled nice, so I thought I would too if I used them. It was still early and no one else had yet come to the washroom, so I said yes.

The water felt good pouring down from my head to my feet. I undid the top of the first bottle and poured some of the liquid into my hand, and then rubbed it over my hair, just as the woman had shown me. Bubbles frothed all over me! When I tried to open the second bottle I couldn't, but suddenly some thick blue liquid squirted out onto my belly. It foamed and I rubbed that all over me too.

When I heard someone calling my name I turned the water off and put my towel round me quickly. I stepped out and waited to get dressed until the next person went in. No one saw me bare.

When I was dressed I gave the bottles back to the woman and she made me sit on the edge of her bed. She took another towel – I don't know where she got all these towels from because no one was given more than one – and began to rub my hair dry. She went at it so fast at first that I had to hold on to the bed, but then she slowed down and spread my hair out and patted it. When she stopped I thought she had finished, but she poured some cream into her hand and then she worked it into my hair with her fingers, right down to my scalp. She had very long fingernails but she didn't scratch me at all. She massaged my head: the very top, the sides, my temples, above my ears, behind my ears and right down by my neck. I was surprised how noisy my hair sounded when she rubbed it. Sometimes her fingers were pushing my skin, and sometimes they were pulling it. They were both soft and hard, gentle and firm. I shut my eyes and I felt sleepy, although it was the morning.

When she began to brush my hair I heard people talking and I opened my eyes again. Several people were watching us, and they seemed pleased the woman was doing this. Then it was over, and they all laughed, and someone pointed to the mirror. I looked at myself and saw my shining, flowing hair, not like me at all! One of the women came close and sniffed me, and then they all did and everyone was laughing. I was very happy because it was good to start my new life with beautiful hair and a good smell, after all those dirty times. And I felt too as if all those women liked seeing me change from one Khadija into another, even though I was still the same inside.

Then we had breakfast but I couldn't eat much. After I had packed my things I was ready to go, although I knew I would not leave until the afternoon. The gloves Grace had given me were at the bottom of my bag. It was cold but I was not going to wear them because I didn't want to lose them.

Then I took the towels back to the laundry room and the woman with the scar was there and she smiled her uneven smile as she spread a cloth over the line. When she reached out to straighten it I saw her hands clearly, and I saw the hand where the little finger was missing. I couldn't not look at it. She saw where I was looking and she held her hand out in front of me.

Then she mimed a big man, a group of men, soldiers with guns, coming to her house by a river. She mimed holding a small child, running away, being chased. She mimed a soldier grabbing the child and throwing it into the river. Her face was screwed up as she showed not knowing what to do next, and the soldier grasping her arm and waving his knife. He pretended to cut her arm off but he just cut off her little finger. And then he laughed and waved his knife at her again, so she turned away, but the wide blade caught her face.

And then she put her thumb and three fingers to the scar by her mouth. I didn't know what to do or say. Then she reached out to me and put her arms round me and held me, but not for long. When she let me go and stood back from me tears were running down her face but she was not making any noise. We left the laundry room together, and she walked towards the bedroom. I went the other way, towards the entrance area.

When I got there two of the guards saw me and one I recognised pointed to my hair and clapped. The other one was new that day and spoke quite good Arabic. They were happy for me because I was leaving, and they were telling me I was pretty and I was lucky. I knew I was lucky because everybody had said so – but at that moment being lucky or pretty did not seem to matter.

I wanted to move out of myself but suddenly the radios crackled and hissed and people were hurrying to the door and windows. A group of guards raced past. I was frightened and moved out of the way. Someone said there was a fight outside one of the men's houses. People said there were ten, twenty, fifty men fighting with their fists and their feet, and one man had a knife. Then a woman from my bedroom said it was not a fight at all, just a scuffle, but someone else said a guard was hit to the ground and kicked and her eye was injured, so she would be going to hospital. The staff were trying to calm things down and they managed to get everyone inside again. No, it was a man from Nigeria who had gone to hospital. No, it was not a knife, but something heavy in a sock. Someone else asked how people knew these things, because she was the first outside and saw nothing, only heard shouting. All this was done in a mixture of languages and signs. I didn't know what to believe, but I didn't want to be in a place where there was fighting. I wanted to go to my grandfather and my cousin where I would be safe. I wanted to go.

But saying goodbye was sad. A group of women came outside to wave me off, just as they did when Grace went, and some of them hugged me. The woman who had massaged my head and brushed my hair was not there. Then one of the guards took me through the metal gates which he unlocked and re-locked in turn, and on past some trees and along paths until we came to another building where I had to give them my name badge and show what I was taking away with me. There wasn't much, but they went through everything. Then the guard took me and my bag outside to a taxi. He spoke to the driver, and then waved at me when the engine started up. I wasn't sure whether to wave back or not, so I didn't.

It was the first time I had been in a proper car. I sat in the back on my own and the driver sat in front on her own. We did not speak. She just drove and I just sat and looked out of the windows. I knew we were driving towards the east, and that made me happy. My new home would be in the east. It would be in the west, of course, but in the east of the west.

I did not know England hardly had any hills. It was very green, even though it was winter and the trees had no leaves. There were very, very many cars on the roads and they all looked new.

After an hour or two we stopped for petrol and the smell made me remember the times we had stopped to fill up on our journey when I could hardly breathe for the fumes. The driver went inside to pay, and when she came back she drove the car just a little way to a nearby building. She turned round to ask me something, but I didn't know what. Anyway, we went into the building and it was a restaurant. We were shown to a table and given a shiny card with pictures of different food. I didn't know what to choose, so I pointed to the same meal that the driver was having. While we waited she drew a picture of a fish, so I knew we were going to eat a fish, but the driver's fish was not the same as the fish that Grace drew. That one had stripes and a wavy tail, and bubbles coming out of its mouth. When the food came it was orange and did not look like a fish until I cut it open, but it tasted quite good.

Then we had some tea and the driver left me in the café while she went back to the car for a minute. She returned with a book full of maps and there was a map of the whole of England. She pointed to London, then turned to another page where London took up two whole pages of grey and had lots of roads and writing jammed together. It looked too big for me.

Then she turned to a different page and showed me where we had just come from and where we were going. I was beginning to understand maps better by now, and one of these showed the edge of England, and it seemed bigger than on the first map – as if we were getting closer. The big roads were marked in green and red, and the smaller ones in brown and yellow. The rivers were blue. She showed me the road we were on – it was one of the green ones – and the place we were at. Then she traced her finger further along the road until lots of roads joined together in a grey place. When she said the name of that town I recognised it because it was one of the names the interpreter had told me. Then she traced her finger even further along, and there was another town and I knew that name too. It was a long name that stretched out into the sea. And that was the place I was going to.

Soon we went back to the car, and the driver let me sit next to her. After a long time we came to a big junction where she pointed to one of the roads we were not taking, and said "Norwich", so I knew the town called Norwich was along there. And soon she pointed to a big green sign with white letters and said the other long name, the name of the town we were going to.

Ten minutes later we were driving down a road with the sea on our left hand side, and then we turned off right down a small street and parked by a row of houses. This was where I was going to live!

We stopped and I got out and the driver handed me my bag

from the boot. Then she looked at a piece of paper and started trying to find my house. I followed her along the pavement, and she knocked at a door. We waited a long time but no one answered.

Suddenly I thought that everything might have gone wrong, and I was scared.

Then she spoke to a man who was walking past, and he pointed to a gap between the buildings, so we went in there and round to the back, and found another door. She knocked again and this time a man opened it. I knew it was Sarwat! He welcomed us and we followed him upstairs. And there, standing by the window, was Grandfather. He looked very, very old.

I ran to him and held onto him as tightly as I could, and he held as tightly onto me. I could smell tobacco and sweat and wool. I could feel the tears and bristles on his face. We stayed like that for a long time before he let me go and drew back from me. He wiped his cuff across his wet cheeks, then wiped my cheeks too. Then he drew me to him again, held me, and then released me again. I sat down on the nearest chair and pulled my knees up to my chest and cried and cried. He sat beside me, and I felt his hand on my neck, on my head, on my shoulder.

When I looked up Sarwat and the driver were watching us in silence. Then Sarwat moved towards me and greeted me properly. He was taller than Grandfather and dressed more smartly. He looked friendly. Then he spoke to the driver in English, and she said goodbye to us and went downstairs.

Grandfather looked small and bent. I heard him say, "*There is no strength, no power, except with Allah.*"

He began to ask about the journey, where we had stopped, the agent, Fatima, what had happened when I arrived in England, the place I had just been in. I talked and talked and it was wonderful to speak Arabic and to hear Arabic – *our* Arabic – although Sarwat said some things a bit differently from the way Grandfather and I did. I was so, so happy to be in this new place, with my family. Sarwat left us to talk and brought us some tea.

I knew I would be safe in this place. I knew he and Grandfather would look after me.

Later, after more talking, Sarwat went out to buy food and Grandfather told me he wanted to give thanks to Allah for bringing us together. He showed me another room I could go into while he prayed. It was a tidy and clean bedroom, and there were some new clothes hanging up. On a shelf there was an ashtray with some coins, and under the ashtray were some banknotes. I thought Sarwat must have got a very good job to be able to afford that house and those good clothes, and to have all that money.

Then I heard them calling out that it was time to eat, so I found the bathroom and washed my hands, and looked at myself in the little mirror over the basin. I turned my head from side to side so my hair swung. It was still shiny and smooth.

We sat down at the table and Sarwat brought us some parcels of newspaper! He told us the food was inside, and so we unwrapped the parcel and he was right – and it was potatoes cut into long pieces and fish – the same food I had had that day with the driver. Sarwat said English people liked to eat this meal which is called "fish and chips". He made me say those words in English and we all laughed. I don't think Grandfather liked the food much, but he ate some of it and then lit a cigarette in exactly the way I remembered him doing.

Soon I was yawning and Grandfather said I should sleep. He was right, for I felt very tired. Sarwat put a mattress down on the floor by the settee and told us he was going out and would come back later. I settled down to sleep and Grandfather told me he would sleep on the settee. I was very happy to be in my new home with him.

He reached out his hand and gently touched my head. Quietly, to himself, I heard him say again, "*There is no strength, no power, except with Allah.*"

I did not hear Sarwat come in last night, so he must have been very late. But today as usual he was up early. My fingers were buzzing with the sharp prickings again. It was always worse in my left hand and that could have been because of the old scar on my left forearm. I was shaking my hand and squeezing my fingers when he turned on the light in the kitchen and started to cook his slices of bread. Usually he watched the news while he ate but I told him Khadija was still sound asleep, so he should not put the television on, and he did not. He brought me my cup of tea and then left, saying he would be back in a couple of hours.

It had been raining, and I could hear the wheels of cars hissing on the wet road while I drank my tea slowly with Khadija asleep beside me. One of her arms was outside the covers, and her face was half covered by her hair. I could see her chin, her mouth, her nose, one closed eye and its dark eyebrow, one ear, a stretch of neck, her gleaming hair. Khadija was part of me. She was part of my wife, her grandmother and part of my favourite daughter, and so part of me and my parents and their parents and back and back through many generations of the Sheghanba tribe. I would not let her be taken away again, unless Allah willed it.

And Sarwat too was of my tribe. Despite the criticisms I had about him, he was part of me and I was part of him. Khadija, Sarwat and I – we all belonged to each other. I did not choose my family. I accepted those whom Allah sent. Even while I was thinking that, I was conscious of how Sarwat was not always respectful, and how that made me feel weak and angry at the same time.

Khadija was much more grown-up now than when we started on our journey. Then she was a child, but the moment I saw her the previous evening, the moment when she ran to me and hung onto me, I saw she was nearly a woman, and I had not expected that. Of course I should have thought how much she would have changed. It was so good to see her but I felt sad too because of how we were living our lives. When she was crying I longed for a woman – my wife, my daughter, one of my daughter-in-laws – any woman, any woman at all who could have comforted her. I was wondering again how – or if – she could live in England, amongst men and with no other women, especially now that she was at this growing stage of her life.

Then I got up quietly and washed and dressed before I put my prayer mat down beside her.

After my prayers I made myself more tea and sat there for a long time. It felt good to watch over Khadija while she slept. I thought of all the places she must have slept in during the past eighteen months. I thought of my journey and of her journey and recalled the dangers we had gone through.

As I lit my third cigarette she woke. She smiled at me but she was not sure if she should get out of bed, and I was not sure what to do either. She had never slept in a room with a man before, and I had not ever been in any situation like this. My world kept on changing and it was difficult to know what was right.

My stomach ache was returning. It was like an enemy, coming up on me at unexpected times. I bent forward with the pain.

"What is the matter, Grandfather?"

I said I had a pain in my belly and Sarwat was trying to find me a doctor. I did not tell her everything. I told her that for some reason – I didn't know what – it was difficult to arrange to see a doctor. She was looking at me in such a way that made me think she thought I was old. I did not know what to say to her and she lay down again.

Then there was a sudden noise. Someone was knocking on the door. The person knocked again, louder. I went downstairs.

It was the woman who had visited us to talk about Khadija coming here. She was asking me something and I understood she wanted to know if Khadija was in the flat. I told her that she was, and she asked – through her hands and her expression – if she could come in and see her.

I led the way upstairs and into the big room. Khadija was no longer on her mattress and must have gone to the bathroom. The woman looked round, and then Khadija came back into the room. I told her the woman was from the authorities.

Suddenly I was filled with fear because I remembered the new rule about children being taken away, and perhaps this woman had come to take Khadija. But she greeted Khadija in a kind way, and I stopped feeling afraid.

Khadija was dressed by then, and I saw again that she was no longer a child. The woman asked for Sarwat, and I indicated that he was out and would be back soon. She was writing things down in her notebook. Khadija stood by the window, watching us. Then I heard Sarwat coming up the stairs. He entered the room followed by Amir and another friend but stopped sharply when he saw us. He shook hands with the woman immediately, greeted Khadija briefly and told the men to go. Then he invited the woman to sit down. He ignored me.

The woman wanted to ask Khadija some questions, so Sarwat translated them. She asked if Khadija wanted to go to school, and she said yes, but she was worried because she did not know any English. Then the woman asked if she wanted to start school soon.

Sarwat said, "You don't, do you? You want to settle in here first, don't you?"

Khadija hesitated, then said yes, she wanted to settle in.

At last the woman stood up and said goodbye to us and Sarwat went downstairs with her. Khadija was quiet, unlike the day before when she had talked and talked and I had suddenly remembered how women could chatter all day.

When Sarwat came back upstairs he was angry.

"Why did you let her in?"

I told him she had wanted to see Khadija.

"You should not have let her in unless I was here."

I asked him why not, and he explained that it was important to keep on the right side of the officials, and if we did not they could stop giving us money. When I asked why they would stop the money if we were not doing anything wrong, he spoke again in that sharp tone that reminded me of my brother, saying that some of them did not really want to help us, they kept changing the rules and I should never let anyone into the house unless he was there. He asked if I had forgotten that soon he would have to go to a court to try and persuade the authorities to let him stay in England.

"And now that Saddam is not in power they could say it is quite safe for me to go back to Iraq." He shouted at me, "Can't you see what a difficult situation we are in? Aren't I speaking clearly enough?"

I was sorry Khadija was witnessing her cousin speaking to me in that way. It is bad for a girl to see or hear something that is not right. I said I feared the woman had come to take Khadija away, and Sarwat said I was right to be afraid, because it was never possible to know exactly how things were.

"That is why it is so difficult for us. They keep talking about changing the laws so we are never sure what we can or cannot do. People spread stories and even the good people who help us are sometimes muddled themselves."

There was no point in saying anything else. My stomach was hurting, and I wanted to lie down and sleep but I could not, because I had to look after Khadija. That responsibility was worrying me more and more. And so was the fact that I was getting old, and I was very anxious also about my bleeding. It could not be good to bleed from the gut. I knew something must be wrong with me.

Then Sarwat went to his room and changed his clothes and smoked one of his scented cigarettes. When he came back he was no longer angry and he began to talk to Khadija quietly. Then he showed her where the food was kept, and they began to prepare something to eat. Soon, I heard them laughing. I relaxed a little. My stomach stopped hurting.

I dozed off until they came in with a tray of food. Sarwat gave me a plate with bread, onions, tomatoes. He held out a plastic container towards me. Inside there was something chopped up in a white sauce which he said was vegetables, but I did not take any. He persuaded Khadija to try some. When her expression showed that she did not like it, we all laughed, and it was good to laugh together.

Later that day Khadija stood by the window again, looking at the street below, at the sea opposite. I asked her if she wanted to go outside, because I thought I could walk with her for a while.

Before she could answer Sarwat said, "No. You are not to go out until I take you. You need to be careful out there."

I asked him what he meant, because the town did not seem dangerous to me.

"I know, but it could be for a young girl like Khadija. I can look after her, but you are too old."

Khadija looked at him and then at me. She said, "I would like to go out."

"Yes, but you must only go if I take you, at least to begin with."

"Grandfather will look after me, I know. He looked after me in the camp. He's looked after me for almost all my life."

"Khadija. Listen to me. I have lived here for two years. This is not the camp – it is England. I know what it is like. You must do as I say because English men can be dangerous. The newspapers are full of stories of how they hurt women and children – even the ones in their own families."

Khadija turned away from us both and stared out to sea again. She stayed like that until it became dark. She was completely still. I had never seen her – or any young person – be so still. It worried me, so, after ten minutes, I encouraged her to come and sit down. I drew the curtains and she walked across the room to the settee. I asked if she wanted to watch the television, but she didn't. She sat quietly, and after a few minutes I realised she was asleep. That was good, for sleep would help to heal her. I prayed to the Lord of the Two Worlds to keep her safe.

♪

He had booked the concert weeks ago. The words *Concert, Snape 1pm* had sat there amongst the many spaces in his diary, getting nearer and nearer, and now the day had arrived. After a gloomy start as he drove down the A146 towards Beccles, the sky brightened when he entered Suffolk and headed for the coast. He listened first to the News and then to a programme of guitar music.

Since Estelle's death he had been to several concerts on his own, all in or near Norwich. Snape was out of his usual territory but Britten's *Metamorphoses* was the most marvellous piece of music – evocative and poignant and well worth travelling for. The oboist, like all the musicians in the concert, was a student from the Berlin Musikhochschule and Richard was confident he would give a sound performance. He had first heard the *Metamorphoses* soon after starting his training as an architect. Since then he had heard it live only twice, the last time seven or eight years ago at a festival of modern music in Oslo.

He slowed down behind a tractor. Mud was spewing off its wheels and its trailer was piled up with sugar beet. No need to hurry. Even if he was stuck behind it for a couple of miles there would be masses of time for a wander around as well as a pint and a sandwich at The Plough and Sail.

His eye noted movement to his right. Three deer had paused in their run across a field green with winter wheat. They were all facing the same way, their heads raised slightly upwards. Beautiful creatures. Seeing them made him want to go for a walk. He hadn't been on a decent walk for ages.

The tractor pulled in to a lay-by to let him and the line of cars behind go past, and within a few minutes he reached the A12 and headed south. He looked forward to seeing the church at Blythburgh, one of Estelle's favourite buildings. And there it was – facing the marshes and mudflats of the wide Blythe estuary on his left. Perhaps he'd stop there on the way home, but he had not visited it since her death. What would it be like without her? There would be no one with whom to look at the carvings of the deadly sins on the bench ends, or inspect the devil's fingerprints, or climb up to the peaceful Priest's Room.

He came to the turn-off to Aldeburgh and Snape, indicated left and followed the road until he saw Snape church, and then turned right to Snape itself. He drove slowly, enjoying the approach to the Maltings.

There were the masts standing up from boats on the River Alde which he could not yet see. He would have paused on the bridge if there hadn't been a truck right on his tail. As he drove into the car park the pub looked different from last time, but they were always changing something. Benjamin Britten would be amazed if he could see what had been done since the first Aldeburgh Music Festival in 1948.

The concert was not for well over an hour, so he walked round to the front of the Maltings, and then along the quayside.

How did these boats - these ships - ever turn round and go downstream? Then he noticed a foot of wet, green weed on the brickwork. Twice a day or so the high tide must reach up and widen and deepen the river.

He walked along a muddy path right round through the reeds behind the concert hall at the back of the Maltings to the Barbara Hepworth sculptures. Estelle had not liked this *Family of Man* group at first, but it had grown on her. Then, as he headed back past the rehearsal rooms, along the rear of the building and up the steps to reach the Henry Moore, he came across the new sculpture he had read about: *Migrant.* Two bronze shapes that gave the impression of birds in flight stood in a rather murky channel, their leg-like supports bolted solidly into a concrete base.

He looked above and beyond them and the wide reedbeds to a flock of white birds rising up from what looked like a lake set amongst fields but he knew was a meander of the Alde. Estelle would have known what they were. They swept right across the middle distance, disappearing beyond a wood.

He moved on towards the Henry Moore where a notice stated it had been removed for an exhibition. Quite unexpectedly he felt let down.

The Plough and Sail was not at all as he remembered, for it was very modern and light now, and too crowded. Just about every table and stool seemed to be taken. Feeling in the way, he decided to go to the Oyster Bar in the Maltings. It was much better up there, and he bought a salad and a pint of one of his favourite beers. He carried them to a table by the window and had his meal looking out on the marshes.

What an amazing place this was. Immediately in front were the reedbeds, their pale brown fronds waving against a watery blue sky with a bunch of puffy clouds approaching from the north. The distant church at Iken was straight ahead, and to his right stood the *Family of Man*. And only twenty or thirty yards behind him was the concert hall.

Two couples joined him at the table. The bar became more crowded and the level of conversation rose. Then a man walked the length of the bar, ringing a school bell to announce that the concert was to begin.

He suddenly missed Estelle badly. He wanted her beside him and enjoying the surroundings with him. He wanted her to stand up with him, take his arm as she liked to on such occasions, and amble along with him to find their seats. He made himself get up and move towards the hall, then settle himself in his seat to read the programme leaflet. The first item was a Scarlatti keyboard sonata, then it was the *Six Metamorphoses*. Then came a sonata by Malcolm Arnold, and this was to be followed by Bach's *Sonata in G Minor for oboe and continuo.*

He read:

When Pan
thought he had captured her, he held instead
only the tall marsh reeds, and, while he sighed,
the soft wind stirring in the reeds sent forth
a thin and plaintive sound, and he, entranced
by this new music and its witching tones
cried, "You and I shall stay in unison!"
and waxed together reeds of different lengths
and made the pipes that keep his darling's name.

From Metamorphoses, Book 1, by Ovid

On the facing page were detailed notes:

Six Metamorphoses after Ovid, Opus 49 for oboe
Benjamin Britten

The six movements portray well-known characters from classical mythology immortalised in the Latin of Ovid's Metamorphoses.

Pan *who played upon the reed pipe which was Syrinx, his beloved.*

Phaeton *who rode upon the chariot of the sun for one day and was hurled into the river Padus by a thunderbolt.*

Niobe *who, lamenting the death of her fourteen children, was turned into a stone.*

Bacchus *at whose feasts is heard the noise of gaggling women's tattling tongues and shouting of boys.*

Narcissus *who fell in love with his own image and became a flower.*

Arethusa *who, flying from the love of Alpheus, the river god, was turned into a fountain.*

THURSDAY 14 JUNE

CAMBRIDGE UNIVERSITY MADRIGAL SOCIETY

IN THE PARISH CHURCH AT 11 A.M.

Conductor: BORIS ORD

The programme will include works by John Shepherd, Orlando Gibbons, S. S. Wesley, and Benjamin Britten's *Hymn to Saint Cecilia* (words by W. H. Auden)

ON THE MEARE, THORPENESS, 4.30 – 5.30 P.M.
(*weather permitting, otherwise in the Workmen's Hall*)

The CAMBRIDGE MADRIGAL SOCIETY (conductor: BORIS ORD) will sing madrigals, Jacobean part-songs, early twentieth-century and contemporary music.

JOY BOUGHTON (*oboe*)

will include a new work by Benjamin Britten, specially written for this occasion.

The leaflet included a facsimile of the programme of the concert in 1951 when the *Metamorphoses* was first performed, although at that time it was referred to only as "a new work". He also read notes explaining that the intention was that the oboist would be on a raft, and although this had not actually happened, a gust of wind had blown Britten's manuscript copy into the water. And on the following day, Friday June 15th, also as part of the Festival, there was to be a film – *Minsmere Nature Reserve and the Avocet*, with a commentary by Brigadier H. N. Stanford, C.B.E., M.C.

God, how he would have loved to tell Estelle about all this.

A couple sat down next to him, and the seat on his other side was empty. He hoped whoever it belonged to would come soon for he hated being disturbed in the last few minutes. And then it was too late because the lights dimmed, the harpsichordist came on, the audience applauded. Then there was that wonderful moment while everyone waited.

The harpsichordist wore a fitted red velvet dress with red shoes, and her fair hair was short and boyish. As she turned towards the keyboard, she bent her long pale neck. When she drew back from it she raised her head and the smooth folds of her dress rearranged themselves.

It was gorgeous music. It was so lyrical, so gentle. It was over too soon, and the musician stood up and bowed to the audience. On her second bow, as she walked forward, she gave a special smile to a couple in the row in front of him. Richard felt sure that they must be her parents. What pride they must have felt.

While the harpsichord was being moved he looked round to see if any latecomers were being admitted. With all the willpower he could muster, he reached out to Estelle and urged her to appear from wherever she was and sit in the empty place next to him.

The oboist came to the front and the hall was silent again, and Richard waited for the first notes. The sound of the unaccompanied oboe reached into him. He listened to its quiet insistence, its echoes, its plaintiveness. He listened to the little runs and to the held, clear notes. He was close enough to hear the closing of stops, the intake of breath and to see the oboist's shoulders move, his arms rise, his slight lifting and lowering of the instrument.

And then it was over, and he became conscious again of Estelle, the empty place next to him, the concert hall, the audience – he recalled everything.

During the applause he suddenly decided he could not stay. He could not take any more – not any more music and not any more sitting next to an empty place. He hardly thought about what he would miss for he had heard what he had come for. While things were being moved on the stage he took his coat and left the auditorium. Outside it had become overcast and dark although it was still early.

He set off home. He did not put on any music because he did not want to dispel what Britten and the oboist had created. To prevent himself from thinking about Estelle he made himself concentrate on the Greek gods and their complicated, tragic love stories. He tried to go through each character.

Pan. Poor Pan. He loved Syrinx but she did not love him and threw herself into the river to avoid him. What was it about Pan that was so awful?

Narcissus. Who was it who turned him into a flower? And Arethusa. Why was she so keen to avoid the River God?

It was Niobe whom he thought about most. He was not sure why or how she had lost fourteen children - fourteen! No wonder she wept. Was losing all those children not punishment enough for whatever it was she had done? Was it necessary for her also to be turned into a stone?

And what was it about metamorphosis that had inspired Britten to compose this opus? It was pretty miserable stuff, but at least the music was more about love and loss than anger and punishment. It seemed very cruel that Pan and the River God should punish those they loved for not loving them back. But perhaps turning them into something else was better than killing them. Metamorphosis was change, not death, not the end of life.

What might Estelle have been if she had been changed into something else? A tree, probably. Something like a birch. No, a bird, of course she'd be a bird. A swift? No, too fast. What then? A blackbird. Yes, a glossy garden blackbird singing from the top of a lilac bush, even if it was only the males which did that.

Richard soon found himself slowing down for the level crossing at Darsham. And there was Blythburgh again. A slow line of cars in front made him decide to turn in and visit it.

When he walked through the huge doorway of the vast church he felt what they always felt there: delight in the open airiness of it, in its spacious space. He looked up to the marvellous hammerbeam roof. He walked along the ends of the pews to find the small carving of Gluttony, and stroked his smooth, fat paunch as they did on every visit.

When were they last here? It must have been before they moved. He looked up to the angels, for Estelle had particularly loved the angels. It was both easy and impossible to think that about two years ago she was actually here, standing beside him and looking up with him.

The church was almost empty apart from a couple he guessed must be in their twenties who were walking around slowly, hand in hand. The girl kept stopping the boy to point something out to him, and they would talk about whatever it was, and then move on. Had he and Estelle been like that when they were young? He rather thought they might have been. The couple were both dark-haired, as he and Estelle used to be. So, might a son or daughter of theirs have looked like this young woman or this young man?

He went outside again. He got into the car telling himself that she couldn't come back and wouldn't come back. He suddenly felt sorry for himself – sorry for being left on his own, for having to go to concerts and to favourite places on his own. He sat in the car and held tightly onto the steering wheel.

He set off again as the light was beginning to go and soon came back to thinking about children. It was not just that he and Estelle had had none, but that his family would not continue. Earlier in his life that had not mattered, but recently it had. His older brother Ian had married and had a daughter, but the marriage did not last when he and his wife moved to Canada, and Ian's contact with his daughter was almost non-existent. How had he let that happen? How could he have let her go?

Two deer suddenly raced from the verge into the road. The first, a big one, was followed by a younger one and they bounded across straight in front of the bonnet, fright showing in their eyes and the flank of the second one bright and close in the headlights. He braked hard, then drove on more slowly knowing they could easily have been killed, or at least injured, as he could have been. It was mere luck that had saved them all.

Back at home, he sat down with the paper and a cup of tea. He found it hard to remember all the feelings he had had at the concert and on the way home. Musically, the Britten had exceeded his expectations and nourished him, but in terms of thinking about Estelle it had been a particularly bad day.

It was strange, he thought, how he was beginning to think more and more about the children they had not had.

I was not sure about Sarwat. I liked him when I first met him but he could change and I could not tell whether he would be nice or not. That first evening, when he showed me the things in the kitchen, we were laughing when he explained how the cooker didn't work properly. It had four black plates that were supposed to get hot when you turned some switches, but you could only have two of them on at once. Sarwat said he had asked a man who used to make cookers in Kabul to try to mend it.

When Sarwat argued with Grandfather I was embarrassed. I was surprised that Grandfather did not tell him to stop behaving like that, but he seemed to accept it. No one in the camp would have dared speak to him in that way. He was looking ill and old, and he *was* ill and old. I watched him doing up the buttons on his shirt one morning and they seemed to be too difficult for him. I asked if he could see the buttons properly, because I knew he needed glasses, but he told me he could see things that were close and what he could not see were things in the distance. It was his fingers, he said, that were clumsy.

I should have asked Sarwat to take him to a doctor and get him some glasses, but I thought he might be angry with me.

When the Authority woman came Sarwat was very polite, but when two of his friends came here the next night I found out he had lied to her. It was late and Grandfather was asleep and they thought I was asleep too, but I wasn't. Sarwat said he was being given money for me, but the Authority woman had told him I must have a room of my own and he told her I could have his. But he told his friends he was not going to move out of his room for me. He also complained about Grandfather letting the woman in, and called him a fool. Then I heard him say that I would be going to school soon, and he was going to get me to do some of the jobs like cooking and cleaning. I have not cooked anything since I was in the camp, so I was pleased about that.

Sometimes he was quite kind to me. One day he took me out to a huge shop where I saw more to buy than I have ever seen. It was like a giant market and there was enough food to feed everyone, but even when people bought some of it and put it in their carts, and the pile of bananas, or tins, or bread or whatever it was got less, the shop workers came with more food to pile it up again. Sarwat said that in our town there were more shops like this. I did not know why there was so much food in one town, or where it all came from, or how it all got eaten.

And no one was *selling* food. People just took what they wanted, and then they paid for everything at once, before they left. They must have had a great deal of money because their carts were often completely full, as if they were buying food for a whole year.

This was not the only strange thing I saw in that shop. I saw a boy, he must have been about eight or nine like my sister Zaineb, and he wanted a certain food. I do not know what it was but he put a box in his mother's cart. She told him to put it back. He refused, so she put it back herself. Then he picked it up again and held onto it so she could not take it away. She leaned over him and spoke to him quietly but her face was very fierce so he started to cry. In the end, she pulled the box out of his hands and put it in the cart, and he stopped crying. I had never seen a child behave like that before.

Then something else happened. A little girl picked up a bag of sugar for her mother, but she dropped it and it spilt all over the floor and people could not help stepping in it. A man quickly came with a brush and pan and swept it up. I could tell he was saying that it did not matter. A whole bag of white sugar on the floor, and nobody minded!

England was not like I expected it to be, although I'm not sure exactly what I expected.

Sarwat had a lot of money. When he had pushed our cart to the place to pay, he took out his wallet and I could see lots of notes inside. I didn't know where he got them from, because he did not go out to work, and he told Grandfather the authorities did not give him much.

In the evenings he and his friends went out quite late. I didn't know where they went and because Sarwat had told me lots of times that it was dangerous in the town I asked if it was safe for *him* to go out at night, and he said yes, it was - men were safe but women were not. He said that in Moslem countries women were always safe because men looked after them properly but things were different in England. That was why I must never go out unless I was with Grandfather, and even then only during the day. He said that Grandfather was old and ill now so would not be able to protect me at night. Anyway, would I ever want to go out at night? Of course not.

I became brave and asked Sarwat to take Grandfather to a doctor but he said it would be difficult to arrange. So I decided that the next time the Authority lady came I would ask Sarwat to ask her about this. It seemed that he did not want to help Grandfather, and he should have done.

One day we were watching football on the television. Sarwat and two friends were sitting on the settee, which meant there was no room for Grandfather. He was sitting on a hard, upright chair which was a shame because he usually liked to snooze in the afternoons. I was sitting crosslegged on the carpet, leaning against the end of the settee. Amir, who was Iraqi but spoke a little differently from us, asked if I minded if he stretched his long legs out next to me, and I didn't. He was always nice to me and Grandfather and he often joked with us. We all liked him.

The men groaned and cheered and held their breath and sighed with relief as the game went on. Grandfather was watching too, but he did not react as they did. Then one side scored a goal and the three of them jumped up shouting. Sarwat went into the kitchen and brought out some cans, and they pulled the cans open and drank the drink inside. I knew it was alcohol because I had smelled it before. I could tell Grandfather was unhappy they were drinking it, and especially that they were drinking it in front of me. Sarwat did not offer Grandfather a can, but of course he would not have touched it.

Then there was an argument on the pitch, and Sarwat and Amir and Hassan started discussing the players and the referee. Hassan asked if there was any more beer, but Sarwat told him no, it was for later. Grandfather had his eyes shut but I did not think he was asleep because he looked so awkward on that chair. I did not think he could be praying either, not with all that noise. Then I saw he was holding his beads and moving them slowly.

Soon it was half-time and the men calmed down. Amir asked when I was going to school, and I said I didn't know. He told me it would be good for me to learn English, and said he knew a lot of English already and he was getting his papers ready so he could go to Norwich to study. He said Norwich was near and he would go there each day. It was bigger than Great Yarmouth and had a university, and he was going to study law because laws were important. When I asked him what new laws he wanted to make, he laughed and told me that lawyers did not make laws, but they made sure that people were protected by them and that trials were fair. He said that some men who are rich and have a lot of power break the laws or take no notice of them to make sure they stay rich and powerful – like Saddam – and that was wrong, because it means that many people suffer. Although I did not understand everything he said, I thought he would be a very good lawyer.

At last the game was over. Amir and the other friends left and Sarwat told me to come into the kitchen to prepare some food. We cooked some rice and green vegetables, and when I took the cooked lamb out of the fridge I found more beer cans at the back. We took the food into the main room. When I passed Grandfather his plate I noticed his hands were shaking. I asked if he was all right, and he said he was not. He said, quite loudly for him, that he was ill and must see a doctor. He said his belly ached and he was not digesting his food properly. For once Sarwat listened to him, and said he would find a doctor the next day. I felt much better when I heard this, and Grandfather did too, for he ate a little before he went back to the settee. I made some tea and took it to him, and his hands had stopped shaking, but I knew he was still very angry with Sarwat for drinking alcohol and not respecting his wishes.

Much later on, in the middle of the night, I woke up because there was a noise in the street. I looked out of the window and saw Sarwat and Hassan getting out of a taxi. They paid the driver and then they shouted something to someone who was still inside the car. They came across the road and I was back under my blanket by the time they came upstairs.

They started smoking in the kitchen and I could hear what they said. Sarwat had just met an English girl he thought was very beautiful, and Hassan thought so too. He wanted to see her again and was hoping she would be in the same place the following week. Then Hassan started talking about another girl. She worked in a shop and he had gone there several times to buy things he did not need so he could see her. He began to say bad things about her, talking about her body in a wrong way. He said he could not help thinking about her breasts because she wore tight clothes like all the English girls.

Sarwat said it was not easy having Grandfather and me here all the time, even though he got money for us, and Hassan said he wished his family were in England because he was so worried about what was happening to them at home. He said, "At least you have someone from your family here. I do not, and I do not know if my parents or my brothers and sisters are alive. You are lucky."

And Sarwat said he knew he was lucky but he wished he had a job and a better place for us all to live, and he wanted the date for his appeal to be decided so he could plan his future.

Hassan replied, "Amir has been given indefinite leave to remain because his family is one of the families whose applications were delayed. So it's all down to luck, isn't it?"

"Amir is the luckiest man I know. Things always seem to go well for him." Sarwat was speaking in what Grandfather calls his knife voice.

I heard them opening the fridge and taking out some cans. They had been smoking for an hour and must have changed from one brand to another because now the smoke had a different smell.

Then Sarwat said he was surprised when I arrived. He had expected me to be younger. He said I would be going to school soon because unless I learned English I would be completely lost. And then he said he would always have to look after me, because Grandfather was so old and ill that he would probably die soon.

I froze when I heard this. I had never thought about Grandfather dying. I knew he was old and ill, but I did not think he was going to die, not for a long time. Even though he had just said he was lucky to have his family here, Sarwat then said Grandfather had been too old to make the journey, so no wonder he was ill. He should have stayed where he was, and even if he had come he should not have brought me. And then he said, "What can Khadija's future be here, in a place where women don't know how to behave?"

Was it going to be as bad as that? Was it going to be difficult forever? Was Grandfather going to die soon?

I moved out of myself. I rose up to the ceiling and looked down beneath me. Grandfather was lying on his back, stretched out on the settee. Perhaps he would look like that when he was dead. I saw myself lying next to him under my blue blanket, and I could see the shape of my shoulder, my hip, my leg, my foot. I saw Grandfather's two white shoes and my two brown shoes in between the settee and the mattress. I saw his beads on the little table beside him.

The first thing I reached for each morning was my beads. They helped me lose the pricking feeling in my fingers and they helped my spirit begin the day. My fingers knew their smooth shapes, knew the slight clicks they made against each other.

I was thinking back to the previous day when Sarwat drank beer with his friends. He took no notice of me when he should have done, but the more upset I felt the less I was able to do anything. I was angry because he went against the teachings and he did so in front of Khadija. She was not a child any more and was well aware of what he was doing. I did not know what to do except pray. I wished Sarwat would join me in prayer, but he would not. He thought I was too old, or at least too old for this new life.

Khadija was waking up. I heard her stretching, and then I heard her sigh. A young person should not sigh like that. Sighs are a sign of pain, of hopelessness. I reached out and touched her arm, and asked if she slept well, and she told me she had. I asked if Sarwat woke her when he returned home, but she said he must have come in quietly. I was glad, because he had wakened me twice recently and I had heard him speaking bad things. He did not care about the right ways, and I did not want Khadija to hear him when he was like that.

Then I turned away while Khadija slipped on her shoes and took her clothes to the bathroom. She was going to wash, dress and then make tea. She had been washing my clothes for me, and cleaning. She was such a good girl. I hoped Sarwat would take her to buy food again because when she came back last time she talked and talked about what she had seen – the dozens of loaves of bread, the shelves full of bottles, the piles of fruit and vegetables, the red meat wrapped in plastic, the fish lying on piles of ice. She was so alive as she told me and it was good to see her chattering in the way women do.

We passed the morning together and at midday Sarwat arrived back saying he had found a doctor who would see me that afternoon. He said a new clinic had been opened where refugees could get help. He did not know if there would be an interpreter but he promised to translate for me if necessary. Sarwat could be a good man when he wanted. Khadija was pleased too and she was going to come with us.

When we had eaten we put our coats on, for it was cold outside. Khadija was wearing a coat with a fur hood and she had her red gloves. I tried to do up the zip on my jacket, but found it awkward. Khadija saw me struggling and said, "I'll do it, Grandfather." She pulled off her gloves and I held them while she bent her head to do the zip. I looked down at the back of her neck and her dark hair and thought that before long she would be as tall as I was.

It did not take long to reach the clinic. Sarwat gave a small plastic card to someone behind a desk, and they checked it, gave it back and told us to go through to another room where Sarwat said we might have to wait for hours. Apart from when I was in London, the last time I saw a doctor was about ten years ago, after a dog bit my leg, and I had waited for hours then. But now, unexpectedly, my name was called almost at once so Sarwat and I went to the doctor's room, and Khadija stayed behind.

There was no interpreter, and the first thing the doctor did was to ask me my family name. I told him and then he and Sarwat talked and it felt to me as if something was wrong, almost as if they were arguing. They said my name several times. Sarwat took out my card again and showed it to the doctor who looked at it carefully, then shrugged his shoulders.

Then he asked Sarwat about me, and how long I'd had the pains, and if I had lost much weight. How much did I smoke? Were my bowels regular? How long did the stomach aches last? How long did the headaches last? He took my temperature and felt my pulse, he held things against my chest and back, and he made me lie down so he could press my stomach. Then he shone a torch into my mouth and poked inside in just the same way as that doctor on the television had done to Saddam.

I asked Sarwat if he had told the doctor that I sometimes bled from inside myself. He had not, so he did so and then there were more questions. How often had this happened? When had I first noticed it? Was it painful?

I did not like to talk about these things even though I was worried about them. While the doctor was writing things down I wondered if I should also tell him about the feelings in my finger tips, but then he stood up and gave Sarwat the piece of paper he had written on, and we went out.

We had been told we could get my medicine here in the clinic so we took the paper to a counter. Sarwat told me the doctor had not given my illness a name but said that the pills and the medicine we were getting would help me.

He said the doctor had noticed that the name on my card did not match what I said my name was, and that was true, but only because my given and my family names were put down in the wrong order. Also, I had told him all three of my names but only two were on the card. The doctor said I should have had it changed, and Sarwat told him that I could not read Arabic, let alone English, and to try to get something like that changed was impossible. It was better just to live with it, even though it was not the exact truth. Sarwat said that it must have been the first time that doctor had worked with people like us, or he would have known that.

There were two women in the waiting room who did not stop talking for one moment. I had never heard their language before. And then a man came in with his wife and a tiny baby which could not be comforted. Every now and then the man spoke urgently to his wife in a low voice. They were both very frightened and this was sad to see. So I shut my eyes, and the baby's cry reminded me of the cry of my own first born when he wanted milk. I had not thought of that for many, many years.

After a little Sarwat was called to collect the medicine and I suddenly felt grateful to him. Even if some things were difficult he was looking after us, and now he had in his hand a paper bag containing the box of pills and bottle of medicine I needed. I was feeling better already.

But four hours later, in the evening, I was bad again. Sarwat had told me to take two pills from the packet with a drink of water, and to swallow a small spoonful of a whitish liquid. I did as he said. I did not know what these medicines were supposed to do, but I felt hot for an hour and then cold, and my belly was tight.

Then he went out and Khadija made me tea. She seemed very worried about me. This was strange, for usually, although she was always caring if I was in pain, she would just be calm and quiet. But this evening she brought me so many drinks of tea and water that I could not drink them all, and she covered me with a blanket, and asked if I wanted the television on, or off, or on again.

I felt exhausted and could hardly respond to her. My eyes

were closed but I knew she was sitting near me. She would make a good wife, a good mother. I tried to pray, but it was difficult. My mind would not obey me.

♪

Richard arrived too early. He was often too early these days, he had noticed. It was not that he had ever been late for things, but here he was, turning up nearly twenty minutes too soon again. The doors were not even open yet. As before, he stayed in the car and listened to the radio. After a while the organiser arrived and then various other course members he recognised began to turn up.

At seven-twenty he went in. About twelve people were already seated and he hung his coat over the back of the chair half-way down the hall. As others drifted in a woman in a suit was taking papers out of a briefcase. She must be the speaker. He looked at the leaflet again. Today's title was *The Fabric of Norwich – a portrait of Norwich as seen through its textile industry*. It was the fourth of a series about the history of Norwich and Norfolk. Each lecture was given by someone different and he was enjoying them as much for the varying approaches of each speaker as for their subject matter. The lecture on William Kett had assumed a greater knowledge of social and political history than he possessed, but the first one had provided a good, broad brush picture of early Norfolk and its monasteries.

The other reason why he came to these lectures was because he needed "to get out and meet people". Mary and Eric had said this to him often, and although he had not agreed with them at first, he did now. Winter had stopped him gardening and he found that if he did not deliberately arrange some activity outside the house he could end up spending days sitting indoors. So, coming to the lectures was part of his strategy to cope with bereavement. And arriving too early? What did that mean? That he was eager to get out of the house and hungry for other people? Were things that bad?

According to the leaflet, this month's speaker was Eva

Thompson. Richard watched her arranging her papers, then taking off her watch and laying it on the desk.

"Good evening, everybody. Thank you for coming. I hope the title of this talk doesn't sound too dull but textile manufacturing has probably been the most important single industry in Norwich, and we know a good deal about it, and it involved a lot of people over a long period. That's why it deserves a session to itself. It would be harder to justify spending a whole evening on, say, mustard."

A smile went round the room at this reference to Colman's. Eva Thompson had a clear voice, an easy manner. He recalled from the leaflet that she was a lecturer at the University of East Anglia. Richard had toyed with the idea of doing another degree - it was history that appealed to him - but had put off making a decision until too late. Or perhaps it was too early - too soon after Estelle's death - to commit himself to something like that. Did he really want to write essays? Did he want to spend hours in a library? Probably not, and certainly not in summer when his priority was the garden. But he felt an increasing need to do something purposeful with his time. Orchestra was an established and nourishing part of his life, but was it enough to go to a concert here, a lecture there? Yes, of course it was - that was how people ran their lives - they fitted things in when they could. His way of living was no worse than anybody else's.

"... with a stark choice: to remain silent or to resist. They were in danger, and they had to act one way or another. They resisted and it was the Protestants' resistance that eventually resulted in the Dutch War of Independence, and one of the results of that war was that it led to people looking outside their own country to find somewhere they could practise their religion in safety and to make a better living for themselves and their families."

Had he missed anything crucial? He checked the time. She had only been talking for two or three minutes so he couldn't have missed much.

"... not only Norwich, but Colchester, Sandwich, Maidstone and Southampton too. And they were not just from Holland, but from Belgium also. What we know for certain is that by the middle of the sixteenth century the well-established textile industry, built on wool and worsted, was in trouble. The competition from Flanders was producing cheaper, better merchandise.

"One of the outcomes of this was that in 1565 the city authorities asked Queen Elizabeth to allow immigrant workers to settle in Norwich to give local workers a sound injection of vocational training, if you like. She agreed, and thirty Dutch weavers and their families were invited here. By 1600 there were around four-and-a-half thousand of them - making up one quarter of Norwich's population."

This was interesting. These immigrants were the Strangers of Strangers' Hall. He had not realised they had come so early. The lecturer told them how the textile trade picked up speed and then went on to talk about the negative issues surrounding the immigrants. At different times they were suspected of smuggling in radical religious tracts, of hiding weapons, of plotting against the Crown. Richard found himself becoming more interested in them than in the textile industry.

"And, if we leave work aside for a moment, they were very keen on making gardens, and many of them kept canaries. It is said that their singing could be heard above the clanking looms. They bred them and those canaries are remembered today."

Eva Thompson looked round the room hopefully. "Canaries?" she said again.

"Oh!" said a man at the back, "Norwich City Football Club?"

"That's it. It was the canaries brought from the Netherlands over four hundred years ago that gave the Norwich team their nickname. Somehow, breeding and selling canaries became closely associated with football matches. That's why the ground the club had before Carrow Road was called The Nest."

"Really?" said someone. "That's where I work! At Bertrams!"

"And - a useful fact for anyone keen on pub quizzes - the Norwich Fancy and the Crested Norwich are the names of two types of canaries."

How amazing. What lovely nuggets of information. Estelle would have been surprised by this. And so, Richard suddenly remembered, would Harriet's Adam.

It was time for the coffee break. Everyone began to make their way to the tables at the back where tea and coffee were being poured out. He picked up a cup and turned towards the couple nearest to him, telling himself that if he was supposed to be getting out and meeting people there was no point standing and drinking his coffee alone. Mingling was easy today, for everyone was talking about the lecture and the speaker was busy dealing with questions. The woman who worked at Bertrams told Richard she could not wait to tell everyone at work about why The Nest was called The Nest, and was regretting that they were soon moving to new premises.

During the break they looked at copies of documents about the Strangers and a map of old Norwich showing where the textile workers had lived. Richard was particularly struck by the fact that in one of the Books of Orders for the Dutch and Walloon Strangers there were specific Orders for the orphans and for the guardianship of the orphans. How very organised and responsible the authorities had been.

At the end of the session Eva Thompson told everyone that she came from a Dutch family which was thought to have been one of the original families. Of the several wills and other documents that had survived, one mentioned a Jacob Desmarets. Eva's maiden name had been Deswartes, which she said was supposedly a contraction of Desmarets. Once, she said, there must have been many more people with her name in Norwich, and she was proud of that connection to the past. Richard had liked the link too, and so did the others. There she was, like the Canaries and their Nest, joining the present with the past, with her family stretching back through hundreds of years.

Yes, it *was* good to go out and experience different things. He was pleased that he had gone. And he would tell Adam about the canaries.

One morning Sarwat told me we would go to the supermarket. I was ready to go early, but he went out in the morning and when he came home it was time to eat. We were having chicken again because the men he took to the food factory often paid him with chickens. When I had cleared up I wanted to go because it would soon be dark. Grandfather was right – there was hardly any daylight here. It was dark when we got up, and then, after a few hours, it was dark again. I hated it. Anyway, we were soon in the car.

We passed some groups of children who I guessed were about my age. They were all wearing similar clothes and they were going home from school. When we stopped at some traffic lights I looked at them carefully. I wondered if I would go to their school and asked Sarwat if he knew which school I would go to, but he was not sure.

I wanted to learn, but seeing those schoolchildren made me frightened. I did not have clothes like those girls' clothes, or a bag like their bags, and I had nothing to put into my bag even if I had one, and I would not be able to speak to anyone until I knew English.

"Sarwat, did you find it difficult to learn English?"

"No. It is not difficult to learn something if you really need it. I need it, and so do you. No one here will speak to you in Arabic, Khadija. You need English for your future."

We parked in the car park, and the shop was all lit up. High up on the wall there was a huge sign with green letters which must have said "Supermarket". As we got near the doors they slid apart for us which had surprised me when it first happened but I was used to it by then, and as it wasn't busy Sarwat let me wander off on my own. You could buy other things as well as food: flowers and plants, saucepans, books, toys, televisions.

While I was wandering about two girls like the ones I saw earlier in the street were looking at some necklaces and bracelets. One of them chose a necklace, and held it up against herself in front of a mirror. She and her friend put it in their basket and went to look at something else. I wondered if I would ever go shopping with a friend.

I found the place where there were clothes. I saw some that would fit me and I went close and touched them. There were skirts and trousers, and things to go on the top part of your body. And there were women's underclothes too, set out in a place where everybody could see them. Then I noticed two of the shop women watching me, so I moved away. I went on a bit further, but when I turned round I saw they were still watching me. I think they thought I was going to steal something, but I don't know why, because I was only looking at things like the other girls had been doing.

Then I met Sarwat at the place he had told me to go to and we went back to the car. Just as we were loading the bags into it a man parked nearby and called out to us. He was one of Sarwat's friends, but I had never met him before. Sarwat said he and Carl needed to talk privately for a little while, and he told me to go back into the shop on my own and to return in ten minutes. I was surprised because I could not have understood a conversation in English even if I heard every word, but it was clear he wanted me out of the way.

I left them and checked to see exactly where the car was parked, because I had been muddled before by so many rows of them. It was by the third tall post with a light at the top and next to one of the glass huts where people put the empty carts. I decided not to go back into the shop. What was the point?

I wanted to go to a different place. Each time we came here I had noticed a stretch of water across a high bank, and I wanted to walk up the bank to get a better view of it. I looked to make sure Sarwat couldn't see me and it was all right because his car was facing the other way. So I went onto the grass which was a bit slippery, and I climbed up to the top.

There, on the other side straight across from me and to the left, was a river with boats. And to the right was a bridge and beyond that was the sea. I seemed to be at the place where the river met the sea.

I had not expected this. Our flat was close to the beach and although I had not been out much and did not know my way around, I was sure we had driven away from it to get to the supermarket. I am usually good at directions. Fatima was always surprised when I knew which direction we were travelling in, even when we were somewhere we had never been before. The sea in front of me was not like the other, real sea, which Grandfather told me could be very rough. This was a calm sea.

There was a path under the bridge and I wanted to go along it, even though it was just about dark now and I was cold and Sarwat would be angry if I was late. I turned round and looked back at the car park and the supermarket. I turned once more to look at the sea. I liked it. I should have gone back then, but I walked along the path on top of the bank to where it led under the concrete bridge, and went right under the bridge. The traffic roared above and everything echoed and it reminded me of places where we had hidden and waited on the journey. It was not many metres long and when I was through it I saw the calm sea stretched out widely and shallowly over a wide area, as if someone had spilled out a huge bucket of water on flat ground and it had spread everywhere.

Then I ran back under the bridge, down the slope and to the car. Sarwat and Carl were still talking, but they stopped as I came near. Carl got out of the car slowly and looked up and down my body as I stood there waiting.

Sarwat hardly said a word to me as we drove back and I did not tell him where I had been. We went straight home and I saw I had been right about the sea. The sea – the real sea near where we lived – was quite different from the one I had just seen.

I helped carry the shopping upstairs and amongst it I found a whole box of small green bottles. Sarwat took it into his bedroom so that Grandfather did not see it. Then he went straight out again, which was unusual at that time of day. Grandfather and I ate some bread and cheese, and fruit. We had bought peaches and apricots in the shop, even though it was winter.

Grandfather did not eat much. He put on the television to see the Arabic news. There was fighting and there were explosions. Women were wailing. Men in western clothes were shaking hands with each other.

"May the Lord protect us. I do not think the world will get better. I do not think anything will get better. It will get worse." He pushed his plate away. "I am not getting better. I am getting worse." He took his beads out of his pocket and began to tell them. “Perhaps it was wrong to leave the camp. Perhaps I made the wrong decision. I asked Allah for guidance. And now – thanks be to Allah – we are safely here, but it is difficult. I did not know how difficult it would be.”

On the television men in Arabic dress were kneeling down in a mosque and Grandfather began to mumble. It did not sound like praying but he was not talking to me and I think he was talking to himself. He had not done this before.

I went out into the kitchen and washed the plates and put the food away, and then came back. Then Sarwat came in too and he looked at Grandfather and heard him mumbling.

“What’s the matter with him now?” he asked.

I said nothing because I thought he might be angry if I said he was ill or sad.

Sarwat went into his room and took off his jacket and shoes. He came back and sat down with a bottle in one hand and a bottle opener in the other. He turned up the volume on the television. He was not looking at Grandfather, but I was. His eyes were closed and he was counting his beads slowly and his lips were moving.

I could do nothing. There was nothing to do; there was nowhere to go; there was no one to talk to. I was alone. We were each alone. We three people were in that room and we were each quite separate. It was only the television which spoke. I had never, never felt like this in the camp. In the camp I had my aunt Laila and my other aunts, my sisters and my friends, and many neighbours, and Grandfather had not been ill. I had not asked to come here. I had not, I had not, I had not asked to come here, and I did not want to be here.

And so I moved out of my body. I went back to the calm sea. I settled on the edge of the bridge by the car park, and I looked down and saw myself standing on the high bank. I saw myself pull my coat tightly round me. And I thought about walking along the path that led under the bridge.

It was morning. It was still dark but I could tell it was morning because of the number of cars going past. For once, my fingers were fine. Yesterday I had believed I was sinking, losing my way. Perhaps even dying. I did not want to die in a foreign land unless it was the will of Allah. When I travelled here I was thinking about staying alive, about being safe. I was thinking about Khadija's life ahead. During all that planning and travelling I did not pay attention to the fact that I was likely to die far away from where I was born, but as time went on I found I could no longer avoid thinking about it.

Khadija was still asleep. I had been watching over her for an hour. It was late last night before Sarwat turned off the television and left us in peace. Khadija could not go to bed until he had left this room. He was so wrong not to give her his room. And now she was turning her head, and then her body moved under the blue blanket. She was awake. I said her name.

"Yes, Grandfather."

That was our pattern in the mornings. Aloud, we acknowledged each other. In silence, we greeted each other. We, an old man and a young grand-daughter had found a way to get up, get dressed and start the day together. We did not talk much, but we were aware of each other. I could feel her eyes on me when I fell into despair, and I watched her when she hid herself in stillness.

I needed to relieve myself, so I was the first to stand up. The room felt damp, and there was condensation on the windows. I felt better when I returned from the bathroom. Perhaps those medicines were working. I drew one curtain and sat by the window with my cigarette. Khadija's hair spread over the edge of the mattress and onto the carpet. For a second, I thought of my daughter's hair when she was young. She was renowned for her beautiful hair, and it was a joy to me that Khadija had the same hair.

Within a short time we were all up. Sarwat was not in the bad mood he was in last night, for he was off to see Hassan who had just had his appeal hearing. He wanted to find out as much as he could before his own hearing. He left sooner than usual, reminded me not to let anyone in and said he might be home late. I felt relief when he went.

I made myself focus on the good things. There was no blood this morning, neither on my clothes nor in the lavatory bowl – and the sun was shining. I put on a clean shirt, clean underwear and socks, then ate some bread and drank coffee.

Khadija appeared from the bathroom dressed in the same clothes that she came here in. She had little else but she needed ... what did she need? I did not know, but I thought perhaps she needed something else – some women's things. I asked if she would like to go outside with me. She was surprised and pleased that I suggested it, for she knew it was a good sign. She said yes, she would like to, and so we went down the stairs, locking the door with the key Sarwat always left on a hook in the kitchen. I walked the way I had walked before, along the street close to the sea, and Khadija began to smile and to speak of the blueness of the sea that day.

I showed her the palm tree. Unlike most of the English trees which had no leaves, it was green. It pleased yet saddened me. Khadija said nothing, but she looked at it carefully and she too wanted to touch it. Then we walked onto the pale, beautiful sand. The whole long wide beach was deserted except for us and flocks of sea birds.

I told Khadija about my café and said I would take her there, but first we walked past shops and stopped to look in the windows. There were clothes, hats, badges, flags and shelves full of toy animals. Then I saw something I did not understand – a strange shaped cup, with lumps on it. When I realised what it was meant to be I moved Khadija past it quickly. I could not imagine who would make such an obscene thing or who would buy it.

We reached the café but the man I met before was not there. This disappointed me, for I had wanted him to see Khadija and know that I have a family. There were other customers that day, but they hardly looked at us. The woman who served us did not welcome me as the man had done. I drank my weak coffee, and wished again for a cigarette, and Khadija ate one of the cakes. But then, after a while the man came in, and he remembered me at once and came to shake my hand. I was proud he greeted me like that in front of the other people. In Arabic, I told him that Khadija was my grand-daughter, and I could see he understood and thought she was a fine girl and a credit to me and my family.

When it was time to go we walked over to the counter where Khadija started to study the map that was pinned up there. The man pointed out the town we were in, and said that the city called Norwich was over to the left. He indicated the railway line and the rivers, and a sort of lake that lay inland. Khadija was interested in this because, she told me, this was the lake she had seen the other day and which she had thought was another sea. Now she understood this water was not a sea at all, although it was joined to the sea, and she pointed out to me how our town was on a piece of land that seemed to be coming away from the rest of England.

Then I offered money to the man and he took what we owed him. We shook hands again, and went out. It was not so cold that day, and we walked home by a longer way. I decided that next time I went to the café I would tell the man my name and ask him his.

When we opened the door to the flat, there was a white envelope on the mat. I took it upstairs and put the key back on the hook. I was tired by then, but my body felt better than it had done earlier. It was time to pray, and I gave thanks for my improved health and for Khadija's goodness. Soon after that I heard Sarwat's footsteps coming upstairs, and I had a sudden feeling of heaviness. He smelled of beer, but he was in a good mood.

"Here's a surprise – Chinese food! Khadija, fetch some knives and forks. We should use chopsticks, but I haven't got any."

He followed Khadija into the kitchen and I heard him unpacking things from the bag and the clattering of plates. Khadija was laughing when she came back.

"Everything is packed separately in little boxes and bags and containers. It smells different from any food I have ever had!"

It certainly did, and I could not imagine what it would taste like. Then Sarwat brought in plates piled up high, and gave me one of them.

"Is this meat? Or fish?" I asked.

"There's chicken, and lamb, and rice, and many different vegetables."

I looked closely at a piece of meat, stuck my fork into it, held it up and said, "This looks like pork."

"I don't think so," said Sarwat. "It might be beef. Yes, I remember I ordered a beef dish too."

I still thought it might be pork so I left it. But the rice was good, and so were the vegetables and sauces. Khadija was working her way through her plateful and even though I hoped she was not eating pork, I liked to see her eat well. She had definitely put on weight since she arrived here, and that was good.

Sarwat ate steadily but was not able to finish everything. He put his plate to one side and leaned back, stretching. Then he saw the letter on the table.

"When did this come?"

"This morning," said Khadija. "We found it on the mat."

He looked at the address, and opened it quickly. He looked up at me. "It's from my solicitor. She will be there at my appeal to help me. That's good news. Hassan said I would fail unless I had a lawyer."

I asked, "Is Hassan allowed to stay here now?"

"He doesn't know yet. And he told me my hearing will be difficult, even with a solicitor, and even though I can speak English. He had an interpreter, but he didn't think she said everything he said. He thought she shortened it. He said they ask many, many questions. They start with easy ones like, 'When did you come to England?' 'Who did you travel with?' But then they move to harder ones about things you can't remember like, 'Two years ago you told us the names of three men who threatened you. Now you are giving one name which is different. Why have you told us different things?' They ask why you didn't move to another part of your country if you were in danger. And they ask about your friends and family, and why you can't go back to them.

"Why do they ask these questions? Don't they see the programmes showing how dangerous Iraq still is? Hassan said that every time they found some little detail that did not match up with something else, they tried to trip him up and prove he was not telling the truth. He thinks that in the end it all comes down to whether they believe what you are saying about your own life."

Sarwat got up to fetch his cigarettes. "How can they know? They only know about the law. They don't know about fighting and mines and bribes and torture and what happens in *our* lives. They just live in their big houses and think about their money and their United Kingdom. We haven't a hope."

As he leaned over to light my cigarette I said, "Well. I pray for your success. I pray that you will be allowed to stay."

"If they refuse me indefinite leave to remain, my life is ruined. If I have to return to Iraq my life is over, and if I try to stay here illegally I shall never be able to do what I want." He tipped his head back and exhaled a cloud of smoke. "And there is news for you too, Khadija. You are to start school next week."

I could hardly believe it. I was excited and nervous at the same time. I thought it would be the real beginning of my new life in England, and then I remembered that leaving the camp in Iran had also felt like the real beginning, and so did reaching England, and so did coming to Great Yarmouth. And now I was thinking that starting school and learning English would be the real beginning!

Sarwat took me to the school the next morning for an interview. We were introduced to a man who I thought was the highest teacher in the school, the head one, though I was not sure. He asked Sarwat my age and if I had been to school before, and for how long, and whether I knew any English. He wrote everything down and he looked at me when he asked the questions so even though I could not understand him I did not feel left out. If other people in this school were as friendly as he was I would like it a lot. When we left he said goodbye to me and Sarwat made me say goodbye to him. He made me say it twice because I did not get it right the first time. I was embarrassed, but the man smiled. When we walked away Sarwat said the teacher had told him the most important things were that I should learn English and make friends, and he was sure I would do both. I felt very happy that I was going to this school.

Sarwat said that I would have a few English lessons with a special teacher, but most of them would be in ordinary lessons with English children. I thought of the girls I had seen in the school and wondered if any of them would become my friends. Sarwat told me he would drive me to school for the first week because I must not go on my own yet, and later on Grandfather could walk with me.

And then he told me that Amir went to this school last year, and it was a pity he was not still there, because he could have looked after me. When I heard this I wished the same thing too.

In the afternoon the same woman from the Authority took me into the centre of Great Yarmouth. I had not been there before and it was quite different from the part we were living in. She took me to a shop to buy some clothes. She bought me trousers, white shirts, a loose top and trousers (for sport) and socks. Then she took me to a shoe shop and bought me some black shoes and some white shoes a bit like Grandfather's. I did not expect these things. She was friendly and she talked to me in English when I tried things on and looked at myself in the mirrors. I didn't look much like me.

I needed new underclothes too. The woman must have thought of that also because she took me to a different part of the shop and told me to try on some of the underclothes. I said I did not want to but she bought them anyway. Then she took me to buy pens and pencils, and a school bag. I had never, ever been in so many shops. We found a blue bag to carry on my back, although the girls I had seen wore theirs half on and half off.

Then the woman's phone went, and while she answered it I walked on a little way and found a different sort of shop. It wasn't as smart as the other ones and it had a mixture of things in the window. No food, but clothes, books, videos like the ones

Sarwat's friends sometimes brought, pictures, and some cups and plates. It looked as if the things would be cheaper in there than in the big shops.

When we got home I tried on my new clothes and put my pencils in my new bag. Grandfather said I looked nice but his face was sad, and suddenly I felt sorry for him. Of course he wanted me to go to school, but I had only just thought about how much he would be on his own. He would hate it. I thought he was lonely in his life, and sometimes I thought he was quite lost – even more lost than I was.

I knew Khadija was excited about going to school because when she thought I was dozing she spread out all her school clothes on the carpet. First she laid out her new trousers, and then she placed a shirt above them with one sleeve stretched out and the other bent at the elbow. Then she put a sock in each shoe, and a shoe at the bottom of each trouser leg. It almost looked as if a person was lying on the floor. She fetched those red gloves she liked so much and put them in the bag and laid the bag across a sleeve, and sat down quietly on the chair by the window looking at the clothes.

Later, when I asked her if she was looking forward to going to school, she replied quietly, "Yes. But it might be difficult."

Yesterday, her last day before school, we went outside together. Even though it was raining I was going to take her along by the sea, but she said she wanted to show me the big shops. As long as we walked slowly it did not matter to me, so I let her lead the way. The shops were so hot. As we walked in a warm wind hit us. I had to take my coat off and I could not understand how other people kept theirs on. And there was music in the shops, and many smells.

Soon I wanted to go to my café, but Khadija asked if I would go into one last shop, and she took me to one which was much smaller and darker than the others, and there was no music and the smell was completely different. There were clothes hanging on rails, and piles of books, and, in one corner, some shoes. I looked at these because although my shoes were quite new they were no good in the rain. I found a pair made out of leather, and when I picked them up I saw they had been worn, and at once I realised that nothing in the shop was new. The soles were marked, but otherwise they were in good condition. And they were wide, wider than the three pairs I have had since I left Iran. That was good, for my feet are very wide. I thought that the shoes must have belonged to a man who had died soon after he had bought them.

A man came over from the counter. He could tell I was not English and invited me to try the shoes on. I sat down and took my wet ones off and when he saw my socks were wet too he signalled to me to wait. He left me for a moment and returned with a dry pair, so I took off my own socks and put his pair on, and then put the shoes on. Khadija tied the laces for me. They felt comfortable and I wanted them but did not know how much they cost. The man went to the counter and came back with a green banknote which he showed to us, and then Khadija suddenly understood him – he was telling us we needed a banknote like that one to buy the shoes. I had one brown banknote left but did not know if it was worth more or less than a green one. When I showed it to the man he laughed and held the shoes out to me, and I knew he was saying I could buy them. I pointed to his socks, still on my feet, and he waved his hand to say I could keep them, and then he gave me my old shoes and socks in a bag, and five gold-coloured coins.

We were happy as we came out of the shop, and Khadija said, "I'm beginning to understand English people even though I can't understand English. I think Sarwat is right and that learning English will not be as difficult as I think."

Later that evening I was watching television and looking at something going on in Basra, but because of my poor eyesight it was not clear what was happening. I had lived in Basra for two years after I moved away from Amara. Living there was strange because I had never been in such a big city before. I worked in the docks, unloading crates, and it came to be a time of my life when I was content.

Who were these men? Were they the sons and grandsons of men I knew? Did I lift and push crates with their fathers, their grandfathers? I must have done. They were shouting and waving their arms but I did not know why. They were thousands of miles away, yet I wanted to find a face that would remind me of someone I once knew, or the tribe I was still part of. It was painful to watch but I could not bring myself to turn off the television in case I missed a message from my country. So I kept my eyes on the screen.

And then they were showing new banknotes without Saddam's picture. They were carting off the old ones because they were no use any more. Things had changed.

The next day Richard found Seville oranges in the market. How many should be buy? Two pounds – or two kilos? Or ten? He plucked a figure out of the air – five kilos. Then, when he saw the stallholder weighing them he changed his mind and asked for three. Even this meant carrying two bulky bags all the way home and he was glad to drop them at last and rub his fingers where the handles had dug into them through his gloves.

He pulled out the recipe book again and realised he would have to return to the shops to buy two lemons and particularly sugar, because the recipe stated he needed twice as much sugar as fruit, which meant six kilos.

There was a separate paragraph about sugar:

Cane or beet sugar can be used in the form of loaf or cube sugar, or granulated sugar. Preserving sugar can be bought and gives a clear finish (important if you are entering your marmalade at the local flower show!)

He made himself go through the list of equipment line by line. He would need an orange squeezer. Yes. A plastic washing up bowl. Yes. Those waxed paper and cellophane circles. Yes, after searching in the utility room.

Twenty minutes later, after a quick trip for the sugar, everything was assembled on the kitchen table including the big steel preserving pan. All he needed now was music and an apron. He found some Ravel on Radio Three, then put on the stripy apron that Estelle (who rarely wore one) had given him at a time when he had vowed to do more cooking.

Wash oranges thoroughly and put into a covered pan with water.

That was odd. He distinctly remembered he and Estelle slicing up fresh oranges. They had certainly not cooked whole oranges. He read the recipe again and saw there were several ways of doing things. You could cook the oranges and slice them when they were soft, or you could slice them first. He decided to follow the second method.

Cut or mince oranges finely, removing pips. Soak peel and pulp overnight in the water, together with the pips which should be tied in a piece of muslin.

Muslin? How had he missed this? How about the foot from a pair of Estelle's tights? He found some, cut the foot off and put it on the dresser. Later he would tie the ankle end with string. Now he was ready. He cleared a space on the table and set things out 'for ergonomic advantage', as Estelle would have said. Washed oranges to the right, chopping board straight in front, squeezer slightly to the left, a pyrex basin behind this for the pips, and the plastic bowl on the left-hand side of the table.

He held one of the oranges and looked at it closely. It was more uneven than most oranges, and the skin was rougher and less orange. Parts of it were quite green. It was completely different from an orange orange.

He sliced the first one carefully, cutting across the segments, cupping his hand round one half and pushing it down onto the squeezer. The juice ran out and he emptied it into the plastic bowl. Then, with his finger, he scraped out the pips from the bottom of the squeezer and tipped them into the pyrex basin. Next he chopped the empty hemisphere of peel into thin slices and scraped them into the big bowl with the knife. The smell was strong and when he licked some juice from his hand it made him wince. Maybe all that sugar was necessary after all.

Seville. They had been to Seville in 1992. He remembered the smooth Guadalquivir river which they had to cross to reach the Expo site, and the Alcazar built by Moors for Christian kings, and their hotel which was full of Finns.

Cut in half, squeeze, separate pips, slice, tip. It was satisfying to do such practical work. It reminded him of digging. He had dug his way through his initial grief, and now he was cutting up oranges to deal with the next stage. Perhaps he would always need things like this to get him through. Better than alcohol, anyway. He stood up straight. Now it was time to measure out the water. He converted pints to litres and realised he was going to need eight litres. He poured the sixth one in cautiously, but there was no room for any more. Never mind, he would add the rest during the cooking.

And suddenly it was Monday and I put on my new clothes. I looked in the mirror and brushed my hair. I said goodbye to Grandfather and went downstairs with Sarwat, and he drove me to school. Many children were arriving at the same time as we were and each one was dressed in black and white, as I was.

I was terrified.

Before we got out of the car Sarwat gave me some money. I did not know why I would need money in a school, but I put it in my bag with my plastic food box. He made sure I had the number of his mobile, then took me in and left me with a woman we had not seen before, saying he would come in the afternoon to collect me. Then he walked out of the door where dozens of children were coming in, and I was left behind. Although the woman was nice, I wished I wasn't with her but with the teacher I had met before.

I was feeling sick in my stomach as I followed her through

long corridors and doors that swung open, and past lots of children but not many grown-ups. I was in a sort of daze. It felt as if I would never know my way around there. She took me into a classroom full of children about my age and introduced me to the teacher. Then she left me standing by his desk, while everyone else was taking off their coats and sitting down.

The teacher called out to a girl who came over to us. He said something to her and the girl smiled and said her name – Carrion – and I said mine. She beckoned to me to sit in the place next to her, and everyone watched as I followed her, put my coat on the back of my chair as she had done, and sat down.

The class was quiet and the teacher began to talk. I had no idea what he was saying. He might have been talking about history, or geography, or science, but I couldn't tell. Then he wrote something on the board – it was a *white* board - with a thick blue pen. He wrote quite a lot of lines and they all felt the wrong way round to me. Then he told a boy to give out a pile of books. This boy looked at the name on each book and took it to the person, then suddenly he threw one to someone at the back of the room, and some of the boys laughed. The teacher was cross, but only a minute or two later the boy pretended to throw another, and more people laughed. The teacher didn't say anything.

I did not have a book at all, so Carrion went to fetch me one. Then all the class began to copy from the board or from a paper they already seemed to have. As I couldn't do either I thought I would write my name on my book, but then I was not sure whether I should because I could only write it in Arabic, so I didn't.

Things were quiet then, and the teacher walked between the rows to the back of the room. He passed me and saw that I was not writing, so he pointed to the board. I didn't know what he meant. Then he picked up my pen and made writing movements with his hand, and I knew he wanted me to copy the work too.

So I tried. It was so difficult. I tried to focus on one shape or line, but they all ran into each other. Some letters went down low, and some reached up above the others, some were curved, others were spiky. It was quite impossible. By the time the teacher told us to stop I could see that Carrion had finished, I had not done even one line. And then that lesson was over, and everyone was moving.

Carrion beckoned me to go with her and she took me into another room, where there was another teacher. I understood by then that Carrion had been told to look after me, and I was pleased or I would have been completely lost by then. Perhaps she would become my friend. This time we all had books to work from, but this writing was numbers, not letters.

The teacher came up to see me. She was a good teacher because no one was talking or moving about. I liked her and I think everyone else did too. She gave me paper to write on, and she watched as I started to copy from the book. It was much easier than copying from the board, but after a moment she stopped me and gently pointed out that I should have started on the left hand side, not the right. And then I remembered that in the last lesson I also copied from the right. That made me feel stupid, although I knew I was not stupid.

I badly wanted to go to the toilet, but didn't know what to say. Luckily we had a break next and Carrion took me along the corridor to the toilets, and I sat in the tiny room and put my head in my hands. I did not want to come out. But someone knocked on the door, so I had to. We went to a big hall where lots of children were collecting meals and eating. We just sat there and ate our food because we couldn't talk to each other. The hall was very, very noisy. Then some of her friends sat down with us. They were friendly and asked me my name and told me theirs, and I knew they were asking Carrion about me. Perhaps she was telling them about how I wrote the wrong way. I didn't know, but anyway, soon they were just talking to each other. One of them had a magazine and they passed it round, taking turns to read it.

Then Carrion took me to a classroom where there were only a few other children, and I realised they were not English. There were four of them, and they were lucky because they could speak to each other in their own language. I wished so very much that I had someone to talk to in my language.

Khadija Khadija

Khadija Khadija

Khadija Khadija

Khadija Khadija

Khadija Khadija

The teacher asked us our names, and where we had come from. I had never heard of the country where the others were from. Then she showed us cards with pictures on, and we learned the names of some things – dog, baby, tree, house, ship; and then we practised saying 'Hallo' and 'Good morning' and 'Goodbye'. I liked this lesson because it reminded me of Grace and I could do everything the teacher asked me to. We copied the words down into a book, and it was better than that morning because everything was quieter and slower and we only had to do one word at a time. Next, the teacher asked me to write down my name, so I did, and then she wrote it in English. It did not look like my name at all and although I knew I would have to write it like that I did not think I would learn it for a long time. But I practised it, and even after four or five tries it looked better than the first time.

Amir came to the flat after tea. It was very good to see him. We talked about the school and he said my first days would be very difficult but it would get better. He said he hated the first weeks but that gradually he began to make friends and settle in. It took him about six months before he could speak and understand English properly. Six whole months.

He told me he made friends by playing football, and that it was probably easier for boys, because they all play football. Then he talked about the teachers and said that many English children did not respect their teachers or even their parents. I could not understand this, and nor could Grandfather, but Amir said many people in England do not seem to know what respect means.

Later, I sat watching television with Grandfather because I was tired, and Amir and Sarwat went into the kitchen. I knew they were drinking beer, and they were talking very quietly. I did not think they wanted Grandfather to hear what they were saying. I thought they must have been talking about the appeal because Sarwat was really worried about it. He had phoned his solicitor that day and she had muddled him up with another Iraqi with a similar name, so he was angry and upset.

Sometimes when we were watching the News there were

pictures of Iraq. Grandfather liked to watch without any sound on, and that was what he was doing now. I used to think he was dreaming when he saw Iraq. Once, there was a film of a place where men were wearing dishdashas, and he said he wished he could still be wearing one. He did not like to watch Iraqi people getting hurt or fighting. He wanted peace in Iraq. He said unless the film showed something close up much of the screen was blurred to him, and this was all right because he had no wish to see war clearly.

When I went to bed I lay awake for a long time thinking about my day. I wished again that Amir still went to my school. Even though he had tried to encourage me, I was scared about tomorrow and next week and all the weeks of all the months it would take me to learn English. And even if I knew English, would anybody want to be my friend?

It seemed as if Carrion had lots of friends already and didn't need any more.

I was tired of hearing Sarwat talk about his appeal. Amir had recently been to a hearing with a friend, and he spent the whole afternoon with Sarwat explaining yet again what would happen when he went to his. Sarwat was convinced they would say that because Saddam was no longer in power it was no longer dangerous in Iraq. He was particularly depressed by the fact that none of his friends knew anyone whose appeal had been successful. Every single person had been refused.

Amir wanted to talk about his own hopes and plans for work and study, but Sarwat was too tied up in himself to listen, and I could see that sometimes he was jealous of Amir. He said if he was allowed to stay he would do his very best: he would work hard, start up a business, employ workers and help people. He wanted to have a sports shop, and I believed he could do this. But, if he was not allowed to stay, he said his life was over and he might as well be dead. He said he was not prepared to go on living his life in difficult circumstances.

But that is what I had done for all the years since I was young. That was the life Allah had given me, and it had value. Sarwat was wrong to say his life would be worthless. Was he thinking like that because he was young, or because he had completely lost his faith?

When I asked him what he would do if his appeal failed, he told me he would disappear and live in hiding, but Amir said that would be worse for him. Sarwat did not argue with Amir, but he would have done if I had said the same thing. Then he said he would buy a false passport and go to another country. He said he felt like a rat in a trap.

I did not dare say words of hope to him for only Allah knew what would happen.

Then Khadija asked him about the future because she had heard the rumour that children might be taken from adults who were told to leave England but refused to go. She was worried that if Sarwat refused she might be taken away and so she asked us why the authorities wanted foreign children. Amir explained to her that they did not want the children, but they told foreigners this to make them go home.

"What will they do to the children they take?"

"They won't hurt them," he said. "They'll just keep them."

"But where will they keep them and what will happen to them?"

"They might send them to the place you were kept in before. The detention centre."

"For ever?" she asked. "Will they keep them there *for ever*?"

Neither Sarwat nor I knew how to answer her. Khadija did not say anything else after that, but it made her even more upset than she was already.

I too feared her being taken away. I feared it so much that I dared not think about it. I could not bear to lose her again.

Those first days at school tired her out. She would come home complaining that her head was ringing from hearing English all day long and from being with hundreds of people. She would curl up in the corner of the sofa and close her eyes. She looked exhausted. When we sat down to eat she said she would never be able to learn English, and she was angry with herself because Sarwat and Amir and millions of other people had learned it, and so she should be able to as well.

Then Sarwat said, "Well, let's speak English here at home, and then you will improve fast. I'll teach you some new words now." This made her get up from the table, run to the sofa and cover her face with her hands.

I tried to hide from her how much I was missing her when she was at school and how worried I was to see her like this. I could not forget that one of my main reasons for bringing her to the west was in order for her to go to a good school, so I sat down next to her and said that there was no hurry and she had plenty of time to learn English.

I could not hide from myself the fact that I did not have plenty of time. My gut was bad again.

Next day Carrion was not in her usual place. She had moved to sit next to Debbie and she looked as if she had been crying. Something had made her unhappy, and most people seemed to know about it because I could see them talking about her. I sat down in my usual place and there was a space next to me. As soon as the teacher came in I knew I was going to have another bad day. She was the most difficult teacher because she talked very quickly. It was hard to hear her words and it was impossible when she was writing on the board and had her back to us. Most teachers turned round to talk to the class but she didn't, so I was completely lost.

After this lesson I went to my special English teacher again, and we did more words. This time we learned numbers, and I liked doing that. This teacher spoke clearly, so I began to feel a bit better, and she told me I already knew more than some of the children who had been there longer than me.

At breaktime I tried to find Carrion although I thought she was supposed to find me. She was with Debbie and another friend, all holding hands and sitting close together. They didn't make room for me. Carrion was still crying but I still didn't know why. Then I saw she was holding a photograph, and I realised she must be upset about the person in the photograph. Perhaps someone was ill. And then a teacher came up and asked what the matter was. Debbie answered because Carrion was blowing her nose, and the teacher listened and looked sympathetic. I wished they could tell me what was wrong.

Then one of the other girls passed the photo to the teacher, and I got a look at it. It was a picture of Carrion with a man and a woman who I thought must be her parents and a boy I thought must be her brother. They were all sitting under a tree, and there was a dog in the photo too, and a cat. Perhaps either her mother or father was ill. Perhaps one of them was even dead, like my parents were. I knew the word for father, and I said it quietly to one of the girls. She did not answer, so I said "Mother?" Then she suddenly understood me and said, "No. The dog." I knew the word dog, but what did she mean? She pulled me away from Carrion and said, "Her dog is dead."

I understood what she said but I still did not understand why Carrion was upset. A dog had died. There were many dogs in the world and one of them had died. That was all. Dogs die all the time.

Carrion went on looking miserable all morning, and her friends went on fussing round her. But I didn't, and they looked at me strangely, as if I had done something.

In the lesson after lunchtime there was nothing to do. The teacher talked to us, then asked some questions, and then read to us. All I could understand was: "Sit down," "Be quiet" and "Stop talking." But I knew quite a lot of names by then, although when I said "Carrion" at lunchtime, two of her friends turned on me and said, "It's not Carrion, it's *Kerry Ann.*" I supposed they were cross because they were feeling sorry for Carrion – Kerry Ann – but I didn't think the way they said her name was much different from how I said it. And I could not think of one single English person who said *my* name exactly right.

So I left my body sitting there at the desk, and I moved myself to above the clock on the wall. I looked down at the back of the teacher's head, and I saw the whole class facing the front. Almost everyone was wearing dark trousers and a white shirt and a dark jumper, but each person was different. I saw myself dressed in the same clothes, those clothes I had been pleased about buying and wearing, but I was looking unhappy. My head was bent forward and I was making little marks on the book on my desk. I was writing out one of the ayyás from the Koran. My teacher in Iran would have been pleased to see how well I was doing this. There was an empty place next to me, and it felt as if there would always be an empty place next to me.

♪

Orchestra was at seven o'clock. Richard decided he should eat something before he went, so set about making cheese on toast. As he checked on the progress of the melting cheese under the grill he noticed the bag of pips still sitting in its basin. He would put it into the plastic bowl with the peel when he had eaten.

Within ten minutes he was driving into the car park of the school where they rehearsed, and drew up next to Harriet who was just getting out of her car with Norma.

"Hallo there, Richard. How are you?"

"I'm fine, thanks. God, it's cold. Come on, let's go in." He held the door open for her and Norma and followed them through to the hall. Most people were there already, taking off their coats, putting up stands, taking instruments out of cases and generally readying themselves for the Scheherazade rehearsal.

He chose a reed, and told himself he must remember to make some new ones. His clear, steady A was taken up by various instruments. Because the hall was cold it took everyone longer than usual to tune up but gradually the sounds settled down and Alan rapped the front of his stand with his baton.

"Right, everyone. I want to take this straight through from the top, movement by movement. Strings, please be careful about your entries. They need to be softer and more prompt. You're a little slow off the mark in some places."

And so they started off going right through it. It went well, and when the woodwind had a pause Richard rested the end of his oboe on his knee and watched the players opposite. He watched Harriet leaning forward with the slower music, and then gently raising her bow from the string as the violin part ended. She was wearing a red jumper and black trousers, and when she pushed her hair back he recalled how Polly had done that in just the same way. He turned back to Alan, watching for his signal to come in.

What joy it was to make music with friends. Playing an individual part to create something whole and moving, what could be better than that? It was one of the very best things in life. He used to wish that Estelle had played too, but had long ago concluded that what he shared with musicians was quite different from what he shared with her, and that he was lucky to have both. He and Estelle had once watched a family performing: the mother played the piano, the father and the elder son played the fiddle and the younger one the cello. Estelle said she thought they must be the happiest family in the world.

Then the third movement ended, and people shuffled around and rearranged their music.

As they began the fourth movement Richard went back to thinking about Estelle's comment, 'It's a pity we didn't have any children.' This had been running round inside his head. Had he misread how she felt about children? He had taken her quietness as a sign that she had accepted the way things were, but perhaps she had wanted the initiative to come from him. Could she have wanted tests and examinations and medication? Perhaps they should have done more, or perhaps he should have done more. Perhaps they should at least have done something, instead of just agreeing to what life had – or had not – presented them with.

Damn. A look from Alan told him he was late coming in. He tried to focus on the phrases and recognised that, very unusually, he was not concentrating fully this evening.

In the break Chris announced that it was his birthday the next day and he hoped people would celebrate with him, so after the rehearsal a group of them made their way to the usual pub. Richard ended up at a table with Chris, Alan and Ian and suddenly wished he had gone straight home because Ian could be so overbearing. Despite this, he settled down to enjoy his pint and after ten minutes Harriet arrived and squeezed in next to them. He had assumed she would not be coming and was pleased when she reappeared.

"I had to take Norma back and then pop home. Adam wasn't asleep, though at least he was in bed, and Polly was working on some project for school. She's far better on the computer than I am. All I can do is what I need for work, which is only wordprocessing."

"What is your work?" asked Ian.

"I work in Social Services."

"I never know exactly what they do?"

"Well, my job is mostly about linking schools and healthcare and housing needs, and at present we're focusing on travellers."

Ian leaned forward. "Why?"

"Because they're hard to reach."

"That's not surprising, is it? If they sent their children to school as we do, or made appointments to see doctors like everyone else, things would be better for them."

"It's not as simple as that."

"Then tell me," he said, sitting back, "what's so complicated about it?"

"Who'd like another drink?" asked Alan, "Harriet, what will you have?"

Richard saw Harriet look at Alan gratefully and decided to help her by changing the subject.

"I've found out something about Norwich City that I think would interest Adam."

She smiled. "Really? Good. I'm not sure that there's anything he doesn't know about them, unless it's news of a top-secret transfer. He's over the moon about them beating Ipswich 2-0."

Richard told her about the Strangers and the canaries, and it interested everyone except Ian who knew it already and said that canaries actually came from the Canary Isles. Then Harriet had to leave, and when Richard saw it was already half-past-ten, he decided to go too. They said goodbye to the others and walked out together.

"How's Polly getting on?"

"She's doing fine. She's more confident now. I think she'll pass."

"When's her exam?"

" Next Tuesday."

"Tell her I wish her luck."

"Of course I will. Oh, I've got some jam jars for you. I nearly forgot." Harriet took out a box of jars from the boot of her car.

"Just in time. I'm cooking and bottling tomorrow. Thanks a lot. I'll bring you some marmalade next time."

Richard let Harriet drive out onto the street first, and he followed her to the end of the road and then moved into his lane at the traffic lights. Harriet waved him a quick wave as she turned left and he turned right. Lucky Harriet, going home to two children.

As he opened the front door he smelled the smell of oranges. He hung up his coat and went into the kitchen. There on the table was the little basin with the bag of pips he had forgotten to put into the liquid. He lifted the tray off the plastic bowl and dropped the bag in carefully. The level of the water rose a fraction, and the submerged orange slices shifted slightly.

Amir came to our flat the next evening. He was very happy. He was usually cheerful, but that night he was laughing, and I was glad because he made Khadija smile. When she came back from school she did not say much and curled up on the sofa as she had started to do as soon as she got in. I think she even went to sleep. But when Amir arrived she recovered her usual spirits. I gave thanks for the way Amir could bring out the best in each of us. Khadija changed out of her school things and brought us some tea.

Amir announced he had some good news, and Khadija begged him to tell us. I thought she might succeed because he could hardly hold in whatever it was. She was hoping that Sarwat would hurry up and come back with the Indian food he had gone out for, and Amir refused to tell us until he returned. So she talked about school and told him about the teachers, and they agreed who the best ones were. Then they talked about how some children did not work and were rude to the teachers, but I did not believe them. Although I had never been into any school I knew that pupils were not allowed to behave badly.

Then Khadija told us about a girl in her class who was very upset because a dog had died, and Amir explained that English people keep dogs in their houses and treat them almost like children. He told her to look out in the supermarket for the rows and rows of pet food, and pet toys and pet collars. I did not know about those things, and then I remembered that in London I saw a man with a dog on a kind of rope, and the dog was wearing clothes – a sort of coat over its back. There are some strange things in this country.

When Amir asked Khadija if she had made any friends she talked fast, telling him about some girls she knew – but then her voice gradually became quieter and slower, and she said she was lonely at school. Amir listened to her carefully and said he knew how difficult it was. He told her that he used to sit in the library on his own at break time because he could look at the books and learn from them. He said he felt less alone in there and it was better than standing around in corridors while everybody rushed past with their friends. I could see Khadija was thinking about what he was saying. Amir said the most important thing was that she learned her lessons. In order to encourage her he turned to me and said, "And you agree with that, don't you? It's important that she learns English and all the other subjects and then passes exams, isn't it?" I nodded, but I was again full of doubt about whether I had done the right thing.

And then we heard Sarwat coming upstairs. I knew he would talk yet again about the appeal because it was to be held in two days. He unpacked the food in the kitchen with Khadija, and then Amir produced a bottle of wine. I was very surprised, but he said to me, "I know you don't approve of alcohol, but I have something to celebrate, and we are in England, where people drink to celebrate. Please do not be offended."

He spoke with a smile and I could not argue with him. I said,

"Years ago, when I was in Iraq and there was a wedding or something special going on, we fired shots into the air - even through the roofs! As we are here, perhaps it is better to drink wine!" We all laughed as Amir opened the bottle.

He poured out wine for himself and Sarwat and water for Khadija and I. Then he announced, "I've got a job. A real job. Not a chicken factory job."

"What is it?" asked Khadija.

"It's in a hotel. I'm going to train as a chef, in Norwich."

Sarwat congratulated him. "I hope you become the best chef in England. Instead of killing chickens, you'll be cooking them!" We chinked glasses again and drank again, and I was pleased that Sarwat was generous towards Amir at a time when he was feeling so anxious.

"I thought you wanted to be a lawyer," said Khadija.

"I do. But I can't get into university until I have more qualifications and more money. A chef can earn good money, and you can always get a job cooking. And the hours I will work in the hotel mean I can have time off in the day to go to college. I don't mind waiting before I study law, as long as I can do it in the end."

He was a very good boy, this Amir. Although he was drinking alcohol, and although he had killed chickens the wrong way and had probably eaten and would cook meat which was not halal, he would do well. I hoped Sarwat could do the same. I watched these three young people. On that evening Amir was proud, Sarwat was tense, but not as tense as I expected him to be, and Khadija was more cheerful than she had been since she had started to go to school. I counted myself lucky to be with them, and gave thanks that Allah had willed it. Then, out of respect for me, Sarwat and Amir put the cork back in the bottle of wine, though they would probably drink more when they thought I was asleep. Khadija made us tea, and we sat and watched the television news, and saw pictures of a red desert with rocks. They said it was the planet Mars.

Later on Khadija asked Amir when he would begin his new job.

"Next week. On Monday."

"And you'll go by train?"

"Oh no. It's a hotel. I have to cook breakfasts, so I shall live there. I will share a room with another kitchen worker."

"But when you were talking about university you said you would travel there each day."

"I probably would, but I must be in the hotel kitchen by six each morning, and I will often work late at night."

"So you won't be coming to see us any more?"

"Khadija," said Sarwat, "Amir's got a new job. Of course he can't see us if he's at work."

"I'll come and see you when I can." Amir stood up. "Anyway, I must go now, but I'll be back the evening after your appeal."

He said goodnight to me and to Khadija, and Sarwat went out to the top of the stairs with him. I heard Amir wishing him luck.

Khadija tidied up the things in the kitchen without saying a word and Sarwat came back into the room and pulled out the mattress for her as usual. Before long she was settled in under the covers.

I leaned over and said, "Goodnight, Khadija."

She answered me very quietly. She was sad again.

♪

Richard went through into the living room. He began to collect up all he needed to make new oboe reeds: cane, staples, thread, scraping knife, mandrel, plaque, cling film, cutting block, nail varnish. He switched on the lamp above the table and changed his glasses to the ones he used for close work. He was feeling low again and needed something to prevent him from fretting, and he was counting on reedmaking to take all his attention.

First he tied the red thread securely to the door handle. Old pieces of thread hung off it like a straggling beard of thick red and blue hair. Carefully, he carried to the table the glass of water in which the canes were soaking. Each cane was folded so it resembled a pair of tweezers that had opened up. Then he opened the box of staples – thin metal tubes fixed into pieces of cork. He chose several of the ones which had been used before and cut the old cane and twine off each of them in turn until he was left with the bare staples. Now he could begin.

He picked up the first one and pushed the spike-like mandrel into it to give him a firm grip for when he tied the cane to the staple.

He picked up the first piece of soaked cane, folded the ends towards each other so they were parallel, and placed them over the part of the tube sticking out of the cork so they enclosed it. With a ruler, he checked the distance from one end of this new reed-to-be to the other, and then turned towards the door handle. He took up the thread, held it tight and began to wind it round the lower ends of the cane, binding them to the staple. He worked towards the top of the staple, and then wound back in the other direction, keeping the winding even and straight. He bent forward to inspect the reed to ensure that the sides of the cane had closed up round the staple. All was well.

Now he looped the thread in a half hitch over the cane, looped it again, knotted it. Then he examined it. This one was fine. He removed the mandrel. So, that was the first one done.

He moved his chair back six inches and worked on: folding the wet canes, binding them to the staple, tugging the thread tight, checking them, knotting them. He ended up a couple of feet from where he had started, with the thread stretched out from the door to his new position and the reeds hanging from it like a sort of kite tail.

Then he cut them free, put a blob of nail varnish on the knots to secure the binding and laid them on the table with their still bent pale canes at one end and the ends of the brown staples at the other. He stood to stretch his back after leaning over for so long, pulled his chair up to the table and sat down again. He then took his Gregson knife, the one Estelle had given him when he retired and which - unlike his last one - was a dream to sharpen. Supporting the cane with his forefinger, he firmly scraped the bark off the reed in tiny strips, concentrating on the tip so it would be thin and flexible enough for him to cut the tip open on his cutting block. Sometimes he would leave the cane to mature until the next day, but he decided to carry on.

Once the tip was cut open, he inserted the plaque between the newly separated blades of the reed to support it while he focused on the fine work. His smaller scrapes produced shavings like thick dust and he blew this off before urging the knife carefully to create a shallow U-shaped depression at the back of the scraped part of the cane. The reed was slightly dry by then, so he put it in his mouth and moistened it. Then he concentrated on the back, sides and tip to ensure the scrape was in balance. He was careful not to take too much from the heart of the reed.

This was always a good point to reach – when from being staple and cane and twine, the item in his hand was becoming a finished reed that he could crow. He loved hearing that first sound it made, loved knowing that he had created it. Estelle had always said that opening the tip of the reed reminded her of slicing open the pages of those old, unopened books they sometimes found in second-hand shops. She used to say that cut reeds let sound out, cut pages let words out. He started on the next one, and worked on, forgetting the time.

He was on the last one already. Damn. This one was not, he could see when he inspected it, as good as he had hoped. It looked as if the sides were not completely closed. The time was getting nearer, he realised again, when he would have to buy a magnifying glass. He tore off a scrap of clingfilm and bound it around the upper part of the thread and the lower part of the cane. Then he painted it with nail varnish. With luck, that would do the job and stop it leaking. Well, he would know before long.

At last all three reeds were done. Now came the real test. He took the first one and put it to his mouth and blew. It crowed well and he was pleased. Then he tried each of the others. One was a little resistant and he scraped it again until the crow was more free. Then he placed each of them in his oboe in turn and played a scale. They were not a bad lot at all. He switched on the Seiko tuner and played an A. The central green dot glowed and the two red arrows lit up for two of the reeds. Richard adjusted the third in the oboe, pulling it out slightly. This still did not bring it into tune, and it remained sharp. Even so, two out of three was a good result. The next day he would go on blowing the third one in, in the hope that it might improve.

He tidied up his things and remembered to turn off the tuner.

He laid the new reeds safely in their box, each one in its little fold of red velvet.

The red velvet reminded him of the harpsichordist's dress at the Snape concert, and he recalled how he had longed for Estelle to appear that day. Perhaps, it suddenly occurred to him, she *had* been there – not in the empty place next to him but metamorphosed into the music itself.

Oh Christ, there she was again, coming back into his thoughts within moments of finishing a job – even while he was still doing it. He did not know whether he felt resentment or grief, but whatever it was he hated it and found himself asking, Why can't I have peace of mind? Is this going to go on and on and on? He did not know who he was addressing these questions to but heard himself saying aloud, Why won't you let me get on with my life? Go away. Go away and leave me alone.

He leaned forward and sank his head into hands. No, don't go away. I'm sorry I said that. I want you back. I want you back so much. Come back, please come back.

He pressed the heels of his hands hard against his cheek bones and looked down at the reeds in their soft red bed, at the small, bright knife.

No one will notice I've gone. I walked out next to a lorry delivering things to the kitchen. While the driver was talking I squeezed down by the side so he could not see me in his mirror. And now I'm out here, out of school. I try not to hurry too fast until I get to the end of the street, but when I reach it I don't care any more and I run.

I run and run and run. I'm running away.

Last night I could not sleep. Grandfather and Sarwat were in the kitchen, and they were talking yet again about what will happen if the appeal is refused. The truth is, they don't know. Grandfather says he does not worry about this because Allah will provide. But Sarwat is scared and angry at the same time. He said that he just needs to know one way or the other so he can get on with his life. Grandfather wants it to be over too, because Sarwat is so on edge.

I can't stop thinking about Amir. He is going away. I like him coming to see us because he is so easy to talk to. I can talk to Grandfather, but there are some things in my life he does not know about and cannot understand. He has no idea how difficult it is for me to go to school. How could he? And I can talk to Sarwat sometimes, but not when he's in a bad mood. I'm going to miss Amir so much. I shall miss laughing with him. I shall miss him sitting on the settee with his long legs stretched out and getting in the way.

This morning I felt miserable when I got to school, so I did what Amir suggested and went to the library. He is right. It is quiet there, and there are many things to look at. I got interested in some books about the moon and stars and forgot the time. Then a teacher came in and pointed to her watch, and I realised I should have been in a lesson.

I walked into the maths class late but the teacher just waved me to my seat. Debbie was still next to Kerry Ann and in the place next to me was a boy called Connor. Nobody seems to like him because there are little scabs all over his forehead and cheeks and chin. My face was like that for weeks during the journey, and I could not help it so I don't expect he can either. They all watched me walk to my place and sit down. I just opened my book and tried to listen to the teacher.

But I couldn't. My mind went off everywhere: to Amir and his new job, to Grandfather sitting at home alone, to Sarwat worrying about his appeal. And then I thought about my home in Iran, and my favourite aunt Laila who looked after me when I was little, and my other aunts, and Zaineb and my little sister Alia who must be quite big by now. And I thought about Fatima and the journey, and then I remembered Grace, and the woman with the scar on her face and only three fingers on one hand. Those were the people who were *not* with me.

I looked around the room at the people who *were* with me. There was the teacher at her desk, with a group of children round her. Some others had their heads down and were working, and some were by the bookshelves. Next to me

Connor was doing his workbook, and Debbie and Kerry Ann were whispering. I wanted to move out of myself, but I didn't. Moving out of myself makes things better for a while, but when I come back everything is the same again – nothing changes.

I decided to write down what I wanted in my life, and so I wrote: see Amir, look after Grandfather, learn English, make friends. Then I wrote down what I did not want in my life: I did not want to go to school, I did not want to be with these people, I did not want to feel the way I was feeling, I did not want to be put back in the detention centre. Then I thought about how to get the things I wanted and get away from the things I did not want.

Just at that moment the teacher called me and asked to see my work. I had not been copying anything, and there were my two lists, written in Arabic. She said something with the word 'English' in it, which must have meant, 'You're supposed to be learning English,' and she tapped her finger on my workbook. Debbie was listening, and when she got a chance she leaned over to look. Then she went back to whispering to Kerry Ann.

But I didn't care any more because, quite suddenly, I knew what I was going to do. I was going to go to Norwich. In Norwich I would find Amir, and he would be my friend and help me make other friends and help me learn English and make my life better. In just a few moments, everything seemed clearer. I would take Grandfather with me, because I couldn't leave him alone with Sarwat. And we would walk there. I remembered the map in the café exactly, and I knew we could walk to Norwich. We would follow the river from Great Yarmouth and go inland, away from the sea. If it took less than an hour in a train, it could not take long to walk there – a day or two at most – and as we have travelled across much of the world already this last bit will be easy.

And so I'm running along the street, but slowing down a bit now because I'm out of breath. I've got to sit down and make a proper plan. I'll have to explain to Grandfather what we are going to do. I'll need to collect some food and clothes, and bed-clothes too. I must remember to take Grandfather's medicine. We'll go tomorrow.

I'll need money. I still have a little of the money that Sarwat gave me for school, but I don't think it's very much because Kerry Ann said she needed some, so I gave her what she wanted. I know Grandfather has some too. And I know where there's more – in Sarwat's bedroom, under the glass dish. I'll borrow it, and pay him back later on when everything is better than it is now. I have just one day to get ready and start. This is the best chance I'll get. Tomorrow Sarwat will be leaving early to go to the appeal because it's nowhere near here, and he won't be back until late. He's already told Grandfather to walk with me to school and come and collect me. We'll be a long way away by the time Sarwat gets home. So what I have to do now is collect what we need, and hide the things somewhere, and then get back to school in time for Sarwat to pick me up. Then, as soon as he has gone in the morning, I'll tell Grandfather what we're going to do. And then we'll leave and buy the last things at the supermarket. I pray that he will be well enough to walk for a couple of days. Surely he will.

I am going back to the shop where we bought the shoes for Grandfather because I saw some thin blankets there. The ones at home are too heavy, but we must have something for the night time. I go in and see it's a different person behind the counter today. She is writing on black and white squares in a newspaper. Here are the two blankets I saw before. They'll do. Then I search amongst the men's clothes for a warm jumper for Grandfather. He has a winter jacket, but he needs more. I'll be fine because as well as my coat I have all my new school things and even a bag to carry them in. Then I notice a row of scarves hanging up. Amir has a nice scarf, and he says it keeps him very warm when it is windy, so I choose two.

While I am looking for more warm things I see a glass case full of necklaces and earrings. I must not waste time on these today, but I can't help wishing I had something pretty. And then, on top of the case I find a book of road maps, just like the one the taxi driver had. It's almost new. I turn the pages until I find the one with our part of England. Here's Great Yarmouth, here's Norwich, here's the inland sea, and here's the river we are going to follow.

I do not have enough money for everything. I look to see what the woman is doing at the counter and see she's gone out to the back. Quickly, I tear the page out, fold it and stuff it into my jacket pocket. I put the map book down again and go up to the counter just as the woman comes back. I hold out the blankets and scarves and offer money in my hand, just as Grandfather did at the café. She takes three gold-coloured and two silver-coloured coins and leaves the brown ones.

Then she reaches down for a roll of black plastic bags like the ones we put our old tins and dirty paper in and she holds it open so I can put the things inside. I go out into the street with my arms full. What I can do with this bundle? If I go home now, Sarwat might be out, and I could hide it in the flat. But he might be there. I can't be sure.

So where can I hide it?

As I stand there two men carry a cooking stove – it's a bit like ours – out of a doorway and onto the pavement. It looks new and I wonder why they are taking it out of a house. They put it down for a moment and then heave it up and over the side of one of those big metal containers for rubbish. It falls in with a crash. Why are they throwing away a shiny new cooker? Grandfather is right when he says that the people here do some strange things. Then they throw in a couple of chairs, and a lamp, and some full black plastic bags. Seeing those bags makes me realise that my bag of blankets looks like a bag of rubbish, and that if I put it somewhere out of the way, it probably won't be touched.

I decide to go to the supermarket because I dare not take these things home. I set off at once because it's quite a way, and I haven't much time. Carrying the bag in front of me is awkward, but it hides me. Tomorrow I will fold our things up carefully and pack them into my school bag so I can carry them on my back.

It takes me twenty minutes to reach the supermarket. I look round the car park but don't know where to leave the bag. Over on the far side a few trolleys are standing out in the open where people have left them. Sometimes men come and collect them, but I decide to take a chance that they won't do that this evening or tomorrow morning. I end up putting the bag right inside a trolley, so it is off the wet ground. I am glad the woman gave me a plastic bag, for I had not thought about keeping the things dry. I pray it will still be there tomorrow and race back to school. I arrive just in time, for Sarwat is not yet there and I end up waiting for him.

But then a car draws up near me and the driver calls my name. I hesitate, and the man calls me again. I go towards him slowly, and when he leans across from his seat I see it is Carl, the man I met with Sarwat at the supermarket carpark. I think he is asking if I will take something to Sarwat for him. He makes me understand that it is important and I must be sure to give it only to him. He says, "Hassan – No. Amir – No. Abbas – No. Sarwat – Yes". Then he passes me a small packet. As he hands it to me he spreads his fingers round mine and tries to pull me towards him. I snatch my hand away quickly. He calls out after me, but I don't look at him. I put the packet in my bag and walk back to where I was standing. I remember I did not like him the first time I met him.

As soon as he's gone I see Kerry Ann and Debbie. They're about to cross the road but they turn back when they see me, and I'm sure they're going to ask me where I've been. Just at that moment, Sarwat arrives and I jump into the car. To stop him asking me about school I ask him if he is ready for tomorrow. He says he heard today about a man whose solicitor did not turn up to the appeal, and someone else whose case took so long they had to stop and go back five weeks later. He says it is all a nightmare even before his case is heard. But he is pleased that the News today showed another explosion in Iraq, and more fighting, and more people injured.

He said, "They can't send me back when everyone can see how dangerous and chaotic it is, can they?"

While he's telling me this I remember I forgot to buy a jumper for Grandfather.

Then a boy riding along the pavement suddenly rides off the edge of it and there's a bump. Sarwat brakes hard and I feel my seat belt hard across my chest. He tells me to stay in the car and he gets out. The boy is older than I thought – about sixteen. He looks all right but he's shouting and pointing to his bike. The front wheel is twisted. Then a man who saw what happened comes up and all three of them talk together at once. After about five minutes, Sarwat takes some money out of his pocket and gives it to the boy. The boy does not thank him and is still looking angry but he starts half carrying, half dragging his bike back along the pavement.

Sarwat gets into the car and slams the door. "I gave him money in case he reported me to the Police. It was lucky that man turned up. He knew the boy and told him it was his fault for riding into the road without looking. He's made a deep scratch but at least there's no real damage."

Then we hear a short, sharp noise behind us. We both turn round and see a long crack across the back windscreen. Sarwat says "Shit" and "Fuck" and hits the steering wheel with his hand. Behind us the boy is standing by his bike and holding his middle finger up like I have seen boys do at school when they are being rude. Sarwat drives the rest of the way in silence and I do not dare or want to say anything. I have already decided to watch television all evening, in case he or Grandfather notice that something is different.

The evening passes quietly and at bedtime when I go into the bathroom I look in the mirror and smile to myself because I've got a plan.

♪

Harriet brings the coffee into the living room where Richard is watching the football results with Adam. Depending on what is announced, Adam gives a yelp of surprise, or a groan or a "Yesss!"

"How much longer does this last?" asks Harriet.

"Only a few more minutes. Anyway, it's not just me who wants to see the scores. Richard does too, don't you, Richard?"

Richard smiles at Harriet and says, "Uh-huh."

"See! He does!"

After ten minutes Harriet despatches Adam to get his things ready for the next day.

"Where's Polly this evening?" asks Richard.

"'Out'. That's what she tells me now when I ask."

"So where's 'Out'? Do you know?"

"Yes. To be fair, I think her saying 'Out' is a gimmick to create an effect, not to prevent me from knowing. Tonight she's with some friends watching a video – she's only in the next street. I insist on knowing where she will be and who she'll be with. She's got her mobile and she's pretty sensible, but that doesn't stop me worrying sometimes."

Richard wonders whether to ask about Polly and Adam's father. No. Not yet. There will be a better occasion. Most of his friends have not split up, but nowadays it seems to happen all the time. Anyway, Harriet appears to be coping well with the children, and they seem fine. He opens the conversation on safer ground.

"Tell me about your work."

"Well, I work with families where there's a child at risk."

"What sort of risk?"

"Of being physically abused, or sexually abused. For example, there might be a couple who have neglected a child, or one of them might have hit a baby. Our job is to pay attention to the whole family – that might include grandparents and siblings – so we can support the family and protect the child."

"Do you see them in their homes?"

"No. My job is to liaise with all the agencies involved – I spend most of my time on the phone – schools, education authorities, clinics, health visitors, foster parents. Lawyers and the courts sometimes. It's interesting."

"And you said the other night you worked with travellers."

"Yes. And that's hard."

"Harder than with other people? Why?"

"Because they don't trust gorgios."

"Gorgios?"

"People like you and me. People who live in houses."

"Are their children more at risk than anyone else's?"

"Probably not. But communicating with them is difficult so we don't know much. And because child protection is so high profile at present, one of our priorities is hard-to-reach groups like travellers."

"Are there many in Norfolk?"

"About a thousand or fifteen hundred perhaps, although it depends on who you count, and when you count them."

Adam's head appears round the door. "Mum, where are my trainers?"

"On top of the washing machine."

"They're not. I've looked."

"Sorry, Richard." Harriet gets up and goes out, leaving him sitting in the armchair finishing his coffee.

He is in a longish room with curtains almost the full length of one side. He has never seen these open as he has never been here in daylight. The piano is this end of the room and at the far end is a dining table with things piled on it, including such a permanent looking load of ironing that he thinks it can only rarely be used for meals. The settee he is on faces the piano and virtually divides the room in two. The music stand has been moved from where it was last time. A not-very-modern television and video sit in the corner together with about twenty videos. Most of their labels are written in a child's hand: Man U v Arsenal, Wolves v Newcastle, Everton v Man City.

He gets up to look at the photos on a shelf above the fireplace. There are several of Adam and Polly at different ages. There is one of a long haired woman which he takes a moment or two to realise is Harriet. She's holding a black and white cat which is just about to jump out of her arms, and she's looking a bit surprised. Here are all three of them looking very smart – the photo must have been taken at a wedding. A football trophy for the Under-11 Runner-ups stands on the mantlepiece. Things are untidy and cluttered. He sits down again, enjoying the feel of the place and hearing odd words of a conversation and then the sound of someone running downstairs.

Harriet comes back in and slips off her shoes. "They were under his bed." She settles herself back into the armchair. "So, what have you got on next week?"

What has he got on? Not much.

"A walk, I think. I haven't been for one since well before Christmas when I drove to the coast and walked in the pouring rain. I got absolutely drenched. When I got home I headed straight for a bath and a glass or two of whisky. God, it was awful."

Harriet throws her head back and laughs. "Why did you go if the weather was so bad?"

"I'm not sure really. It seems strange, but I had just decided I needed a decent walk, come what may, and I took no notice of the weather. It was stupid, because I could hardly see anything, let alone identify any birds."

"Are you a bird watcher?"

"Not really. But Estelle was, and recently I went through all her books. It's made me interested." He pauses, thinking about what it is that he means. "Before, I'd go with her because she was keen. I went along because she wanted me to, and because I liked the places we went to. But when I was looking through all her books I found myself wanting to know more about birds for me, not for her.

"Things keep changing in my head, in how I look at things. She died about eighteen, twenty months ago, and I still keep on thinking about everything. Things I haven't thought about for years. Our marriage. What we did together. Things we said and didn't say. Things I thought I was sure about."

Richard picks at a piece of fluff on his knee. "You won't want to know all this."

A door bangs at the back of the house.

"That's Polly."

They sit in silence until Polly comes into the room.

"Hi, Mum."

"Did you have a good time?"

"Yup, thanks."

"Did the exam go OK?" asks Richard.

"Yes, it did. I don't know what marks I got, but I think I passed."

Polly takes off her coat and goes back towards the hall. "I'm going to finish off that Spanish." She pulls the door to behind her.

Richard hears the hall cupboard opening and shutting, and feet running upstairs.

Harriet says, "Sorry she's a bit brusque. She's a little put out, I think."

"What do you mean?"

"By you being here. She's not used to me entertaining a man."

"Really? I'm sorry .. I didn't..."

"It doesn't matter. She'll be fine."

Richard is astonished. This is new territory. How should he respond?

Harriet carries on, "When things change, that's when you start to see the past differently."

She is sitting with her feet tucked up under her. She seems very young.

Then she says, "I've been thinking about choices. Sometimes, we don't think we've got choices when we have."

He waits.

"Polly. Polly was a mistake. We both thought we wanted to get married, and when I found out I was pregnant, that seemed to confirm it. But it shouldn't have done. We shouldn't have let it. Anthony and I were very attracted to each other, were in love, but it wasn't the right thing to get married."

"You couldn't have known that then. You can't blame yourself for that."

"I can." She pulls her knees up and hugs them. "And I do."

She has on the same red jumper and black trousers that she wore to orchestra practice, and her socks are red too, but a different red. She looks like a student.

The sound of pop music reaches them from upstairs. Harriet sighs. "She always works with music on, but it's no good her starting to finish off homework at this time."

Should he try to continue the conversation or not? He's not sure.

A door opens upstairs, making the music louder. Polly runs down and puts her head round the living room door.

"Please can you come and help? We're doing ser and estar, and I'm confused. How can there be two verbs for to be?"

"It's too late, Polly. You should have done it earlier."

"I should be off now, anyway," says Richard, standing up. "Thanks for supper."

Harriet uncurls herself and gets to her feet. "Thanks for the marmalade. We'll open it tomorrow."

He pauses in the porch, and Harriet stands in the doorway, the light behind her.

"Do you speak Spanish?"

"Yes. Part of my degree was in European Studies and I spent six months in Spain as a student."

"Where were you?"

"Seville."

"Really?" Richard smiles. "When we get a decent day, would you like to come for a walk?"

"Thanks. Yes. I'd love to."

While I'm getting the last things in the supermarket, I pray that Grandfather stays where I've left him by the trolley, and when I come out I breathe a sigh of relief and hurry to tell him we can really start now because we have everything. I've already folded the blankets and his prayer mat as small as they can go and pushed them into my school bag. His pills are in a small polythene bag in my pocket with the money and the map and the number of Sarwat's mobile, and I'm carrying a bottle of water and a bag with the food from the supermarket. And I've still got the packet Carl gave me. I didn't mean to keep it, I meant to give it to Sarwat, but because of the accident with the boy and the bike I just forgot, and now there's nothing I can do except look after it and give it to him when I see him again.

I lead the way under the bridge and Grandfather follows me.

As we come out from under it, there, to our left is the big lake. I can see now it is not a sea, because there is land ahead of us as well as on the other side. The lake is shallow and spread out but does not look as if it is going to the real sea under the bridge, which I know it does. It doesn't look as if it is going anywhere because it is completely still. Birds float on it, and some are standing in it, pecking at the mud which lies between us and the water. The mud is so wet and shiny that at first I thought it *was* water. I stand still and point out to Grandfather where we are going.

There is only room to walk singly along here and I set off in front, eager to get away from the bridge, from the supermarket, from Sarwat, from school, from the first part of my life in England. I look up to the road running over the bridge and see a big notice there. It is a road sign and I realise I can read the word Norwich on it. To go to Norwich cars must turn left – and that is the direction we are going in. It is so good to know we are going the right way.

After five minutes I hear a call and turn round. Grandfather is a long way behind. He's not keeping up with me at all. He waves at me to wait, and I do, although I'm so jumpy and excited I could run all the way to Norwich without stopping.

Behind him I see the bridge, the town's tallest buildings, a high chimney with smoke coming out. To my left there is a noisy line of cars driving away from the town. I'm not worried about being seen because it is very unlikely that anyone we know would be here. I go back along the path to Grandfather. He tells me his shoes slip on the mud and that walking is difficult on the uneven path. He doesn't want me to go too far away from him, so I slow down and keep turning round to see how far he's come. We have only been going for a very short time and he's already struggling. We walk on and my mind and body begin to calm down as I get into a rhythm. It's slippery for me too, but I know it must be harder for Grandfather, so I make myself go at his pace, make myself breathe steadily instead of fast.

I woke early this morning and got up when it was still very dark. I made tea for Sarwat and wished him luck. I felt very guilty about leaving him because it didn't feel honest. At least I did not take any of his money, because there was none there. He must have taken it all with him.

Grandfather was very confused. He took ages to get washed and dressed and to say his morning prayers. When he was properly awake and Sarwat had gone I told him what we were going to do. He did not understand, and when I told him why I wanted to go to Norwich – to get away from all this, to find Amir, to make things better than they are – he said that we must trust in Allah. I did not say another reason is that I want to look after him, because he still thinks he is looking after me.

Suddenly there's an unexpected, loud noise. It's a train, and it's on rails right next to us. There are just two carriages, and Grandfather says it's the one he came here on. And he came from Norwich, so this train must be going to Norwich. I wonder if Amir could be on this train. I want to look into its windows in case he is on it, but it is already a long way past us.

And of course I wish we were on the train. It would be much easier to get to Norwich like that, but Sarwat might go to the station and ask if we had been there, and find us and make us come back before things have had time to get better. It will only take us a day, or perhaps two, to walk there, I'm sure. Anyway, I don't have enough money for tickets.

It feels as if this is the very first time in my life that I myself have decided to do something important, and it is a good feeling, even if I am scared. I keep on walking, glad that our path is leading us the same way as the road and the railway lines because it makes me feel as if we are not completely alone, although we are really. Everything is grey or white: the sky, the water, the mud. Even the birds are grey and white. Looking far ahead I can see a faint thread of pale smoke in the sky.

Grandfather is walking with his head down because he doesn't trust the path. I wish he would go faster. I shift the bag in my arms to a different position. It is awkward rather than heavy, but we will need every single item I have packed. I made sure Grandfather put his warmest shirt on, and when I did his buttons up today I saw his ribs showing through.

And now we begin to move away from the road that's been running alongside. The road goes straight on, but our path bends left, around the side of the lake. As we get further away I can still hear the traffic roaring but gradually it's becoming quieter.

Then Grandfather calls out again. I go back twenty paces to him, and he tells me he is tired. Tired? How can he be tired? We've only just set out.

We cannot stay here, so I urge him on. I suggest he goes as far as the next place where a fence crosses our path, because there is a little ledge there to help people climb over, and he can rest on it. He doesn't say anything and keeps on going. He's looking at the ground in front of him, his head bent. I keep having to make myself slow down so I don't leave him behind. The path stretches out ahead of me and it's pulling me along. We're high up and have a good view of the green fields on our right hand side and the lake on our left.

And now we become separated from the railway line too. It goes straight on, just like the road did, and again we turn towards our left. It's getting even quieter, though I can still hear the cars, but there are different sounds now: the wind, the sucking of my shoes in the mud, birds calling.

I keep checking to see if anyone else is on the path, either in front of us or behind us, but there's no one, even though the path has many footprints from shoes and from what I think must be dogs' paws. These prints look quite new, and this worries me. When we reach the next place to climb over the fence I'm over in a moment and going on, but Grandfather calls me back and reminds me that this is where I said he could rest. The ledge is too small for him to sit on, and he wants to sit on the ground, but I daren't let him in case he can't get up again. So he leans against the fence and looks back to Great Yarmouth.

He is silent for a while but then he asks, "Why are we walking away?"

I am astonished. Has he forgotten what I said about leaving, or has he not understood?

"So we can get to a better place, Grandfather."

He doesn't say anything else, and he turns round to face forward. I know he cannot see much except the muddy path and the grey water and the green fields. The wind is blowing his hair back from his head, and I can see all the lines on his forehead. Suddenly, I know I should not have brought him. He is too old. He is too ill.

But I have brought him, so after a few minutes I tell him we have to keep moving. He slowly stands up straight and slowly climbs over the fence. I'm angry with him for being so slow and with myself for having brought him.

"We'll rest when we get to the next fence," I tell him.

He follows me steadily for a while. Sometimes, when I turn round, I see he has stopped and is looking inland towards the flat fields. Once when he does this I wait, and when he catches up with me he says, "The water is like a knife." He points to two stretches of water lying in a low part of a field. They gleam in the grey light. Does he mean they are the colour of steel?

"That one is the shape of a knife blade," he says, "and that one is curved like a sickle."

I am still worried about meeting someone, so my eyes are on the path. Then I see a small hut by the water. No, it's not a hut. The bottom part looks like a boat, but the top part is a sort of shed. It's joined to the bank by a few thin planks. Is there someone in it? There might be. But there isn't. It's all closed up, though it looks as if someone could live in it. And then I begin to think seriously of where we will sleep tonight. I have no idea at all, and I have not made any plans. All we have are some black plastic bags, a few extra clothes, two thin blankets. We are not cold now because we are walking and it is the middle of the day, but at night it could be freezing.

Then I hear Grandfather say something. I look round and see that a man and a woman have just overtaken him. They must have greeted him and he must have answered, and now they are nearly level with me, and they have a dog which runs up and sniffs me. I step back and the woman calls it and it runs past me. She smiles at me and says something, and I think she is saying that the dog won't hurt me. When they've gone I ask Grandfather if they spoke to him but he doesn't answer, he just keeps on walking. Anyway, the couple did not seem interested in us, and I feel better when I see them going away.

Now I notice a grass track running below our level, at the edge of the field. This could be easier to walk on, so I go down to it. It is a bit better on the grass but there are cows down there, and I'm not sure about them. I climb back up the bank to our path, and decide to stay here. It feels safer here because I can see all around, and I want to be as close as possible to the edge of the lake.

Grandfather slows down and stops.

"It is time to pray," he says.

Surely he doesn't want to stop again? "You can't pray here. You can't pray here on this path, out in the open."

"Why not? I have prayed in many places. I shall pray here."

He asks for his prayer mat, and there's nothing I can do but unpack it. He spreads it out on a dryish part of the path and then goes down to the edge of the water to drink and wash. I look up and down the path. He does not care if anyone else is nearby, but I do. No one is in sight, and I wait while he kneels and bends and stands and kneels again. I realise that he is going to do this at least three times a day - something I had hardly thought about before and can hardly bear to think about now.

While he is praying I'm wondering where we will sleep, what Sarwat will do when he finds we have gone, whether Grandfather's health will get worse, what Amir is doing today and whether I have done the right thing. I don't think I have done the right thing, and now that I have stopped walking I am becoming cold and worried and angry. When will he stop praying? He's taking so long about it. I feel all tight and shivery. Oh why can't we just *go*?

At last he comes to the end and begins to roll up his mat, but just as he does so I hear a strange noise, like nothing I have ever heard. Then two huge white birds fly past, low over the water. They have long necks and their wings sing as they beat.

Grandfather stays where he is, with the rolled up mat in his hands, watching them until they are out of sight. Then he says, "Let us follow those birds which Allah has sent to us. But there is no need to rush. Take your time."

Take my time? How can I take my time when I'm carrying an awkward bag along a slippery riverbank on a winter's day with an old man who is ill and walks as slowly as a child? It is all Grandfather's fault that this is happening. If it hadn't been for him I would be back at the camp with our family, and so would he, and we would be better off than we are now. I don't care if I remind him of my mother. I wish I *didn't* remind him of her. I wish I wasn't his granddaughter. I wish that my life was different.

I'm not going to wait for him any longer. I'm not going to stand here while he gazes around at the river, the fields, the sky, until at last he slowly puts one foot in front of the other. Can't he see it's already getting dark? How does he think we'll get to Norwich at this speed?

I march off along the bank, wishing and wishing.

⁂

Khadija has told me we are going to stay here for the night. I don't know why we are in this place. It is cold and wet. She tells me we are going to another city, but I keep forgetting why we are going there.

She gave me food – those dry dates they have here, bread, cheese – but I have no appetite. She also made me take the doctor's pills, although I do not think they are making me better. She is quiet now. I cannot see her because it is dark, but I do not think she is asleep because she was angry this evening and is not yet calm.

This is a strange building. It is round and tall. There was still some light when we first came in, and right in the middle of it we could see a big piece of old machinery and a huge iron wheel with cogs, and an iron shaft going up to the roof. There were holes in the walls and the roof and the ground was covered with bits of brick and wood. Khadija cleared a space for us, arranged our things and spread out coverings on the floor. But it is uncomfortable and dank in here. I wish I could have a drink of hot coffee or sweet tea, but Khadija says there is none, so I lean against the central beam and light a cigarette.

Where did I sleep yesterday? It was in a house somewhere. When will we reach the west? Our journey goes on and on. Every few weeks or months we are in a new country, with a new language, new streets, new food, new agents, new things to fear. Which country is this?

It is a cold place, and it is quiet. I am sure I am not in Iraq. Iraq has three types of landscape – mountains, desert plains, and marshes. I long for them all but Allah has led me away from them to places I do not know.

And where is Khadija?

I pray for her and hope that Fatima is looking after her well. She is young and, if she lives, she will grow up to be strong and beautiful and good like her mother and my wife. But she is lost and it is I who have lost her. Perhaps she is dead. Many of my family and my tribe are lost, and many of them are dead. But it is I who lost Khadija, for I tried to bring her to the west. These things sadden me and weaken me, and I am already old.

I feel in the dark for my beads, and let them run through my fingers before I begin to work through them, telling the names of Allah.

Earlier, I dreamed that a sheikh invited me to eat with him, but I refused and travelled on to search for Khadija. This was impolite and gave him offence, and now he and his tribe will speak against me and he may send his men after me. I have lost his respect, and it is my fault. My family will suffer because of me. I have failed them and Khadija and my Sheghanba tribe.

I move my thigh because my right foot is full of sharp prickings. As I do so, I feel an object digging into me. There is something with hard edges close up against my skin. I try to move it but I cannot. I want to turn the light on but I do not remember where the switch is. Tomorrow I shall move this thing that is hurting me.

I feel drops of rain on my face. The door must have been left open. I should get up and close it but it is too far away so I call out to the other people, 'Close the door, close the door.' I try to think of the names of these people - of any one of them - but I cannot. I put my hand on the blanket that covers me and it is damp. But it will be hot tomorrow, and the blanket will dry in the sun while we cut the reeds. We will cut plenty of reeds so the water buffaloes will thrive and give good milk. And I shall go fishing too, with the fishing spear that my cousin gave me. He is a kind man.

The next time I wake I hear the cheepings of small birds. It is becoming morning now, and the light is coming in together with rain from the hole in the roof above me. I turn round and there is Khadija, standing at the doorway, looking out at the rain. She is very still, and she will not hear me if I call to her. I used to think she was praying when I first saw her being still like this, but now I believe that instead of opening herself up to Allah she is closing down her spirit. This is not good.

I look round this tower and recall that we came here last night as it grew dark. Yes, we are on a journey. I cannot remember where we are going, but Khadija knows.

The day has begun. I shall get up and pray.

I have moved out of myself to the bank of the river, and I am looking back at myself in the opening of this round building which gets narrower at the top. I see my loose dark hair, my untidy clothes, my pale face. I see the holes in the walls and the broken roof, broken wooden fences. It is pouring with rain. The sky is full of dark grey clouds. It will rain all day. Now I see myself put my hands over my face. I see myself waiting for something to happen. Now I watch myself push my hair back from my face, turn round and go back inside.

Huge puddles have collected round our building, and during the night water ran in to where I was sleeping and made some of my clothes and most of my blanket wet. At least the food is dry because I hung the bag up on a metal bar in case rats ate it. I hope Grandfather is not wet. If he gets as wet as I am he will be ill and he will die. Although it is his fault that I am here, I do not want him to die. I do not know what to say to him this morning. He will not want to walk in this rain, and anyway he would slip on the ground.

But we must eat, so I reach up to get the bag of food and put it on a few bricks I have pushed together. I take out some dates and biscuits and offer them to Grandfather who is drier than I thought he might be. He takes some food and eats it and this is good, even though he is confused about where we are going and why we are going there.

And now we cannot go anywhere, for it is pouring down and I can hardly even see the bank. So I move Grandfather's things to the driest place in the building and he sits down and leans against the wall, facing the old machinery. I change from my wet trousers and jumper into dry clothes that were inside one of the plastic bags. We will wait, even if we have to wait an hour or two. There is no point in going out in this. Last night I was angry and frightened, and I thought someone might find us here. But now I see it is a deserted place, although cows must come in here at times because there is dung on the ground. I still keep my eyes on the doorway but I am less worried this morning.

What I see does not change – the dark grey sky and rain – but my thoughts change all the time. I start thinking about the beginning – even though I can't remember the things that happened when I was very little – like my mother dying, my father being killed, my big brother dying, my grandmother dying. I start with what I can remember clearly in the camp in Iran. I try to remember Zaineb and Aila and our house, and what we ate, and the songs we sang, and my lessons, and aunt Laila and the other children. But in the middle of all this I think about Sarwat, and trying to write the wrong way round, and Fatima's daughter, and the fight at that place with the sharp wire, and the palm tree near the beach, and Grandfather getting ill and tearing the page out of the map book.

I count up how many good things I can think of and there are three. The first is Amir. Today he will be going to our flat to hear how Sarwat's appeal went, and he will find I am not there. I do not know what he will think, but I hope he will want to find me. Anyway, he will be so pleased when *I* find *him* in Norwich! The second is Grandfather, because I am looking after him and I love him and I am not angry with him today. The third is the nice women I met in the place I went to when I first arrived – Grace and the woman who washed my hair. And then I remember the woman who only had three fingers on one hand, and that brings me back to all the bad things. Travelling in a stinking lorry with no seats so we slid across the floor in the dirty stuff when we went round corners. Being frightened of everything. Missing my sisters and aunts. Hiding in that basement. Badly needing to drink. Being sick on the boat. Men banging on our van and dogs barking. Lice. Not understanding anyone.

Wanting to go home. Sarwat being angry. School. Thinking I might be taken away.

Grandfather has shut his eyes but he is not asleep and he is not moving his beads. He might be praying, but I think he is just being. I cannot just be, because I can't stop myself from thinking or doing something. I wish I could do what he does.

At least two hours must have passed, so I get up and look outside. Nothing has changed. We could be here all day.

I get out the map. It's dim in here but light enough for me to see that we have only gone a tiny distance – the length of my thumb. We've come nearly as far as the end of the inland water, to a little mark with a cross on the top. That could be this building. Yes, I think it is, and now I see there are lots of marks like that on this part of the map. But I'm shocked that we've hardly come any distance at all. If we took one day, or most of a day to go only this far it's going to take us a week to get to Norwich.

I feel horrible. We have little food and little money. Grandfather is ill. And we are stuck here because of the rain. How did I imagine that we could walk there? It is far too difficult. Why did I decide to do this? I am so stupid. I put the map away carefully and curl my knees towards my chest, and pull my coat round me. All I want to do is sleep, but I start coughing.

♪

Richard gets up early, makes himself a proper English breakfast and reads the paper. There is a photo of the new *Scallop* sculpture on the beach near Aldeburgh spattered with white paint. Why on earth would anyone do that? What idiots.

Then he practises his scales and goes through his part of Scheherazade twice. That's it now. The concert is tomorrow evening, and he is satisfied that further practice at this stage will not make much difference. He walks over to the window. It is bright and clear outside after a night and early morning of torrential rain.

So, as it is not yet midday, he decides to make the most of it and go for a walk. If he stays out for a couple of hours he will only need a flask of coffee, an apple and a museli bar. However, this time he will not drive for miles or go off to a wild part of the coast. He consults the OS Explorer map and decides on Rockland Broad where he and Estelle have been several times. That will be quite far enough.

Within fifteen minutes he is in the car. He turns off the main road as soon as possible and drives through Bramerton and round onto the road to Rockland St Mary, past the village sign with its picture of a wherry that Estelle liked so much. He follows the village street down to the car park by the New Inn and the little square staithe they were so pleased to discover some years ago.

He changes into his boots before starting along the path. It is squelchy underfoot, but the air smells good and as he walks along the raised path a glossy male pheasant clatters off in alarm, followed by its pale brown mate. Two birds already – that's a start. As he reaches the hide he wonders if anyone else is there. He and Estelle often ended up chatting to people they met in hides, especially when it was raining. But this one is empty, and he opens up a hatch. Rockland Broad stretches out in front of him with its red, green and white markers in the water and little clumps of reeds and a clutch of mallards. It's cosy in the hide and reminds him of the camp he and Ian used to play in. They used to pretend it was a ship's cabin and Ian gave him orders like "Man the foredeck!" and "Pull on the mainsail!"

Now he closes the hatch and goes on round the broad and along a stretch of water the map calls Short Dike. He pauses every now and then to look at the flooded green fields on his right and to the bank beyond the dyke and the high piles of clouds. It does not take him long to reach the River Yare where small patches of ripples are being blown across the surface. He puts his bag on the ground, and squats down to pour himself a cup of coffee. He stands up, cupping his hands round the warm metal beaker. On the far side of the river, to his left, is a small building with a chimney. It must have been some sort of pumping house once. Directly opposite are brownish fields, and there is a church in the distance over to his right. He consults the map again. That must be Buckenham. Much further to his right are some large industrial buildings and a chimney emitting a long trail of smoke, and he looks this up too and finds it is a factory at a village called Cantley. How odd to have a factory in the middle of nowhere.

He pours himself more coffee, feeling contented. As he munches his way through an apple he tries to define what this contentment is due to. Being in the open air, taking exercise, enjoying the natural world, being freed up from the recent, intrusive feeling that he should have done more over those years when Estelle did not become pregnant. And he cannot deny that he is looking forward to having Harriet with him on a future walk, perhaps even the next walk. How will Polly feel about her mother going out with him? Did Harriet really mean she was actually jealous or resentful of him? It sounded like it.

A train trundles across his sightline on the far side of the river.

Harriet had not seemed bothered by what Polly said, but what had she really been thinking? And does Polly know she is 'a mistake'? Richard feels information is flooding in faster than he can process it. How can Polly be jealous? He has only been round to their house twice. Has Harriet said something about him?

He throws his apple core away, causing a long grey bird to fly up from a ditch. A heron. At least he can identify a heron. Estelle loved them and wrote one of her few poems about them, and he wishes he could point this one out to her. Even as he watches, it flies off slowly towards the river, and he realises he has not brought the binoculars. He looks at the slow-flowing water.

Where is this all going?

He decides to follow the path a little way along the river. The wind is fresh and clean and the sun is trying to come through. The water is brown and choppy, and the whole place deserted. Whole areas of fields are covered in water. Here he is, less than ten miles from Norwich, but it feels as if he's in the middle of nowhere. He is completely on his own and there is hardly a house in sight. A pair of coot bob by the bank, and a group of geese – too few to make a V – fly to the east.

He makes his way back to the car, hauls off his boots and drives home slowly with Scarlatti. What will Harriet be doing now? He imagines her seated at a desk and on the phone, and he has an image of the subject of her conversation: a forlorn withdrawn child. Should he phone her this evening? Perhaps it is too soon, perhaps he should wait until he sees her tomorrow at the concert.

I ease myself up from where I have slept because I must pray properly. This morning I did not set out my prayer mat, for it would have become sodden, but now it has stopped raining and there is more light. I slip my shoes on, tuck the laces in and walk carefully, avoiding rubble and dung. I make my way over the uneven ground to the doorway and see the green bank that lies between us and the expanse of water we are following. To my left three cows stand on the bank. They are smaller than buffaloes, and the sound they make is not as sad as the sound that buffaloes make. The sun is hidden, but brightness is coming from high in the sky, so it must be at least midday. I go back inside for my prayer mat which is in a plastic bag above Khadija, near the food. As I reach up for it she coughs again. She has been coughing all morning.

I walk up the bank and there in front of me is the inland sea. It gladdens me. Because I am old now and my eyesight is poor, the water disappears away in each direction, to my left, to my right and straight ahead. Behind me is the round tower, and behind that are green and brown fields, with their floods that look like wide knives.

I spread the plastic bag on the flat top of the bank, and then lay my mat on top of it. I turn to the south east, kneel and pray. I recite some of the ayyás, and I give thanks to Allah whom I obey in all things. Each time I raise my upper body, the wind blows against my face. Each time I lean forward, I feel it on the back of my neck. When I have finished I shut my eyes and wait. I do not know what I wait for, but something will come. Something always comes.

Wind runs through the grass, and past me, and through the

openings in the round tower. Little rills of water must be curling against the bank because I hear slight, wet slaps. A loose board in the fence is flapping. A train passes in the distance. A cow coughs.

And then I hear geese. I hear them call as they are disturbed and rise up, and I know they must be peeling off the ground to join those already in the air. Their wings approach and their calls fill my ears. I open my eyes and look above me, and there they go in a great mass sweeping across the grey sky.

I lower my head, for I have not heard or seen these things for many years, and I am moved.

To Allah belongs the east and the west.
Whichever way you turn there is the face of Allah.

And then I remember all the geese in all the marshes of my boyhood. I remember punting through the reeds at dawn with my father and brother. Out there, geese would rise up and fly past us at speed, making for the open lake. We would pause and look up at their beating wings, their glidings, the patterns they made against the pale sky.

Yesterday two big white birds flew past us, close enough for me to see them clearly, but I did not know them. They were not storks, or pelicans, or egrets or ibis. I hoped I would dream of them, but I did not. And now I have found geese again, here, in a foreign place where I do not belong. I do not know what these things mean, but they hearten me.

Khadija coughs again. I get to my feet slowly, and pick up my mat and the bag. I must take care of her because she is unhappy. We will eat, and then we will decide what to do. I have begun to enjoy the fact that there are just the two of us. There is no tension between us, as there sometimes is with Sarwat. I am beginning to feel I am myself again.

As I turn to the west I notice something different in the air, in the wind. It is a smell, a smell I know but which I have not smelled for many years. For the moment, I cannot recognise it. But I will remember. Khadija is standing by the doorway.

I say, “Let us eat.”

She says, “I am not hungry, but I am thirsty.”

"I will fetch you some water, but you should eat too."

"I want to lie down again."

"Then lie down. I will be here with you."

"But we should keep walking. We cannot stay here."

"We will walk tomorrow. Rest now, Khadija. Allah will wait with us." I go down to the river and collect water in a bottle for us to drink, and then I see that the level of the water has changed since yesterday.

When I return to her I say, "This inland sea rises and falls with the tide. Tell me if you can taste salt."

We both drink a little of the pale brown, cloudy water, but it is not salty. Khadija puts the bottle to her mouth again and drinks again, slowly.

Grandfather does not care about time. He says we should wait because he thinks I am not ready to move, but he himself is ready. Something has happened to him. Perhaps the medicine and pills are working. Perhaps one of his prayers has been answered. I do not know what it is, but he is stronger while I am weaker. After he told me to rest he spread out his blanket for me. It was drier than mine, and he settled me down on it and told me to sleep. He sat next to me, on a seat he made out of bricks and a piece of wood.

But I did not sleep. My mind was full of everything I have lost in my life. I have lost many people – my mother and father, my brother, my sisters, my aunts, my friends. And I have lost the places where I have lived.

I feel very bad that Sarwat has lost us, and I hope it will not be long before we find him again, when things are better. But I do not want anyone to find us yet. Except Amir. I would like Amir to find us as soon as possible. And now I wish I had talked to him and asked him to help instead of doing what I have done. I wish he was here now.

I open my eyes to look at Grandfather, and my head is level with his shoe and his untied laces.

What have I found in my life? I have found England. I have found Grandfather again, when I thought I had lost him. I have found Sarwat. It seems I have lost many more things than I have found, but of course I have found Amir too.

Grandfather is singing quietly to himself. Or perhaps to me. I do not know which. I have not heard him sing before, and I do not know this song. I can't hear all the words because his voice is not even, and sometimes he turns away from me. It is strange that he is singing here, out by this water in a broken down building, but I like it.

Now I am hot. I feel under my collar and touch my neck, and my skin is so wet my hand slides over it. I am thirsty again, and I ask Grandfather for water. He passes me the bottle and I drink again.

I lie here looking up at the sky through the roof. It is getting darker now. We have wasted a whole day. Sarwat will be looking for us now and we have hardly gone any distance. He will be asking at my school, and searching in the streets. He will be angry. I should have left a letter for him. Why did I not think of that? I was in such a hurry to get away, and now he will be worried. He will be both worried and angry, and even though I knew that he would be, I decided to do what *I* wanted. I have never done that before, and now I see I was wrong, for he was often kind to me. He let me live in his flat, and he gave me money, and he wanted me to be safe. How can I have been so selfish? Were things so bad that I had to run away? Will I always run away if things become difficult in my life?

It is dark now, with only a little light coming in through the open doorway. Grandfather moved away to say his prayers, but now he is back here and close to me. I can smell his cigarette, and I see the tip of it glowing red each time he puts it to his mouth.

Should we go back? This question keeps coming in to my head more and more.

Later I wake because something falls on my face. I brush it off, and hear a bird fluttering in the tower. Right above me I can see two bright stars through the gap in the roof. I am not so hot now, and Grandfather is lying near to me. I hear his breathing, as I did in the flat, but his breathing is deeper and slower than it was there. He sounds as if he will go on breathing for ever, and that makes me feel he is safe, and if he is safe then I am safe. I try to listen for other things. There is no wind. That bird has not moved again. I thought there might be rats here, but I have not heard any.

I look up to the roof and look for the two bright stars. They are no longer there, but some small ones are. They have moved in just that short time while I was thinking about something else. I did not know stars could move so fast. But of course they are not moving, because it is the earth which moves. While I am lying here quite still, the earth is turning and what I see through the hole in the roof keeps changing, but I'm too tired to keep my eyes open any longer.

Fatima is with me and we are in that place with the sharp wire and bright lights. At least we have made it this far. She is drawing a map to show how we can get back across the sea, but I keep telling her there are no boats, and we have no money to buy one. Then she picks up her daughter and shouts at me that I am too much trouble and she wishes she had never agreed to look after me. So I set off on my own, and the guards let me go through every gate and every checkpoint. And there is a taxi waiting for me and it drives me to Denmark and on and on through cities and mountains. But then it stops by a very tall chimney and the driver says I must walk the rest of the way. I don't know which way to go and he tells me to follow the direction of the smoke.

I know that my family and friends are expecting me, so I make myself go on. After a while I recognise the shape of a valley, an outline of hills. It cannot be far now. I meet a man and ask if I am going the right way. Yes, he says, yes, and he points ahead. But though I reach the right place there are no houses, no people, not even a chicken. Everything has gone.

Grandfather goes on breathing in and breathing out. I try to breathe at the same speed, but I can't. I have to breathe more often. His breathing goes on and on and on.

♪

Just before Richard sets out for the concert Eric phones for one of their regular chats. It is usually Mary who calls, but this time she is playing bridge. Richard values the couple's concern for him, but his most enjoyable times with Eric are when they have a bottle of whisky on the table. After a couple of minutes they are running out of things to say. And then Eric says they are going to an exhibition in Ely Cathedral, and would Richard like to come? Yes? Good. And is there anyone he would like to bring with him?

Richard immediately says no, and then, "Sorry, Eric, I've got to go. It's our Save the Children concert tonight. I was just getting ready to leave when you phoned. I'll put February 28th in my diary. Many thanks. I'd really like to go. Give my love to Mary, won't you?"

Yes, he could take Harriet, but no, he is not going to.

By the time he arrives at the hall over half of the orchestra is already there, but Harriet has not yet come. Richard sets up his stand and the music, chooses the best of his new reeds, places it in his oboe and plays his first few little runs of notes to warm up.

He will have to get to know her better before he introduces her to people who will presume he is seriously interested in her.

The audience trickles in as the players tune up to his A.

So, is she someone in whom he is becoming seriously interested?

He feels slightly nervous, as he always does when the oboe has a decent part, and he likes that feeling. He used to tell Estelle that it kept him on his toes. 'On your toes?' she had asked, 'How can you play on your toes?' This led to them referring to an important concert as a Toe Concert. Tonight's concert is, by definition, a Toe Concert.

But where's Harriet?

He looks over to her place and sees Sam moving her chair off the crowded stage. The other violinists shuffle along to fill the gap. Isn't she coming? Why on earth not?

RIMSKY-KORZAKOV: Scheherazade
2nd MOVEMENT
Andantino (♩ = 112)
dolce ed espress. assai
espress. molto
ten.
a piacere
rit. assai
p
accel.
cresc.
rit.

Within a few minutes the lights go down and the audience becomes quiet. Louise, the first violinist, comes on, bows shyly to the applause and sits down. Then comes Alan, beaming as usual. He always accepts the applause before the concert as if he had already earned it.

He starts them off, leading them into the lyrical Scheherazade themes that the audience probably knows as well as they do. It goes smoothly and Richard concentrates on his part with confidence, although conscious that Estelle is not in the audience. Last year he believed he would never be able to play a concert without thinking of her because for decades she had been the most important person in his audience. So he decided to go on playing to her, even though she was not there. He thinks of her before and after playing, but not while he is playing.

But Harriet is not there either and he has to wait until the interval to find out why. Then Norma tells him that two hours ago Harriet had a phone call from her sister to say their mother had been taken into hospital with breathing problems. Harriet let Norma know because she would not be able to give her a lift and also wanted her to tell Alan she could not play at the concert. She said she was arranging for the children to go to their father before she rushed off to Worcestershire.

Richard has an image of her chasing up Polly and Adam, hurrying them into the car, taking them to her ex-husband (or perhaps he is still her husband?) and heading for her mother's. She has never mentioned a mother, or indeed a father, or a sister. How little he knows about her.

He is disappointed, but there is no chance to dwell on it, for within minutes Alan is holding up his baton, and they are onto the next piece. That is what he finds amazing about playing: it holds you, it takes all of you. When he is cutting a hedge, or driving, or making marmalade, there is always room to think. He finds it is easy to do two things at once, even when listening to music. But it is almost impossible to *play* music and think about something else at the same time. That is one of the extraordinary and the best things about playing – it cuts out the rest of the world. At its best it anaesthetises all thought leaving only enough for what is technically required. It focuses on what is right inside him and brings it out to meld with what is inside other people as expressed through their instruments and the score.

And then the concert is over. Alan congratulates him on his playing, and even Ian comments on it for once.

He put his reeds back into their box, and wraps his oboe in its piece of silk before putting it in its case. They are all going to join the audience for refreshments. He volunteers to pour out the wine and does so while wondering whether Harriet will have reached Worcestershire yet, and what condition her mother might be in. He does not have her mobile number, and he has no way of getting it, though it is possible Alan might have it. Or even Norma.

He would like a second glass of wine, but as he has promised to drive Norma home he accepts Sam's offer of coffee and chocolate cake instead. He finds himself standing with a cup and saucer in one hand and a plate in the other – quite unable to eat or drink – and being asked by one of the Save the Children committee members if he knows whether there was a Mrs Rimsky Korsakov or any little Rimsky Korsakovs. This is no place to be. He wants to be home.

After dropping off Norma (who does not have the number of Harriet's mobile) he drives the last couple of miles, parks the car in the driveway and stands outside his unlit house. He hears the engine ticking under the bonnet as it cools down, and notices that the forsythia is just coming out. Above the houses, clouds race past a nearly whole moon.

I am woken by birds. I have slept well, and my stomach is not hurting. Those pricking feelings are in my fingers, but I feel today will be better. Khadija is still fast asleep, and I get up carefully and go right round the central machinery to avoid disturbing her. Outside, the sky is a bright white. I want to see the inland sea, so I climb slowly up the bank. And there it is. It is light grey, and almost motionless. At once I give thanks. Then I see some movement, and realise there are flocks of birds floating on it. The sky behind them is yellowish, and the sun is still below the horizon.

So I wait for sunrise. I stand still in the way that people in the west do not, or cannot, and I watch. Three more of those great white birds go singing past. Nearby, small birds fly between bushes. Something jumps in the water by the bank and I see ripples reaching out. Cows amble towards me and I hear them pulling the grass from the ground and chewing. Somewhere behind me a dog barks. The sky is changing from yellow to orange. There might still be stars but I cannot see them. Then a group of birds rises up from the surface of the inland sea. I hear their feet running on the water and the water falling from them and their wings beating. They do not call out to each other, but they are connected to each other. They are like the birds in our marshlands. Sometimes, if an eagle came close a group of them would splash together to make a wall of water against it. Or they would move away from us as we approached in a canoe, knowing we might harm them. Or they would fly up because they felt a storm coming. Now the top arc of the sun is over the horizon. I can see this clearly. It rises up fast, and I remember how the day used to pass slowly when I was young, but that the sun would appear almost suddenly at dawn and be gone as quickly at dusk.

The sun is halfway risen now and sending an orange glow across the water. Now the birds look black against the orange sea, and I hear the calling of a flock flying off to my right, towards the place where Khadija is taking me. I have forgotten the name of the town, but it does not matter. Allah will protect us.

Now there is space between the sun and the horizon. There is just sky and sun and this inland sea. I breathe the air deeply. This is the best air I have breathed for years. I fill my lungs with it. I walk down to the water's edge to drink. I kneel on the bank, dip my hand into the water and carry a handful of it to my mouth. It tastes good, even better in this calm dawn than it did yesterday. I look into this water that is not real sea, nor real lake, nor real river. Here by the bank it is slow and brown. It is like the water in our marshes.

It is Allah who has sovereignty over the heavens and the earth.
To Allah shall all return.

I turn towards the land, but the land is not like our marshlands. I am standing on hard, solid ground with stones in it. The fields stretch away inland to where there are roads and cities. This building we sheltered in overnight is made of bricks and wood. It is nothing like our homes we used to make out of reeds.

I turn back to the water which is now bluish because much of the sky is now blue. I shut my eyes and recall how I used to go out on the boat with my father and brother. We would set off with only our curved knives and our punting poles or paddles, but when we returned the canoes would be piled high with reeds for the buffaloes. My mother and sisters would greet us and tell us what had happened that day, and we would tell them about who we had met on the water, and where we thought there might be a boar, or a nest with eggs. And at the end of the day the buffaloes would come out of the water on to the platform behind our reed house, and eat and eat and eat.

It is time to pray. I walk back into the round building and before I enter it I hear Khadija coughing. I go in and see she is still lying under her blanket.

"How are you feeling?" I ask.

She coughs again, and says a few words I cannot hear.

"It is a beautiful day outside," I tell her.

She smiles at me. "Good. I will get up soon."

"I shall take my prayer mat outside." I step forward to reach it but trip heavily as my foot catches on something.

"Stop, Grandfather. Let me tie your laces."

Khadija is properly awake now and sitting up. I walk carefully towards her, and she leans forward and ties first the laces on my right shoe, and then those on the left. Then I take my mat and go back to the bank.

I feel bad. My throat is sore and I keep on coughing, and when I cough my whole chest aches as if I am bruised. But I must get up. It is a fine day and we cannot waste any more time. I wish for a miracle that would take us straight to Norwich, and I remember how I used to think the same thing when we were travelling. I used to wish that the next time we got out of the van, or the lorry, or the boat, we would be in the west, and not have to travel any more. But before long I had stopped thinking about where we were going. It didn't matter. My life - all our lives - consisted of being moved from one place to another. When we stopped, it might be for a night, or ten days, or even months, but we knew we would be setting off again at some point. By the end I did not know if we had made the journey to get away from Iran or to reach the west, because all we did was to be moved. And we hardly ever moved ourselves. There were only a few times when we had to make our way on foot. But here, in England, Grandfather and I are walking. And today we must walk much further.

I push back the blanket and stand up. I do not feel clean and for a moment I wish I was back in that place they kept me where I was able to wash my hair and body properly. Then I go outside and round to the back to a private place, even though I know Grandfather will not see me because he is at prayer. Now I shall check to see what food we still have. It will not be enough, and we only have very little money. I start to wish again, for food. I collect two plastic bags, and a blanket and the bag of food, and I take them out onto the top of the bank. Grandfather is still kneeling, so I stay away.

For a minute, when I look at the inland sea, I am confused. Although I can see the buildings back in Great Yarmouth they seem to be much further away than they were yesterday, and when I look across the water I can see the other shore more clearly. This means the other side of the inland sea is getting nearer and it is becoming a river. This is what it is supposed to do and what it does on the map. All at once, I feel better.

And there are other new things too. There are posts out in the water, a long way in front of me, some red ones, some white. Birds are sitting on top of them. And along the path we are going to follow again, I can see more buildings not very far away. One of them, the tallest one, is strange. It looks, oddly, almost like a mosque. Of course it can't be a mosque because it is not really the right shape, and anyway, there would not be one in this place. And beyond that, there is a stream of smoke coming from a tall chimney.

This is the middle of nowhere. Although we have seen a man and a woman and footprints on the path, I am sure we are alone. I know it is still quite early in the morning, but I cannot see any reason for anyone to come here. Perhaps we are safe and will not be seen, but there could be people in those buildings we will be passing. I shall look at the map and see if that place further along the path is a village. If it is, we will have to be careful. I must talk to Grandfather about it.

Before we came here, I thought *I* would decide exactly what we should do and tell him what I had decided, like I did at first, but already I find myself wanting to ask him what he thinks. Perhaps it would be best to walk through the next place at night time, but I am not sure. I do not want to stay here any longer and as soon as we need food we will have to go to where there are people.

And now I start to cough again, and I cough up some stuff as I have been doing in the night. I am glad to get rid of it, but there will be more.

Grandfather has rolled up his mat and is coming towards me. Together, we spread out the blankets on the plastic bags. There is some wind, and I pull my blanket round me, but at least it is not raining.

"I have been remembering the marshes," says Grandfather.

"What marshes?"

"The marshes in Iraq. The marshes where I was born, the marshes I grew up in, where I played and punted and fished and shot and cut reeds."

I had heard about the marshes from people in the camp in Iran, but Grandfather has never spoken about them to me before.

"This place reminds me of them. The water here is brown and slow. There are reeds growing here. There are many birds. The wind is strong."

Grandfather has his eyes shut, and I watch his face. His hair is blowing around his head, and he has stubble on his chin. He is sitting cross legged, which I have never seen him do at Sarwat's, although people in the camp often used to sit like that. He is holding his beads, but they are still. He says, "It is good to be here. We should be thankful."

I look out across the water and see something moving. "There's a boat!"

Grandfather opens his eyes. He says, "I was expecting a boat. I thought to myself that with all this water, there must be boats here just as we had boats."

It is not coming near us so we stay where we are. When I tell him about the buildings in front of us and my worry about people seeing us, he says that Allah will decide what happens, and it will be good. Then he says, "Let me tell you about our boats." He lights himself a cigarette. "There were several kinds. Some were just bunches of reeds tied together, but most of them were made of wood. The wood had to be brought from far away, for we had no trees."

While he talks I eat a few dates, but my throat hurts. It was like this once on the journey, and Fatima looked into my mouth and said I had white spots. But they disappeared, so perhaps if I have any now they will disappear too.

"We fixed planks together for the bottom and sides, and we cut smaller pieces for the ribs. Then we covered the outside with a sort of tar that bubbled out of the ground in certain places, and we let it dry.

"Some of them had a high prow like this." He raised the hand that held his cigarette in an upward sweep, making a thin arc of smoke hang in the air. "Those were the taradas, which could take ten or twelve men. There were bellums too, which were smaller. I was good at paddling, but not so good at punting. It was my brother who was best at punting." Then he is silent for a while, and then he stands.

We collect up our things and continue on our way, with me in front. We get nearer and nearer to the buildings, and now I can see that first we will come to a long house, and then to the tall one like a mosque, and then to more houses. We will have to walk directly in front of all of them. I can see too that the reason why one looks strange and like a mosque is because it has something shiny all over it, almost like a sort of shroud.

And now the water has really changed from being an inland sea to being a river. When I look backwards, it's like the sea, but forwards, it's a river. In fact, it's two rivers, and they either split or join, depending on which way I look at it. The path is very muddy, but what I'm worried about is reaching the buildings. We get closer and closer, and there's a man driving a tractor. We will have to walk quite close to him, and my heart is beating.

And then he waves to us!

Now we are close to the mosque, and Grandfather is right. It is a building like the one we slept in last night, and it is being repaired because all around there are machines and bricks and planks. He says they might have covered it up for winter, but we don't know. There is a notice on the door and Grandfather asks me to go and see what it is. I do not want to and I will not be able to read it, but he wants me to, so I do. It is a picture of one of these tall buildings, but with something like wings at the top. I run back quickly, in case someone sees me, but we do not see a single person.

And then we walk and walk and walk.

We just follow the path, on and on, with the river on our left and the fields on our right, and a far off stream of smoke in the sky. My map does not show anything along here except little marks with crosses on the top. In fact, a lot of the map along the river is white and has no roads. There are certainly no roads here, but we will reach a village later on today because on the map not so far ahead is a place coloured grey, like Great Yarmouth and Norwich, and grey means houses and buildings. But before that village there seems to be a group of yet more of those old tall round buildings. We keep seeing them. And suddenly I realise that these are what the marks with the crosses mean. I remember the sort of wings I saw in the picture – those are the crosses. Perhaps they all had those wings once. We walk on past them and then stop for a rest.

Grandfather is still thinking about the marshes. He begins to describe the houses to me and how they used to cut giant reeds – taller than three men – and how they would tie many of them together to make strong posts of them, but posts that could be bent and joined. They used to make an arched framework and cover it over with mats made out of reeds. "They were huge," he says. "We called them mudhifs, and when a sheikh had visitors – for it was only important men who had mudhifs – they spread out rugs and cushions on the ground."

"Did your family live in one?"

"No. My father was not a sheikh. He was an ordinary man. He belonged to the Sheghanba tribe. And so do I. And so do you."

He pauses, fingering his beads.

"We built smaller homes from reeds, but first we had to make the ground."

"Make the ground? Why did you do you that? And how?"

"The marshes stretch between two great rivers – the Tigris and the Euphrates."

He pointed to the river beside us. "Khadija, this river here is a trickle, a dribble compared to the Tigris and Euphrates. They are *real* rivers."

He paused for a moment, then went on: "In some parts of the marshlands there is always water and when the wet season comes there are floods. There is no real land. It is all water for many kilometres in all directions, but reeds grow everywhere, and the clumps of reeds were strong enough for us to live on. They were like floating islands, and we made them more solid by cutting more reeds and piling them on top. Then we built our houses on them." He explains to me how part of the marshes were open lakes, and parts were full of reeds but there were channels through which they could steer their boats.

As he is telling me this we heard a noise coming towards us and getting louder. We look up and there are dozens of geese flying high above, calling as they fly.

"There they go," he says. "Come on, Khadija. We must go too."

Then we get up and start off towards the village. The food bag is nearly empty, and I hope we will find a shop.

♪

Richard goes downstairs to collect the paper and put the kettle on. He is looking forward to a cup of tea in bed and The Guardian. But there on the mat is the Eastern Daily Press. Damn. He takes it upstairs and gives it a cursory glance, noting the Norwich City win over Sheffield United.

The day stretches out in front of him in an unsatisfactory way. The Toe Concert is over, and so there is no specific reason to practice. He has nothing planned. Harriet has disappeared. He needs a project – something to get excited about. When was he last excited by anything? The concert at Snape, perhaps. Yes, that counted, even though the day was full of Estelle's absence.

In the shower he ponders again whether he should find a job, or do some voluntary work. Now that he is both retired and on his own, going to a certain place each day and having a routine seems very attractive. Mary had said, "Don't dismiss the idea. It's well worth thinking about."

He has also given some thought to VSO. He could be useful in a building programme somewhere. Africa? India? Anywhere at all. He can do anything he wants and he can do it whenever he likes and for as long as he likes. Is this freedom? Is freedom having no one else to think about? If so, does that mean it is essentially selfish? Or is freedom merely freedom from something, like an oppressive person or a regime, or externally imposed constraints? Or is it merely the gap that exists after commitment to one thing and before commitment to something else?

He goes on wondering about this as he puts bread in the toaster. He has been fortunate throughout his life. He has never felt shackled, has rarely felt fear, and never physical fear other than one or two near misses in a car. He, and millions of others, he supposes, take freedom – whatever it means – for granted. But what use is freedom without peace of mind?

This is a hopeless way to start the day. He must get on and do something. First he changes his sheets and puts on a load of washing. Then he puts the rubbish bin out. It is gorgeous outside. Cold but bright and clear. He decides to go for another walk. As he packs himself a lunch he wonders where to go. What about Reedham? Yes. With luck, he might see the swing bridge in action, and he could go across the chain ferry. The river will be beautiful on a day like this, and there are three pubs to choose from. It looks like a good day for birds and this time he remembers the binoculars.

He is in the car just in time for the eleven o'clock News. There has been an accident involving Chinese cockle pickers. Poor sods. How on earth had they got to Morecambe Bay? The weapons of mass destruction story runs and runs. And how will England fare in the Six Nations? He chooses Telemann to keep him company until he reaches the ferry at Reedham. Estelle loved the slow, clanking hulk as much as he did. They rarely took the car on it, but always crossed from one side to the other as pedestrians just for fun. Today the river looks smooth and creamy, like thick gravy, and the ducks hardly disturb the surface.

When he arrives the ferry is on the far side so he has the pleasure of watching it raise its ramp, trundle across, be pulled into place by the chains, and finally lower its ramp at his end to allow its cargo off – one white van. Richard walks on and pays the ferry man, and when the ramp draws up like a drawbridge he enjoys the fact that he is the sole passenger. On the door of the ferryman's cab he sees a small notice advertising for part-time ferry operatives. Now, there's an idea.

He has never found out why the ferry is so far from the village, but there must be a reason. As they cross he looks upstream to the reed lined river and downstream to more reed lined river. He feels the movement of the ferry judder pleasantly through the soles of his feet. He gets off by the pub and turns right so he is walking downriver. He follows the path round to where it goes straight across the garden of a former windmill. Estelle coveted this windmill. She was sure the view from its upper windows would be stunning, and the idea of a pub only minutes away was tempting. Each time they came here she looked to see if there was a For Sale sign. And there isn't one today, either.

He walks for a mile or so, gradually getting nearer to Reedham village. The path takes him away from the river for a few hundred yards, then back down past the boatyard to the street where every house faces the river. He always likes the feel of the waterfront here, and today it looks splendid. Ducks are gathered on the grass, the water sparkles, and there is the metal bridge, firmly spanning the Yare.

It is a shame that today there are unlikely to be any boats passing through that will require the bridge to be turned. There is something satisfying about the basic, practical business of turning it at right angles to allow tall boats through, and then turning back. It makes him think of giant Meccano. As he watches, he hears a train approaching from the far side and in seconds it's there, clattering over the bridge and away.

He walks back the way he has come, looking forward to a pint, and takes the ferry back to where he started. He goes into the Ferryboat Inn and settles with his drink at one of the small tables, not far from an old boy in the corner. He has rarely sat alone in pubs. Today is busy. Almost everyone seems to be in couples, except for a large party of three generations. Presents are being passed to an elderly lady, and now a little boy is giving her a picture of a big red 80 surrounded by blue dots.

Should he have another pint? No. But he does not want to leave yet so sips more slowly. Photos hang on the walls, mostly of the swing bridge or the ferry. One, half hidden behind a curtain, shows a blue boat right against the ferry. He unhooks it from the wall and looks at it carefully. It is not a particularly old photo, but he is surprised by the size of the boat.

The man sitting nearby says, "You won't see her again."

Richard looks across at him.

"The Blackheath. You won't see her again. She's stopped coming. She last went up river about three year ago. They don't use her now."

"That boat, in the photo? Did it come up here?"

"That photo was took when she hit the ferry – in the sixties."

"I'm not sure what it is. Is it a tanker?"

"Yup. She used to bring oil up to Cantley."

"To the factory?"

"Yes. Every few months she came up here from Yarmouth. We had to clear the river to make room for her and they had to lower the ferry chains to the bottom."

"It looks as if she would be too big to make it."

"She filled the river. There were only that much to spare when she turned round above Cantley." The man holds his hands out a foot or two apart. "She was a rare sight, I can tell you."

"Why doesn't she come now?"

"They bring oil in tankers now, by road. Everything is by road now, isn't it? The beet comes in by road, the sugar goes out by road."

So, the factory he saw the other day was a sugar factory. He should have known from the steamy smoke because it was like the one at Bury St Edmunds. He finishes his pint and nods goodbye to the man. As the door closes behind him the family group begin singing Happy Birthday.

He decides to make a day of it rather than return home. He will walk his pint off and find somewhere to picnic. There is no footpath south of the river, so he treats himself to another ferry crossing and carries on walking upstream. Would Harriet enjoy a walk like this? He hopes so.

After a while he sees some sort of monument opposite him on the other side. It is a stone cross and it intrigues him. He cannot think how it could be reached, nor why it is there. A cormorant appears from somewhere and settles on top of it, so he takes out his binoculars. As he watches it spreads its wings and adopts what Estelle would call "its crucifix position." It is such a strange posture, like something primeval, especially bizarre on top of a cross. This is the place to have lunch. Moving slowly so as not to disturb the bird, he sorts himself out so he is sitting on a plastic bag and has his sandwiches, flask and binoculars within reach.

The cormorant hardly moves. But the wind is getting up and the river is covered with little eddies that alter its smoothness and colour. He examines a pair of grebes diving and surfacing and counts to see how long they stay underwater, guesses where they will next pop up.

Should he invite Polly and Adam on the walk? Would that

make Polly feel included or annoyed?

The grebes move further away so, making sure the strap of the binoculars is safely round his neck, he creeps along the bank taking the flask with him.

He would much prefer it to be just the two of them.

When he next checks his watch it is after half past three. He stands up slowly, but not slowly enough to avoid disturbing the cormorant. It launches itself off the top of the cross. He walks back to the ferry. It is on his side this time, but no cars are in sight. What would it be like to work here? He decides against asking the attendant about the job, and is ferried over yet again. Four times in one day – what a treat! Once again he is the only passenger. But more people are on their way, for behind him a man and a young girl are standing on the bank outside the pub. As he watches the girl bends down and kneels by the man's feet. She stays there for a few moments. She must have dropped something.

He hurries to the car as it begins to rain.

We have been passing reedbeds. When I first saw them, there were only a few, but gradually there were more, and now there are wide patches of them. I asked Khadija to fetch a reed for me. I ran my fingers over its smooth segments, its raised joints. I picked at its layers of scratchy casings. I pulled the feathery top through my hand and recalled its softness. And then we saw different reeds, the ones with wider leaves at the top. They are all brown because it is winter, but it is my winter too. These reeds please me.

But Khadija is becoming anxious. When we saw that bridge she thought we were coming into a big place, and there are certainly more houses here than anywhere we have been so far. I had to encourage her to walk past them, and at times we had to go away from the river because there was no path. There were quite a few people around, but no one gave us a second glance. We went past two buildings I knew were pubs, and we could smell meat cooking. Khadija said we could buy food inside, but she did not dare go in herself and I did not want to go in either.

I believe Allah will provide for us because Khadija is weak. She is coughing and she says her throat is sore. I wish she could have a hot drink. I am all right, because although my medicine is finished I have my cigarettes and my beads to soothe me.

We looked for a shop and found two. Khadija was hopeful when we saw the first, but when we got close, it was shut. And the second looked as if it was not in use so we had to keep on walking, and soon she began to tell me about something she could see ahead. It was something that moved, and she thought it was either a machine like a tractor, or a boat.

Now we are right beside it, and I can see it is a sort of mechanical raft that takes cars across the river. It is a clever idea. It cannot be driven up or downstream, for it is on chains that can only pull it to one side or the other. I have seen something like it before.

It is beginning to rain and we need to press on through this place, even though Khadija should rest now. There is a pub here too – they have them everywhere, even out in the country where there are few people – and there are lights on inside. I think we have enough food for one more meal but Khadija shows me the map and explains that we will have to go a long way to find a shop, and that there must be food here. Hunger is making her brave.

"Are we going to beg for food?" I ask. "How will we get it?"

I recalled how, in the marshes, everyone offered food to travellers, especially if they were strangers. People would call out to passing boats, "Come and eat!" And it was rude to refuse, even though the host would have to have chickens killed, and fish caught, and rice cooked. It was a man's duty to invite others to eat, and their duty to accept. That was the way of things. But in the west it is different. Many people eat in restaurants every day, and some eat alone even though they have families, and even though those families are near.

Khadija says, "We have some money. I shall go and ask." So she goes to the door of the pub and tries the handle, and it opens. She goes inside without looking back.

While I shelter in the lee of the wall I notice some big rusty anchors I did not see earlier. They are like the ones I used to see on the ships waiting in the Shatt al Arab by Basra. For a moment I recall how they used to be slowly lowered down on their chains. But I do not understand why these anchors are here because we are far from the sea or any river big enough to carry the type of ships that would need these.

After about five minutes Khadija reappears, and she has something in her hands. She explains to me that there were no customers inside, but a man was wiping down the tables.

"I held out the money and pointed to my mouth. He was not sure what to do so he called a woman from another room. They talked and then she went out again, and the man told me to sit down. It was warm in there. Then the woman came back with this," Khadija held out the packet she was holding, "and gave it to me. I held out the money again, but they did not take any."

As we walk on looking for somewhere dry to sit I give thanks, because there are good people everywhere. The ground is slippery but we continue along the path. I am in front now and I see something shining on the ground ahead. Is it a bottle? A can? I stop and point forwards. "Khadija, what is that?"

"I don't know."

I let her pass me and she hurries on. She stops and picks it up. "It's a container, a sort of jug with a lid that screws on. Sarwat had one in the back of his car, but I never saw him use it. It's for keeping drinks hot." She unscrews it and puts her nose to the opening. "It's coffee! Hot coffee!"

Further on we can see a metal bridge across a dyke, and we decide to go on as far as that. We can sit and eat and drink there. Allah is with us, because it stops raining when we reach the bridge. Khadija opens the pack of food she has been holding underneath her jacket to keep dry, and she brings out slices of bread with meat between them. I ask if it is pork, but she does not know.

She says, "It is dark, so I do not think it is pork or chicken. I think it is beef. Or sheep." She bites into it.

I take a piece of the bread but there is the juice of this unknown meat on it, so I ask Allah's forgiveness. We eat in silence, and the food is good. Then, Khadija opens the flask, pours some coffee into the small metal cup which is the lid and passes it to me. It is hot and bitter and good. I pass it back to Khadija and she drinks some too. We sit there, warming up inside although we are wet outside. Khadija is getting a little colour in her face. I stand up and realise how dark it is already. "We must find somewhere to sleep. It is getting late."

"We should go back to that place I have just been to. It has places where we could shelter. And if they found us I do not think they would hurt us, for they are kind people."

Khadija stands up next to me and we look ahead. She tells me she can see the shape of another round tower though I can't make it out well, but then she points to a big, brightly lit group of buildings to our right.

"It must be a factory," I tell her. "Look at all that smoke."

Khadija says, "Well, we will not go near it because it is a long way from the river."

"Then we could go on to that next tower. We could go inside it and make ourselves comfortable."

"It won't be comfortable, will it?" she says, "It can't be comfortable. It will be cold and wet again."

"I shall make a fire."

She turns to me. "How can you do that?"

"Because I have made fires from reeds many, many times in my life."

"These reeds are all wet. They will not burn."

"I can make them burn."

And so, unlike Sarwat, she accepts my decision with grace, and follows me on the last part of the day's walk.

We were lucky to find the coffee jug. Someone must have dropped it, or left it there by mistake. I shall use it for fetching water. And we were lucky too to be given food. The man in the pub looked at the money in my hand, and I am sure it was not enough to buy what we needed. He and that woman were good to me. My throat is better since the hot drink, but I am often coughing

I have worked out how to find Amir. I shall go to each of the hotels in Norwich in turn and ask for him. Now I have asked for food, I can do anything, even without English. I wonder how many hotels there are? Three or four, perhaps, but I'm not sure. There could be more. Amir will be so happy to see me and Grandfather. When he is looking after us I shall phone Sarwat. I have got his number and it cannot be too difficult to use those phone machines. I want to apologise to him. But what if he has been sent away? I need to find that out from Amir. I don't think the English people could take me away from Grandfather. And if they tried to I would not let them. I would fight them.

I am not sure where we will live in Norwich, but I expect we can find a room. Amir will help us. Grandfather is so much healthier now he might be able to get a job, like Amir. And I know I must go to school again, even if I don't like it.

Grandfather has stopped walking and is bending to pick something up from the ground. He shows me a small orange object.

"It's a cartridge, from a gun."

"A gun?"

"Yes, for shooting wildfowl. They must shoot ducks, here, or geese, or coot – just as we used to. I was a good shot when I was young, even better than my elder brother. I could shoot straight even when the boat was rocking."

The cartridge worries me, but we have not heard any shots so we walk on in the dusk towards the tower. We are nearly there. Then I see that the factory with all the lights is ahead of us now, not to our right. That's something I've noticed about this river – because it keeps on curving, when there is something ahead, like one of these round towers, I can't tell which side of the river it's on, or even how close it is to the river. It only becomes clear when we are very near.

Grandfather is ahead and has already reached the tower. He is trying to get inside, but the door is locked shut. I am very tired now, and when I get there I just curl up by the wall and close my eyes.

What if Norwich has twenty hotels? How will I find them all? And what can Amir do to help us? After all, Sarwat helped us a lot. What more can Amir do? I know I am expecting him to help us because I want him to and he is a kind person. But perhaps I have not thought things through, and perhaps going to Norwich may not make anything better for anyone.

At least Grandfather is better off. He seems to be happy. I did not expect this at all. I thought he would find the walking difficult, and perhaps be ill. I even thought he might die. But here he is bustling about in the darkness, quite content. He's trying to make a fire, but everything is soaking wet. There is some food left, even though it's not much. There's some bread, and meat, and three apples. The cheese is finished. And I think there is a little bit of coffee too, but I'm going to save it until the night when it's very, very cold.

I'm cold already and I ought to take the blanket out of my bag and wrap it round me, but I don't want to move. So I stay in the same position, sitting on a bit of wood and with my back against a wall. I am looking up at a huge white moon in a nearly black sky. When I look away from the moon I can see stars. There are so many of them. The more I look the more I can see, and some of them are moving across the sky. I am millions of kilometres away from them, down here on the earth, on this small spot of the earth that I have walked to from another little tiny part in Iran. I should not be here. I have made the wrong decision. I have travelled across half the world and then done the wrong thing by walking away to yet another place. I am a stupid, bad person.

I move out of myself and go up onto the bank and look at myself. But this is too near so I go up to the moon. Then I look back. I look away from the blackness and the stars and down towards the round earth. I see land and sea, and I look towards a particular piece of land, to an edge of that land, to a river near that edge of land, to a round tower. And there I am, at the foot of the tower. I am as small as a baby. I am sitting leaning against the wall, with my knees up. Next to me is my bag. I look cold and unhappy, but I do not feel that coldness or unhappiness while I am in the moon. I shall stay here for a long time.

♪

To Richard's pleasure and surprise, Harriet phones, but her news is not good. It looks as if her mother, who is seventy five, is going to have to stay in hospital for two or three weeks. She is still having problems with her lungs and they are doing tests. Her other daughter lives near her and is therefore the one who visits her most in the ordinary course of events. Because Harriet knows she has done less than her sister, she wants to do her fair share while all this is going on, and there is a brother in Wales who can be there for a week later on.

"I'm going to take some time off now while she needs me. The children can stay with Anthony, thank God. And he's OK about that."

Richard asks whether he can do anything. No, there isn't anything, but thanks. Anyway, she'll be back in ten days and the family will take it from there. She's sorry if she sounds a bit frenetic, but she feels a bit frenetic.

He puts the phone down, pours himself a drink. He is coming to see what Harriet's life consists of: single-handedly managing work, children, the home - and now an extra responsibility. Estelle always recognised her privileged lifestyle - a husband with a good income, part-time work which she did only because she enjoyed it and help in the house. She had always said, "I'm so lucky. We both are." And she was right.

He is delighted that she phoned. He had told himself that she would not have his number, and would be totally occupied with her mother in any case. He found himself wondering when Harriet might last have been taken out to a restaurant or to the theatre? Did she and Polly and Adam ever go on holiday? He recalled her telling him how much it had cost to have her car repaired. Things must be pretty tight financially.

Just as he sits down with his looked-forward-to drink before his meal the phone goes again. He looks at his watch and knows it will be Mary, for she never seems satisfied with news reported via Eric and always seems to phone when it's inconvenient. Well, at this precise moment, he is not going to get up. After all that fresh air and exercise and a shower he is relaxing, and nothing is going to delay him from this glass of wine. She will leave a message and he can phone her back later. Perhaps he should invite Mary and Eric for a meal. They'd like that, and so would he. That's interesting, because since Estelle's death he has not yet cooked a proper meal for guests. He thinks wanting to do this must be a good sign.

As he takes his first mouthful of Chablis it occurs to him that Harriet might have a partner. She's young, attractive, free. How could she not have someone interested in her? Perhaps because Polly gets upset, the man does not go to the house much. So when a new man - Richard - turns up, she's jealous. Brooding on this makes Albinoni seem a good idea. And another glass of wine.

But why, if there was someone else, would she be phoning him, when they have only just begun to talk to each other about anything other than orchestra?

Later still, as he passes the flashing light in the hall, he is reminded of the message waiting for him.

"Hi Richard. It's me again. Where are you? You were there a second ago. Anyway, after I put the phone down I realised there *was* something you could do for me, if you wouldn't mind. It's Adam's canaries. It's a bit complicated to explain, it would be much easier to tell you about it. Can you call me this evening or, if you've just gone out, tomorrow morning? I won't be going to see Mum till midday. I'll be sorting out her washing and things here. Thanks a lot. Cheerio."

So, here's Harriet again, turning up when he does not expect it. It is hard to interpret that call as anything other than a request for help from a friend, and that friend is him. She's chosen him. Yes, she sounded a bit frenetic and was speaking faster than usual. But that's not surprising. When Estelle was in hospital he only had her and himself to worry about. No dependents, no work, not even a cat. On the other hand, there was no one else to help. Of course, there were friends who visited, but people seemed to find it difficult to see her when they knew she was dying. Even Mary and Eric shied away.

But Estelle just accepted it. "It's too hard for people. They don't know what to say. It's easier to stay at a distance and send cards and flowers."

And so, for the last couple of months, he had been virtually her only visitor in a room where he had been both pleased and distressed to see dying flowers constantly being replaced by living ones.

Should he phone Harriet back now? Why not?

"Hallo. Sorry I missed you. I was here, but I thought it was someone else, so I left it."

"Don't worry. It's just the canaries. They only need feeding once a day so I hope it won't be too onerous. I've given Anthony a key, but I can't expect him to keep running Adam backwards and forwards to do it."

Richard is surprised to find himself thinking, Why not? They're his children too, aren't they?

He says, "Not a problem, except that *I* haven't got a key."

"There's one in the shed, on a hook under an old raincoat behind the door. It's our emergency key."

"OK. What do I have to do?"

"The canaries are in Adam's room and the food is in a packet right next to their cage. I've forgotten how much they need, but Adam wrote some instructions out when he went to football camp, and they're pinned up on his board."

"Can I leave it until tomorrow morning?"

"Of course. That'll be fine."

He does not want to finish this conversation yet and says, "I don't want to finish this conversation yet."

Harriet chuckles, "Then don't!"

He pauses before asking, "Are you OK?"

She hesitates. "Yup. I think so. But it isn't easy."

"No. It can't be."

She pauses again, and her voice is slower now. "I don't know what's going to happen. They – the doctors – they don't know either." She sniffs. "Thanks for asking. I'm going to go now. I haven't forgotten that walk you know. I'd like to get away from doctors and wards and tests and into some fresh air. That would be good."

"Then that's what we'll do, just as soon as you're back."

The fire is alight! I felt my way around the ground until I found dry things: dead leaves from a corner, pieces of broken wood, twigs. There was not enough fuel here to keep it going all night, so I moved further from the tower and found piles of cut reed. When I pushed aside a layer of them from the top, the ones underneath were dry. I carried armfuls of them to where we were sheltering and made a dry bed for Khadija to rest on. Then I made the fire, carefully at first, so the thin dry reeds caught alight from my match, and then the thicker ones. A fire is a marvellous thing. I think of the fires we used to make from rushes and pats of dung. I have sat by so many fires like this one, watching thin wisps of smoke.

It was hard to get Khadija to move from where she was sitting. She had become very still in that way that she does, and I had to rub her cold hands and help her to her feet. She started coughing at once, but now she is settled here by the fire away from the wind. I made her take her shoes off and then pulled her blanket and the dry reeds round her, like a nest. Now she says she is warmer but she is still awake, looking into the glowing ashes. I shall sit with her all night and tend the fire. There is no food left except some of the bread we were given today, and we have finished the coffee. After this cigarette, I have only three left.

It is already very cold tonight, but it will not rain for the sky is quite clear. I have been telling Khadija the names of the stars. She says today has been like school, because I have told her so many things. There is much more to tell her about the marshes, and if I don't nobody will, and then the things I have lived and known will be forgotten. I want to show her how we wove reed mats and tell her about the storm on the lake which nearly drowned us, and about how the boys would dance and how we had to be wary of boars. I shall show her the scar on my arm. But she is too tired for any of this now.

And now it is just me and the moon and the night. But first I must pray, for today I have missed one prayer time and so I need to say more prayers than usual. It is good to feel myself well in spirit and body. I roll up my mat and walk up to the bank. The water reflects the moonlight. The river curves away in each direction. There are tiny ripples here by the edge, but out there it is quite flat. We are alone. I feel safe, and I wish I could stay here. I do not want to go to the city. I do not want to travel anywhere other than along this river, because this river has brought me to where I want to be. I am as close as I can be to the belly of the marsh. It was in the marshes that I began my life, and if Allah wills it, I shall be close to them for the rest of my life.

If you reckoned up Allah's blessings, you could not count them.
Allah is forgiving and merciful.

Khadija coughs again. I go back to her but she has not woken. Her shoulder moves slightly with each breath she takes. I know she will be a beautiful woman. The women of the Sheghanba tribe were renowned throughout the marshes for their beauty. I sit close to the fire and feed it with more sticks. They catch alight and send out sparks. In the ashes are little curls of red, all that is left of each twig or reed before it disappears. They remind me of the shapes in writing. Later, I will collect more fuel, and this moon will shine all night and draw the tide, so tomorrow there will be more wood on the bank. I will be cold, but I have endured cold many times in my life. I sit and doze, but every now and then I rouse myself and stretch my legs and my back and make sure Khadija is safe. How blessed I am to be able to watch over her while she sleeps. It is good to watch over someone you love.

Before dawn I wake because there is a wind rising. It is coming from a different direction, and it brings the smell from the factory. Sugar! That's what it is! I knew I knew it. Of course it is a sugar factory. How could I not have recognised it? I look at it again now, and can make out the towers and the chimneys. It is like the one I worked at in Majar al Kabir. That was the first job I took outside the marshes. It was noisy and it had this same rich, damp smell. It was hard to be inside a building for most of the day and not out on the marsh, but it brought me money, and I was able to buy a new boat and then go back to the marshes for many years until things changed.

It was a terrible time when Saddam drained the floods and put chemicals in the water. I do not know why he could not let us live in peace. He would not let us live at all, and we had to hide ourselves in the marshes or move away. That was when my son was killed, on the day before his wedding. My only son.

We had to decide what to do, and it was a hard choice, and in the end we were destroyed. We were forced out of the marshes. That was when I went first to Amara, and then they told me there was work in the docks in Basra, so I went there. Many of us moved to the cities, but we did not know how to live in them. We only knew how to cut reeds, and fish, and shoot birds, and make boats and reed houses. We knew little about money, and streets, and the laws of the city, and we still had to hide from the authorities. And we were separated not only from the marshes but from our families and tribes. That was why many of us decided to flee to Iran where we could stay together.

I still do not know why we were hated so much. We had done no harm. And now I have been told that the marshes themselves are destroyed, but I do not believe it, for the marshes stretch out for many, many kilometres. Not even Saddam could destroy such a big area. We used to punt and paddle day after day and still go through new waters. There were millions of fish, of birds. Eagles, ibis, kingfishers. Boars, otters, terrapins. And the buffaloes! Every man owned buffaloes! We cut reeds for them and they gave us milk to drink and we used their dung for fuel. I can recall exactly how they would lumber slowly into the water and swim in that sinking way, with only their heads above the surface.

And now dawn is coming. The moon is still up but there is a pale glow on the horizon across the river and the tide is turning. Before Khadija wakes I shall pray, and I shall build up the fire. When the sun is up I shall tell her about these things.

I wake coughing. I find I'm in a pile of reeds and do not know why until I realise that Grandfather must have covered me with them in the night. They have scratched my legs and arms but as soon as I push them off I miss their warmth. I cough up more stuff from inside me. I try to bury myself in the reeds again, but they slide off me.

The fire is burning well. Grandfather is not here but he will not be far away. I do not want to get up. I do not want this day ahead of me. I want to curl up under my blanket and the reeds, and sleep. Although I have only been awake for a minute or two, my mind is racing off into a muddle – the money under Sarwat's ashtray, being seasick, the café where Grandfather took me, Kerry Ann's dog, the spoilt boy in the supermarket. My head is not thinking straight and I can't sort it out.

I have to get up, and when I do I feel dizzy. There is a strange smell and something is wrong with me. I try to walk forward but I lose my balance and can't stop myself falling to the ground.

Then there is shouting. Grandfather is calling and I am crying out because of a bad pain in my ankle. Grandfather pulls me away from the fire, and he pours water from the metal flask over my right foot. He is praying and talking to me at the same time, but I do not understand what has happened. Then he hurries to the river to fetch more water.

When he comes back he is breathing heavily and he pours the

water over my foot. He says he saw me stand up and sway and so he ran to me but I fell into the fire and burned my foot. He is very upset now, blaming himself for leaving me, for building the fire up, for letting me be so close to the fire. I still feel dizzy, and he tells me it is because I have not eaten. The skin round my ankle bone is burnt. It looks red and open. I have never seen a burn before, but Grandfather has and says this is a bad one.

But there is nothing more to be done so I doze off again against a pile of reeds. I leave my foot open to the air so it can heal. It becomes numb with cold but I don't mind because this stops it from hurting.

Grandfather has gone away again to find something, anything, for us to eat. I am half asleep and half awake, and I suddenly remember the package I was supposed to give to Sarwat. I had completely forgotten about it. It is at the bottom of my bag and I hope it is still safe.

If I had one wish now I would wish that Amir was here.

When I wake up again the fire has good-sized flames and Grandfather is back and looking pleased with himself.

"I promised you food, and I have found food!"

"Did you go back to where we went yesterday? To that pub?"

"No. Allah sent us this!"

He holds up a thin fish nearly the length of his forearm. He says, "It's an eel." He explains how he was walking quietly by the edge of the river when he heard a rustling noise. He turned and saw an eel – he thought it was dead – slowly sliding down a bank towards the water. He knelt down and grabbed it, and then stayed quite still for he knew that something like a heron must have caught it. Within a minute an animal like an otter had appeared.

"But it wasn't an otter. It was too small, and its head was more like a rat. Even so, Allah willed that it should provide our meal!"

As he tells me this story he's laughing and scraping a space in the hot ash. Then he places the eel in the ash, and covers it over. I want to try to walk, but he says I must eat first, so we wait for the eel to cook. Soon we can smell it and I can't wait for it to be ready.

When he pulls it out with a stick a piece of it breaks off.

"That's good. That means it's cooked." He pulls it out carefully and tears off a small bit with his fingers, and passes it to me. I brush off as much ash as I can and put it in my mouth. It is delicious. Grandfather says that in the marshlands no one ate eels, but now he needs to eat, and so we eat every single bit of it except the bone. Grandfather offers me the head, but I don't like the look of it, so he has it.

When I stand up my foot hurts a lot. It does not feel as if it is part of me and when I begin to make a step the skin pulls round my heel and the burnt part at the back of my ankle. I can't put my shoe on properly. Amir would know what to do.

"Grandfather, we can't stay here. We must go on."

"You must not walk on your bad foot. Wait till tomorrow."

"No, I want to go now. Please. I want to get to Norwich."

"Well," he hesitates, "we will walk a little way and see how you are." He comes over to me and I pull his laces taut and tie them firmly, then pull the ends of his coat zip together so he can do it up.

And then we set off slowly, with him in front now, and me limping behind with my right foot only half in the shoe. It's painful, but the worst thing is not being able to walk properly. It's so tiring. I dread to think how long it will take to get from here to the next place. And as we walk it becomes clear that the factory is right by the river after all, so we will have to pass directly in front of it or behind it. But I'm thinking that I might not even get as far as that. And I'm noticing the smell too, the smell I smelled this morning. It is getting stronger and stronger. I don't mind it, though. In fact, I quite like it.

Every now and again Grandfather asks if I want to stop. I do, really, but I say I don't. The important thing is to reach Norwich, and we won't be able to do that if we keep on stopping. On the map it seems as if we're about half way from Yarmouth to the edge of Norwich. If only I hadn't fallen into the fire. I've promised myself a rest when we are on the other side of the factory. It's not late yet, but we are going so slowly. Grandfather goes ahead, looking back often to see how I am. It's exactly the opposite from when we set out. On that first day it was me in front looking back at him and hoping he'd keep up.

He told me this factory makes sugar. I wish we could have some of it. I've never stolen anything - not since the time Aunt Laila was angry when she found me with bread that I took from our neighbour - but now I could easily steal food, now that we need it badly.

We are very close to the factory and the path has become a track, and there are signs on posts and we're suddenly walking straight towards the buildings across a big area with cars and trucks. The buildings are huge. I forget about my foot when some men come out of a doorway in front of us, but we do what western people do and look away from them. And they don't take any notice of us either so we pass directly in front of the factory, keeping to the river wall, and then back onto a grass bank again, and we follow this out past another house which they are working on, and then we're back into the country.

Now that we're safe I suddenly feel dizzy again and I want to stop as soon as possible. There must be a shop near here, and we *must* buy food.

I've begun to think about what's inside the package in my bag. Carl said it was important. Perhaps it's money. If it was money, would it be all right to borrow some, and pay it back later? I'm not sure.

I think it might be.

Richard decides to feed the canaries first thing in the morning. He collects the key, lets himself in, picks up the post from the mat and goes upstairs. It feels very strange to be in the house of a family he hardly knows. It does not feel right at all. Upstairs, a door is open to what is clearly Polly's room. Harriet's room must be that one on the left.

He goes into Adam's room. Delia and Darren perk up at once and start hopping about from one perch to another, giving out little chirps. He cannot help thinking how much Estelle hated to see birds in cages. There is the Norwich FC poster on the wall, and on the desk is a Norwich City Annual and a dictionary. A grubby pair of trainers poke out from under the bed, and an open cupboard holds models, toys, boardgames. Richard has been told that every child of this age has its own TV and computer, but there is no evidence of these here.

The pinboard is by the window, and he finds the instructions for feeding half hidden by a newspaper cutting about Adam's school play, an invitation to a party and a Post-It which says DON'T FORGET MUM'S REAL BIRTHDAY. He changes the water and pours in some birdseed, and the two yellow canaries immediately peck at it. Though they have perches, a bath, a mirror and a cuttle fish bone, he reckons they would be better off back in the Canary Isles.

He goes downstairs again and puts his head round the door of the kitchen. Almost every horizontal surface is covered. There are papers, boxes, a pair of shin pads, a radio, a crumby toaster, a leggy hyacinth, washing powder. A box of empty bottles stands next to the bin. A peg holding some coupons hangs from a hook. Another holds a council tax notice. He hesitates before looking at the calendar, but concludes that calendars in kitchens do not contain confidential information. It has entries on almost every day, written in three different lots of handwriting : Polly/dentist, Maisie here, frame/pic, PTA meeting, Footie tourn. For today it says Hair appt. and he wonders if Harriet has cancelled it. On the last day of the month it says: Mum's 11th birthday. What on earth does that mean?

He drives home thinking of his own kitchen, and how he likes everything to be in its place. Compared to this kitchen, his is almost empty. Compared to this, his life is almost empty.

Once home, he brings in from the car his things from yesterday's walk. He puts the wellingtons in the utility room and takes the rucksack through to the kitchen. He goes out again to fetch the thermos and his map.

That's odd. The thermos isn't in the boot, and it isn't on or under the front passenger seat. Damn. Where is it? Exactly when he did he last have it? On the walk. He spreads the map out on the kitchen table. That's it. He had it when he was just there, by that stone cross, watching the cormorant. What a pain. It's a decent one, one of those smart metal ones. Estelle bought it a couple of years ago when he dropped and broke their plastic one, and he wants it back. He reckons that he should be able to find it, but that the longer he leaves it the more likely he is to lose it, so he makes an instant decision to go now.

This time he takes the car over the ferry, so he can come back a different way rather than drive along the same roads for the fourth time in two days. It's bright but bitterly cold. He parks by the pub and goes straight to where he was the previous day and there is the stone cross, just peeping above the reeds. No cormorant today. Only some mallards, processing in an untidy line by the far bank.

He finds the spot where he sat to have his lunch, and then goes to the place he moved to but there is no sign of the flask. Could it have rolled down the bank? If it has, he's lost it for good. But the ground is not a smooth slope so it can't have rolled. After a few minutes he gives up, disappointed and somehow feeling as if he has let Estelle down. When he reaches the car he switches on the engine at once and turns the heating up. Despite the welcome warmth, he can feel himself sliding back into a negative frame of mind, and all because he has had a glimpse of Harriet's busy, useful life and has lost the thermos Estelle bought. Is he so fragile that small things like these can knock his confidence?

So. Concentrate on something positive. Make a decision. He drives off from Reedham thinking – One: invite Mary and Eric for a meal; Two: do something for Harriet's birthday on February 29th . It was only an hour ago that he worked out that if her 'real' birthday was on February 29th, it would actually be her true eleventh birthday this year. She must be about to become forty four – fifteen years younger than he is. And Three: an instant, unplanned decision – go and have a look at the sugar factory. He had been interested to learn about the Blackheath, and now that he has half an hour to spare he will pay Cantley a visit.

He turns off left towards Limpenhoe and follows the signs to Cantley. The factory lies there to his left: a pale, spread-out site with steaming chimneys. He has to go round three sides of a huge square to reach it and he joins a stream of lorries laden with sugar beet all making their way slowly towards the entrance. He passes a railway station and a level crossing but when he realises that every vehicle entering the site has to check in, he decides to follow a rough track leading to a pub by the Yare.

He hears the roar of the factory as soon as he gets out of the car. He tries to imagine the tanker he has seen in the photo coming up here, and docking, and being unloaded. The man in the pub had said it turned round on this bit of the river, and he can see now how it must have taken up the whole width of it – it must have been an amazing sight. But the river today is empty except for gulls.

The pub is in the throes of renovation. One sign still bears the name The Red House, while a new notice announces it as Reedcutter. He notices a line marked on its wall, showing where the 1912 flood reached. He did not even know there was a flood here then.

The water is such a beautiful steely grey he tells himself there is no need to go back at once for there is nothing at home that can't wait. A group of black and white birds flies over and he is fairly sure they are lapwings, but cannot be sure because the binoculars are in the rucksack on the kitchen table. He decides to walk upstream a little way and back here for a beer before driving home.

He is feeling pleased he is beginning to know the Yare. Each of his three recent walks here has been similar but not the same. The river is always slow and the path is always empty, but there is always something going on. Like those three swans keeping an eye on him. Or this tree, whose pussy willow buds are just beginning to show. Or the curve of the river itself, the way it leads round to yet more river bank.

Ahead of him he hears someone coughing and he suddenly sees two people sitting on the ground. They are just sitting – not eating, not bird watching, not talking. They are facing the fields, and have not yet seen him.

He slows down. He finds himself slightly reluctant to pass them, but as he approaches they turn towards him. There is an older man and a young woman – a girl really. They are sitting on black plastic bags. The man has a moustache and a bit of a beard. The girl looks cold and tired, and one of her shoes is lying in the path. The man's skin is quite dark, but the girl is pale. They look pretty rough. Although Richard feels no sense of threat, he is nevertheless uncomfortable. He greets them as he passes and they nod a response. He does not smile, and nor do they. He walks on, thinking that he will have to walk back past them.

He continues for ten minutes or so until he sees a wood ahead, but he no longer feels like going on along this lonely track. It is time to make his way back. He keeps his eyes on the path, wanting to see the couple before they see him, although it occurs to him that perhaps they will not be coming in this direction.

But there is the man, standing alone. As Richard comes nearer he sees the girl kneeling at his feet. What on earth is she doing? Then she stands and they set off but hesitate as soon as they see him. They move to the side to let him pass, and as he does so he notices the girl is trying to walk with her left foot half in and half out of her shoe and that the man is holding a metal thermos flask in his hand. He realises that this is the couple he saw yesterday by the Reedham ferry.

He phones Harriet early in the evening, hoping she is not still in the hospital with her mobile switched off.

"Harriet? It's Richard. I've got something to tell you about, but tell me first how your day's gone."

"Well, my mother's a bit better. The test results aren't through yet, but she's perkier than she was, and she's made friends with the woman in the next bed. They both used to love country dancing, so they're exchanging memories of the Circassian Circle and Strip The Willow. Did you find the key?"

"Yes. The canaries are fine." He pauses a moment before saying, "Something happened to me today that you might be interested in. I came across some gypsies." He recounts the story in some detail, finishing up by saying that he thinks the girl did not look well or happy.

"So, what made you think they were travellers?"

"Because they didn't 'fit' the situation. They weren't out for a walk as I was, with proper coats and boots. They looked dishevelled and dirty, almost as if they had been sleeping rough. They had dark skin, or the man did, at least. And they had picked up the thermos I had left on the path."

"Are you sure? It could have been theirs."

"Yes, it could. But it wasn't."

"Anyway, if you're right, and they *were* travellers, what of it? After all, anyone's allowed to walk along the river path. And they didn't actually steal the thermos, did they?"

"But there was something wrong with the girl. Why was she kneeling at the man's feet, twice?"

"I don't know, but if she was doing that out in the open – especially by the ferry where there are people around – it can't have been anything much, can it?"

"No, I suppose not, but the more I think about it the more I think something was wrong. Why didn't she have her shoe on properly, if she was walking a long way?"

Harriet pauses before asking, "So, what are you going to do?"

"I don't know. I hoped you might have some ideas."

"Well. If you are really worried about them, or at least about the girl, you could tell the Police. I doubt if they'll be interested. Most of them have a pretty negative attitude to travellers and aren't likely to do anything unless the law is being broken. Do you think a law is being broken? "

"I don't know. Probably not. But I haven't been thinking about laws. I've been thinking about the girl. I remembered what you said in the pub about child abuse."

"Do you think she's being abused?"

"All I know is she didn't look well or happy."

"If you want to do something, the obvious thing is to go to the Police. Social Services can't just turn up and say, 'So what's going on here?'"

"No I can see that. But that's why they get it wrong, isn't it? All the criticism they get is about where things have been missed, or not acted on."

"True. But they still can't just bowl in because of someone's suspicion."

"Well, they ought to be able to. Don't you think so?"

"Usually they investigate more – with teachers, or health visitors, or at clinics."

"But you can't do that with gypsies, because they don't go to school, or have health visitors or go to clinics. You said yourself that they are hard to reach."

"You're right."

Richard heard Harriet sigh, so he asked, "What are you going to do this evening?"

"First I'll phone Polly and Adam. Then I'll phone Sadie, my sister, and Neil with an update. Then I'll pour myself a big glass of red wine and collapse in front of the TV. I haven't had so much time to myself for years! It's a very strange feeling – not having to check homework's been done or make a meal for the following day. I feel quite guilty."

"Then you shouldn't! Do you eat anything or are you just living on red wine?"

"I usually have cheese on toast. Tonight I'm going to have scrambled eggs."

There is silence between them for a few moments.

"Well, I'm going to sleep on it," he announces.

"Good idea, but tell me what you decide to do, won't you?"

"Of course. Well, I hope things go on getting better at your end. How are Polly and Adam?"

"They seem OK. Adam says they've been to McDonalds twice, so he's happy. And apparently Polly has a boyfriend. Not that she told me, but Adam said she spent ages choosing a Valentine's card."

"Let's hope she gets sent one too. And don't worry about the canaries. You can tell Adam he can trust me."

"I've told him already!" Harriet pauses for a moment. "Thanks for phoning. You know, it's odd being on my own all evening. I feel lonely. I hadn't expected that."

"I know what you mean."

"Yes, you must do."

"I'll phone you again tomorrow. Sleep well." He puts the phone down and goes through to the living room.

He reflects on the conversation. It consisted largely of questions and answers, partly because of what he told her. That's

OK, but he wants more than that. It was so easy with Estelle. They just grew towards each other over the years, so conversations and silences and touches just happened without thought. Will this be possible with anybody else? With Harriet?

Grandfather's gone off to find food while I rest. He's taken the bag and left me here by this little brick building. I'm sitting on a concrete step with our blankets. It's not far from the factory and I'm just hoping no one will come past. At least that man has gone. He looked at us in such a strange way, as if he knew something about us. I was scared he might say something, but he only greeted us.

My ankle is hurting a lot now, more than it has done since I first burned it. The skin looks horrible, and there is dirt on the raw part. I can't keep it out of the mud unless I walk on the tip of my toe, and that's impossible.

I've checked the map. We have walked more than half the distance to Norwich but there is still a long, long way to go, and now we are much slower. Also, there are no more grey bits that show villages so if we don't get food now things will get worse. I hope Grandfather has found a shop or another pub. He could have gone into the pub we just saw, but he thought that man who passed us might be in there.

I'm looking back at the factory. We can't smell it any more. The steamy smoke is pouring out of the tallest chimney as if it's being pushed out. Then it gets blown sideways, away from here to where we've come from, in a sort of long tube of whiteness, and then it opens up, goes darker, breaks into thin clouds and disappears. Smoke's coming from other parts of the factory too, but not in the same way. Grandfather said it smokes all night long.

Norwich. I know we're going there, but it's easy to forget that. I can't imagine Norwich at all. I suppose it will be like any city, but I am worried about this, because if it has too many people and streets and buildings it could be very difficult to find Amir.

There are lots of these seabirds here like there were in Yarmouth, and I like them. It's a shame Grandfather can't see well. He wants me to describe every bird I see in case he knows what it is, and he knows lots of the water birds, but he has never seen the huge white ones before, the ones with the long necks that run on the water to take off and fly low and smooth with a strange noise. If they're not too far off he can see them out on the fields or in the river, especially when they open up their wings. He says they spread out like lily flowers, but I've never seen a lily flower. At first he asked me about the river and what I saw on it, and I told him there were more birds on the land than on the river. There are hundreds of them on the flooded fields, and I think they are eating the grass. Grandfather has told me about a special bird he calls the Sheikh's daughter. He said it's very beautiful and fast and has bright blue and brown feathers and a strong beak for catching fish. I hope I see one.

Here he comes. He's just coming round the bend, but I can see already that he is looking worried, so perhaps he hasn't got anything. But when he reaches me he pulls out a plastic box.

"I stole this. There was a boat outside the pub, a big flat boat and a floating platform with a crane on it. The men who work on the boat were talking together by the pub. Then they went over towards the factory, and while they were there I saw this box lying on top of their boat. It was easy to reach over and take it."

I open the box and there are two apples, some bread and cheese, two chocolate bars. I start eating at once, and pass the box back to him. He takes an apple and eats it slowly and in silence. He feels bad, and I do not know how to comfort him. But the food makes me feel better and warmer, and soon I am ready to start walking again, so we set off. He leads the way and I try to keep up with him. Yesterday's high tide lifted old reeds and bits of wood and rubbish up and almost onto the path, and many of the growing reeds have been flattened down by the strength of the water.

We keep on walking. I'm just looking at the ground now, counting the little mounds of black earth that Grandfather says must be made by an animal, though he doesn't know what. Thirty six, thirty seven, thirty eight, thirty nine. I'm ready for another rest after an hour, but just as I am about to say I need to stop, we hear a different noise. I look behind and there's a mechanical crane sticking high above the river and moving towards us. At once, we both squat down so we can't be seen.

When it's safe, Grandfather stands up straight and goes on plodding along the path. We go on and on, and there's another round tower on our side and then a house ahead, on the other side, with some boats moored near it. We pass them and just keep going, but suddenly there's a loud crashing in some reeds by the field, and a brown animal races out and away and is gone.

Grandfather cheers up at once. "I thought for a moment that was a boar! It sounded like one, but it was some sort of deer. Look, there it goes!" He points, and we watch it bounding across the field. I wish I could run like that.

"Have I told you about the boar in the marshes? No? There were many wild boar living there. They were very dangerous, and could kill a man easily. Once, when I was about twenty, I was in a boat when one came charging out of the reeds and into us. It knocked the boat right over and we all fell in. Its tusk caught my arm, but luckily it was frightened and swam off. Look at this scar." He pulls his cuff back to show me his left wrist and forearm, and there are two red lines running towards his elbow. In between them the skin is sunken in and stretched.

"It tore the muscle, but it healed, and that arm is quite as strong as the other one. It is only the skin that looks bad."

When we go on walking I think about the woman with the scar on her face. I am glad it is my foot that is hurt, and not my face.

After quarter of an hour Grandfather says, "Wait a little. I need a drink." He goes to the edge of the water, and stoops to dip his hand and carry water to his mouth. He prefers this to using the cup from the flask. While he does this I decide to go on ahead.

And then I see the soldier.

There is a tall soldier standing on the path looking out to the river. I'm sure he hasn't seen us. I hurry back to tell Grandfather, and we crouch down.

"A soldier?"

I describe the man to him, including his brown and green clothing and fur hat. I have seen films about soldiers like this one at Sarwat's flat.

"Is he alone? What is he doing?"

There were no others with him as far as I could see, and he was just looking at the river - not across it, but *at* it. I tell Grandfather to stay hidden while I stand up carefully. When I do I see that behind the man is a big green umbrella. This is strange. It is not raining, and he is not holding it. It seems to be fixed to the ground.

"A soldier with an umbrella? Can you see a gun?"

"No."

"Then let us go on. Allah will protect us."

So we go on, but I am very worried because this is the first soldier we have seen in this country.

When we get near Grandfather turns to me and says this man is not a soldier and he is not in uniform - he's just dressed in green clothes, and the umbrella is to shelter him. And then we see his sticks. He has four sticks pointing out over the water. He is fishing! Grandfather is so curious that he slows down when we go past and the man says something to him. Grandfather points to the sticks, and asks the man, in Arabic, about the fish he catches. Of course the man does not understand, so Grandfather spreads his hands some distance apart to show the size of a fish, and then the man laughs and goes over to his umbrella. Under it he has many things: a chair, plastic containers, a metal flask like ours, a raincoat. I notice that he has a big knife too. He opens one of his boxes and takes out a book. Inside there are photos of him holding up huge fish. He is very proud of these photos, and Grandfather is interested in them.

And then we go on, and Grandfather has to stop himself from walking fast now so he can tell me about how he used to go fishing with a spear, and how some people in the marshes killed fish by poisoning them, and there was one tribe who used nets. And he said the fisherman we had just met was a good fisherman because he had a decent sized knife and this is the first proper knife Grandfather has seen in England.

I can't keep up with him. I want to stop walking and rest. Perhaps we will have a fire again. Now there's another building ahead of us and it looks like a small house with a tall chimney. It's too far away for Grandfather to see clearly so I tell him about it and say I'm not going further than that. I can't be certain which side of the river it is on, but I hope and hope it is on our side. As we get nearer I start to set myself something to reach. I choose a bush or a post, and make myself walk to it, and then choose another object. I notice that while I do this I often start thinking about something else, and that helps me go further. Another thing I do is to count my steps. I decide to walk thirty steps, and then another thirty.

And now I can see that the house is on our side, although it's not a house after all and the chimney is not part of the main building. It looks in quite good condition, so we should be all right here. But when we climb over some bars to reach it Grandfather finds the whole place is locked up. There is no way in at all. Worse still, all the way round the outside it is muddy and wet so we will not even be able to shelter beside it. Then I see a sort of bench right by the river, and I go over and sit down. My foot is aching and burning and stinging all at once. I daren't look at it. I gaze across the river at the woods. A few ducks are swimming away from me, leaving overlapping Vs behind them on the surface of the water, like the outline of mountain peaks.

I don't know what we will do now.

Richard is looking forward to Mary and Eric coming for a meal on Sunday evening. He decides to do a proper roast dinner and takes care in choosing a decent piece of organic pork. He buys sweet potatoes as well as carrots, sprouts and potatoes. Estelle introduced him to sweet potatoes years ago and he loves them roasted round the meat. What wine would they enjoy? He buys a Californian Chardonnay and a South African Pinotage, knowing one of those will certainly do. That's the first course sorted. But what about a dessert? Chocolate mousse?

Something more elaborate from one of Estelle's cookbooks? He settles for fruit salad and a couple of good cheeses.

It feels strange going round Tesco's with a trolley after all this time with just a basket. He loads the shopping into the car and drives home with the News on. The main item is about more bombs in Iraq, but he misses parts because he is thinking about Harriet. He won't phone her for an hour or two until about eight thirty. There's a lot to tell her.

After stacking the plates from his supper into the washing-up machine he checks the time. Only seven-thirty. He had hoped it might be later. Will she have had enough time to unwind? Or might she still be phoning her brother and sister, and Adam and Polly? Does she talk with her ex-husband as well as the children? What must that be like for her? How has their marriage ended? Are they still friends? Does Anthony have a partner? And is Harriet wondering about him and his life the way he is about her and her life? He decides to wait another half hour.

"Hallo Harriet. It's me. Tell me first if I'm too early. Have you made all your phone calls? Have you had your first glass of wine?"

"Yes. I'm OK, but only just, to be honest."

"What is it? Has something happened?"

"Yes it has." Now she sounds upset.

It must be her mother. He waits for her to speak.

"It's Polly. Or rather, it's Anthony. Did I tell you she now has a boyfriend, Lee? Well, Anthony allowed her to go with him to a friend's party last night. He didn't tell her when she had to be back by, and she stayed out till past one o'clock. I can't believe it. She's only fifteen, Anthony doesn't know anything at all about Lee, and the girl friend who should have been going too didn't go, so Polly went off in a car to God knows where and came back drunk."

Richard does not know what to say.

"Anthony just doesn't think. He has no idea about teenagers. She could have been given drugs, or anything could have happened. It was Adam who told him she is only allowed to stay out till eleven with my permission, and that she has to tell me exactly where she is and who she's with."

"Is she OK?"

"She is actually, but she stayed in bed all morning because she had a hangover, or that's what it sounded like. When I spoke to her an hour ago she said there was no need for me to worry. Yes, she had been out later than usual, and yes she had had a drink or two, but she was fine, and Anthony's 'friend' has been looking after her this morning. But no one was looking after her last night, were they? And she knows darned well what the rules are. I don't know whether to be angry with Polly or Anthony."

"You sound angry with them both."

"I am." He hears her let out a big sigh.

"And how's things with your mother?

"Better, thanks. She's more comfortable, and they don't seem to have found anything alarming. They'll let her come home when they've sorted out some drugs – I dread that for her because there's always side effects, aren't there? And Neil, my brother, he's already here, and that feels better."

"So when are you coming back?"

"As soon as possible. Monday at the latest. I just want to get Polly and Adam home as soon as I can and get back to normal. I've only been away for six days, but it feels as if my life is out of control." She draws breath, then says, "But that's enough about me. How about you?"

"I'm all right. And I'm looking forward to seeing you."

"Are you? That's nice. I hope I won't be as miserable as I feel now." She pauses again before saying, " Richard, do you know you have a really nice voice?"

This puts him off his stride. "Do I?"

"Yes. It's sort of reassuring and steady."

"I've never really thought about it."

"I haven't either, but just now I realised how much I like it."

He's not sure what to say so brings the conversation back to what's easy. "Do you want to hear what I've been thinking about the people I think are gypsies?"

"Yes, of course I do. I've thought about them too."

He tells her again about the couple on the path and describes in detail their unkempt appearance, the girl's limp and her expression of fear.

"I'm sure she's frightened of something - perhaps the man - and I think she's in pain or even ill."

"How old is she?"

"Thirteen? I don't know. I can't tell the difference between girls who're fourteen and those who are twenty."

"Younger than Polly?"

"Yes. She must be. It's hard to say, but yes, I'm pretty sure she's younger than Polly."

"Have you decided what to do?"

"I'm going to find them once more, and then I'll either tell the Police, or leave them. But I'm not sure what's likely to happen if I tell the Police."

"I expect they'll listen to you, but I doubt if they'll go and look for them unless they think a young person could be at risk."

"But suppose they *did* go to find them - what would they do next?"

"It depends on so many things. If they are travellers - which, to be honest, I doubt - they'd probably just get them back to where they belonged. But you don't know what's happening, do you?"

"Not really. Anyway, I'm determined to go back tomorrow."

"Good luck. I want to know what happens."

They finish the conversation with Harriet saying she is going to phone Anthony again. Richard wishes her luck and tells her he will talk to her tomorrow.

He puts the phone down. What was it she had said? "I really like your voice"? That was a surprise. He reflects again on the fact that he is fifteen years older than her. It seems a lot. Estelle would probably say it was too much. And so, he was sure, would - or does - Polly. And what does Harriet think about it?

Later that evening, as he sits with his whisky, he goes on thinking about Harriet and her children and her ex-husband. There must always be something going on in families. Two people are manageable, but once there are four or five, there must just be so many things happening. From the outside it was easy to think that having children was straightforward and enjoyable, but here was Harriet upset and angry - moods he has never seen her in at rehearsals and concerts.

The girl by the river must be younger than Polly, surely, but while Polly is getting drunk and going to parties, the girl seems to be living rough on a river bank in midwinter. He must ask Harriet about that when she is over today's upset. She had sounded pragmatic rather than sensitive about the girl, but how would she feel if Polly was living like that?

He pours himself his second drink. Forty-four. It's very young. Then he thinks again about the Reedcutter pub. He liked the sepia photos of men cutting reeds, stacking them, loading them onto carts, and the one of a long flat boat laden with tied bundles of reeds was particularly evocative. That life was like something out of another world, but not so long ago it had been going on here, on the Yare.

How had she described his voice? Reassuring and something. Reassuring and steady. Yes, that was it.

Khadija limps across the grass towards the fire I have made. Thanks be to Allah. I was worried seeing her sitting for so long and feared she might fall in the water when she stood up. But now she has got up and is coming over here, and I point to a platform I have made from some bricks and wood so she can be off the ground. I set aside a little bread for the morning and then give her some cheese and the last apple, and she takes a piece of the chocolate. It is so sweet she needs to drink water with it, so I fetch her some.

Then we sit in silence, listening to small noises. We are close to trees, so we hear the wind and the whistles of night birds. A bird of prey screeches. We hear the river too. Animals and fish and birds move in it, causing ripples and small splashings. Further off is the sound of traffic and trains.

Khadija tells me we are not so far from Norwich now, but I know this last bit will be the hardest. While it was still light I made her show her foot to me. It is bad. The flesh above the back of her ankle is open. The skin round her ankle and over her heel is covered in blisters. All of it is covered in earth and she says her whole foot throbs.

And I too am ill. There are days when I do not bleed, but I did yesterday, and I did today. I want to eat real food – rice and lamb and good fruit – not English bread and cheese and chocolate. Even though I needed food today it was not good to have to steal it. Although my father taught me not to steal, I was not devout until I became older and my life became so difficult. It was then that I wanted to learn more about the true ways.

I thought about how I accepted it when Amir and Sarwat drank wine, even while Khadija was there, and I am noticing that because I am in a foreign place I am doing some things which I would not have done before.

At first I thought this was bad, but I am not sure now. It is not that I choose to ignore the teachings or customs, but I find myself in new circumstances and so have to do new things. Do all those who move away from their homelands do this? Or do they hold tight to the truth and their own ways? It seems that both these things happen. I think again about Sarwat being disrespectful to me, and about the men he takes to their work where they kill chickens in the wrong way. If a man moves away from his home and his people, is it possible for him to remain the same?

And how much does it matter? Sometimes I think that it matters less for me than for Sarwat and Khadija. I shall not live for many more years, but what will happen to them if they lose the ways of the families they were born into? Can they become part of another tribe, another people?

Perhaps they have lost their old ways already. I think they have, for Sarwat has no idea about the marshes and nor had Khadija until these last few days. But if I believe the next generation should know about the one before it, then it is up to me to tell them. At least we can speak together in Arabic. When people leave their birthplaces there must be a generation which knows two languages, but then the next generation may not learn the language of their grandparents. That seems to me to be a situation of great sadness and great loss. Amir told me that now he thinks in English for most of the time, and that many people can think in another language. How can they do that? I cannot imagine thinking in anything except Arabic, but then I recall that I learned enough Farsi to make myself understood by Iranians. Sarwat sometimes spoke to his friends in English when I was there and I think he did that when he wanted to say bad things, or things he did not want me to know about. So being able to speak another language may not always be good.

Khadija is asleep now, leaning back against the wall. She looks uncomfortable but this is the best place I can find for her. Her leg is stretched out in front of her and her foot rests on a plastic bag.

When we started walking along this slow river I was not sure where we were going, or why, but Khadija led me and I could do nothing but follow her. We are walking upstream, away from where the river meets the sea and towards its source. Then I found my memories of the marshes which have been there inside me for many years, although they were hidden. I have been on so many journeys in my life, especially this long one to the west. Where have I come to?

I look out at the glint of the river. The clouds are moving slowly across the sky. Sometimes the moon shows itself, sometimes it remains covered. The tops of the reeds rustle a little, for they are dry and old, but there are new green reeds growing close to the water, and today I saw another sort of reed – the ones with tops like the brown tails of an animal – hard at first but then soft when they break open and let their pale seeds blow into the marsh. The trees near us are dark and the shapes of their bare branches are black against the sky. Some of the bushes have new buds and some have tiny yellow flowers hanging from the twigs. One type of tree has white buds as soft as a duckling's down.

It is He who sends down water from the sky
with which He brings forth the buds of every plant.

Khadija wants us to go to the city. She is young, and she wants to live her life. Even if I tried to, I would not be able to stop her. Perhaps I love her especially because I know she will not give up. It was my idea to come to the west. She did not want to come. I did what I did for the best. But *was* it for the best? I have seen how sometimes people choose a course of action but later they are not always sure they were right to choose it. That is why

I pray. It is not easy to make the right choice alone, so I ask for guidance.

Allah will decide about our progress, and Khadija's foot, and my illness, and Sarwat's appeal. His decisions will be for the best. I do not know why He let our marshes be ruined, our houses be burned, or many people be tortured or killed in war. He has His reasons.

Now Khadija is slipping sideways. I try to make her comfortable on the wooden platform by putting one hand under her instep and one under her knee and lifting her leg up gently. Then I cover her with blankets. I put more wood on the fire and go on listening to the sounds of the night.

It is very grey and cold this morning when I wake. My leg is aching and feels fat and hot as far up as my knee. I pull up the leg of my trousers to look at it. It is worse than it was yesterday. I will not tell Grandfather this, for he will make me stay here longer. We cannot stay here. We *must* get on and reach Norwich and find Amir. It is not far now, and I am hoping we can do it. Grandfather is praying, so I get up carefully and bring out the last of the food, but there is less of it than I thought.

When we have eaten we must move on along the river path, but at our next resting place I shall open the packet that Sarwat's friend Carl gave me because I realise now that it must have money in it. I do not know why I did not think of this before. I am sure we will reach a shop now because we are getting close to the city, and Grandfather will be able to buy food.

Last night I had a bad dream. I couldn't find Amir. I went to many hotels, but each one said he was not there. Then I sat down by the road and asked people who were passing, but none of them understood Arabic. So I stood up and tried to walk, but I could not. And then I cried. I do not cry often. I have not cried much since the day I came to Yarmouth and found Grandfather again. But this dream was wrong, because I *can* walk, even if it hurts me.

When we set off I do up Grandfather's shoes and he goes in front. After only a minute of two he turns round to watch how I am getting on. He comes back to me.

"A stick. You need a stick. I will find you one."

I wait, standing with almost all my weight on my good foot, while he goes into the woodland close by us and the path. Soon he returns with a stick he has broken from a tree. He is breaking twigs off it. When I try walking with it, it helps me keep my balance. This is good, for I have already nearly fallen. He wants to find more sticks to make me crutches, but I want to get on. So we keep walking, and the stick makes it slightly easier for me, especially when I pause for a minute or two. But I still go on counting steps and telling myself to reach a certain bush, or get level with a particular tree. It is not so open here and I feel a bit safer.

Grandfather walks slowly but steadily. He always looks around – at the river, at the opposite bank, back towards me and to the places we have passed. He does not seem so ill now, even though we are cold and wet and hungry. He points out to me that the factory and the smoke are no longer in sight, and somehow this makes me feel sad. I liked that smoke and I shall miss it.

Most of the time I keep my eyes on the ground to make sure that I do not trip. The path is uneven and muddy. Sometimes I suddenly find I have caught up with Grandfather because he has waited for me, and each time he asks if I want to stop.

This time I tell him I will stop after another hundred steps, so he goes on ahead and finds a good place for me to sit. By eighty steps I am out of breath and sweating and my leg is very bad, but I do what I set myself.

When I am sitting down I pull up my trouser leg and see that the whole of my calf is red. I drink some water from the flask and look back, but we have hardly gone any distance at all. The group of trees where Grandfather found me the stick still seems very close.

I suddenly turn sideways to vomit into the grass.

Later, I hear Grandfather is saying my name again and again. I lift my head and open my eyes. Have I been asleep?

"Khadija. I have found a safe place for us to go. It is not far. I can carry you there."

I face him and let him lift me up, lean me over his shoulder and carry me a few paces. He is panting with the effort and soon puts me down.

"It's difficult, but I will do a few steps at a time."

So he picks me up again, struggles on for few steps and then lets me down to the ground. It is too difficult. Then he tries walking next to me, half holding me, with my bad foot next to him. This is a little better. We do ten paces then stop, then another ten, then another. And after fifty paces I look up from the ground and see that ahead of us things look different. The grass has been cut. The path is clearer, neater.

"There are more marshes here. Look." Grandfather points to the reedbeds on our side of the river and on the other side. Small pools and stretches of water lie between the clumps of reeds. There are no buildings in sight, but the train sounds close when it passes, and we come to a wooden bridge. We are both out of breath, and we lean against the side of it and relax.

"How much further is it?"

"Not far at all. About the same distance we have just come."

And so we get up again and go on and he leads me down a grass path away from the river, and along another path in between reedbeds, to a wooden hut.

"There it is. It is quite dry inside and we can sleep there."

There are lots of footprints outside the door, but I don't care any more. Grandfather goes in first and helps me in. It is dark, but he makes it light because parts of the wall can be opened up, like windows without glass. He fixes one section of wood up so it stays open. Outside is a lake with wild birds. It is a good place, but I am shaking. Grandfather is tired and he lies down across the floor with a blanket. He is asleep at once, for I don't think he slept last night and he told me his stomach was hurting again.

I sit on a bench, leaning on a ledge and looking out of the window. Then I pull Carl's packet out of my bag and put it on the ledge. It is very small and light, so it must be notes not coins. It is wrapped up tightly in plastic which is a good thing or probably the money would have got wet by now. I have to tear it open with my teeth. There's more plastic inside, wrapped over and over.

But it's not money. It's powder, rather like salt, or sugar. I lick my finger to taste a tiny bit of it. I have no idea what it is, and there's not much of it anyway. For a moment I am puzzled, and then I realise what has happened. Carl must have owed Sarwat money, but hoped to trick him. That was why he gave *me* the packet instead of taking it to Sarwat himself. Carl would have disappeared by the time Sarwat understood he'd been tricked. So now, except for one bar of chocolate, Grandfather and I have only a few coins to buy food. We have almost nothing at all.

All at once I feel so angry. Carl is a thief, and he has tricked me as well as Sarwat. And we need money badly. I want to eat, I want to eat proper food and drink something hot. I want my foot to be better. I want to not walk any more. I want to go home. I want home but I do not know where home is. And I want Amir.

But I can't have any of what I want.

I stand up on my good leg and throw the packet as hard as I can out of the opening in front of me, but it falls down into the water close to the hut. Some powder spills out and settles on the surface for a moment before sinking in amongst the reeds. The bag stays floating on the surface. I am shaking, and I feel myself beginning to cry. And I *do* cry, but Grandfather does not wake up. I sit sideways and bring one knee up to my chest, and stretch my bad leg out along the seat. Like this I can see right across the lake. There is a big group of geese on the far side, and high above is a large black bird which slowly flaps and glides, flaps and glides.

There is no point looking at the map any more. I know there are still hours and hours of the day ahead. It starts to rain and I watch patterns on the water changing as the wind blows the rain across it. Grandfather is snoring quietly.

I do not know what will become of us. I lean back against the wall and move out of myself.

♪

Richard has forgotten how enjoyable it is to make a meal for friends. He decides to do the job properly – he rubs salt into the pork and brushes it with olive oil to make crisp crackling, then peels and chops the potatoes and arranges them round it. He puts it all into a very hot oven. He will add the sweet potatoes when he turns it down later. He makes a point of slicing the carrots lengthways rather than into common or garden roundels, and, after taking off the outer leaves of the sprouts, he cuts a small cross into the base of each one as his mother used to do. Poulenc accompanies him as he cuts the grapes in half and takes out the pips.

Now for the table. When was the last time this striped cloth was used? Certainly not since Estelle's death. And here are the napkins, of which he will only need three. He hesitates when it comes to laying the places round the square table. Which side will he leave empty? In their last house he always used to sit in the same place so he could reach the wine from behind him on the sideboard, and Estelle always sat nearest to the kitchen. They have only had one dinner party here, and that was also with Eric and Mary. He remembers the conversation he and Estelle had about who they would put where. And now there are only three of them. He decides to put himself nearest to the kitchen, facing the empty side. Seven-thirty exactly. He polishes the glasses and pours himself some white wine, and here they are already.

It is good to see them. Mary pushes a big bunch of red tulips at him before hugging him. Eric hands over a bottle. "You'll like this, I guarantee." Then he too puts his arms round Richard's shoulders and holds him. "Good to see you. We've missed you." They shrug off their coats.

"The house looks *lovely*," says Mary.

They settle down with a drink, exchanging news about Aylsham and how the concert went, and how their grandson is. Mary pulls several photos out of her bag and passes them across to Richard. He looks at them in turn. In one, a baby peeps out of a snug little cocoon, held by their daughter.

"You can't see much of Jack there, but it's a nice one of Rachel, isn't it?"

He nods and looks at the next. Here Jack is sitting propped up in the corner of an armchair. He stares at the camera with a solemn expression. The third one is taken at bathtime. A man's hand supports Jack's head, and the baby's podgy knees poke out of a heap of bubbles.

"You must be enjoying Jack a lot." He leans back in his chair and feels himself beginning to relax for the evening. But then he sits up again, saying, "Hang on, I need to put the vegetables on."

He hurries out to the kitchen, feeling unprepared for entertaining his guests and dealing with the meal simultaneously. He pours boiling water on the carrots, and returns to the living room with the white wine from the fridge.

"I'm making you responsible for the wine, Eric. I'm not capable of topping up drinks *and* seeing to the vegetables *and* making gravy. Shall we open the one you brought?"

"No. It's been shaken up in the car. Keep it for another time. Can I start on this Pinotage?"

"Go ahead. It's been open at least an hour."

The meal is a success, except that he forgot completely about apple sauce. Afterwards Mary and Eric go back into the sitting room and Richard disappears to make coffee.

When he returns with the tray, he finds Mary by the music stand. She has picked up his box of oboe reeds. "I've never looked at these properly before. Aren't they strange?"

"Well, not to me. They're tools of the trade for me."

She picks one up. "I mean that they look strange. You wouldn't expect something like this to make music, would you?"

"It takes other things as well to make music: the oboe itself, the blowing - even spit - and the score, of course."

"Even so, without this reed, the oboe wouldn't work, would it?"

"No, it certainly wouldn't. You're right, the reed is crucial."

Eric pulls a book out of the shelf and leafs through it. He says, "Last time we saw you, you were dreading sorting Estelle's things out. How are you getting on?"

"Not too badly. I need to take a final load of clothes to a charity shop, and I should phone two of her friends because I've kept a few things for them. There's a college photo which I think one of them should have. And a memento from Greece where she and Frances went on holiday before I met her. It will mean more to Frances than to me. But I've sorted the bird books. That was easy - I decided to keep the lot, and I've even been out doing some birdwatching myself.

"In fact," he continues, "I want to tell you about something interesting that's been going on in my life." Immediately he notices Mary glance at Eric. This causes him to hesitate, but then he launches into the story about the man and the girl by the river. He mentions Harriet, but when he does so it does not elicit any further sign of particular attention.

There is a silence when he finishes. Then Eric says, "So you've decided to go back there? Are you sure?"

"Yes. I really think that something is wrong, and I think the girl is ill."

"But surely the Police should be dealing with it, not you."

"Harriet seems to think they won't be interested."

"But have you phoned them?"

He shakes his head.

"Why not?" asks Mary. "In fact, why not do it now?"

Eric agrees. "That's a good idea, you know. It sounds dodgy to me. You've used words like 'desperate' and 'rough'."

Richard demurs, then admits, "I suppose I have."

"Go on. Phone them now. You've got me intrigued, " says Eric.

"All right. But I'm going to have a refill first. Who'd like some more?" As Mary holds out her cup he asks, "Is it sensible to do this on a Saturday night? Wouldn't tomorrow be better?"

Eric says, "If something's wrong, the sooner they know the better."

Mary looks up the number in the phone book, and Richard goes into the hall to make the call. He is back within a few minutes.

"They wanted to know whether an offence was being committed. I said I didn't know, but that one *might* be being committed. Then they asked what offence, and I didn't really have an answer. I said I thought the man might have hurt the girl, but they said they could only act when an actual offence was reported."

"I don't believe it! I thought they were supposed to *prevent* crime," says Mary.

Eric asks, "Didn't they want to know anything else?"

"Not really. They took my name and phone number, but I got the distinct feeling that they were not going to do anything. They probably think I'm some mad twitcher. So I'm definitely going back tomorrow."

"You shouldn't go on your own," states Mary, "but I'm afraid that tomorrow we've promised to see Eric's aunt - Joan - the one you met at Christmas. It's her eighty-fifth and we can't let her down."

"That's OK. I'll be fine on my own. Don't worry about me. I've met them twice already, don't forget."

It had been a good evening. Quite a watershed in one way - inviting friends for a proper evening meal. He thought that he would miss Estelle more, but they talked about her quite easily. In fact the hardest thing was trying to do everything at the same time on his own. At one point he felt really rushed, and he had never experienced that as a host before. It was strange how things turned out not to be as you expected them.

And the photos. Seeing those photos of the baby made him think about all of his and Estelle's photos. The ones taken from before they were married, across the nearly thirty years of their life together. It wasn't that they had taken a great many of them, rather that there were some special ones. Like that one on their wedding day when the sun came out in the courtyard just in time for the reception. Or the one in York, on Estelle's birthday, and the one on the mantlepiece of them at that summer ball.

And what would happen when he died? He had put off altering his will since Estelle's death. Should he leave everything to a charity? To the new cancer support centre being planned in the Norfolk and Norwich Hospital? Or should he leave it all to Ian, his brother, whom he hardly knew? Oh God, it was so difficult. But the photos. Who else would want them? No one. Why should they? And yet the thought of them being thrown away is appalling. He makes himself think about something different.

He remembers Mary's give-away look to Eric when he said he had something to tell them. He was sure her ears pricked up because she was hoping to hear about some female friend.

So. Harriet. It is true he has begun to think about her differently. Until very recently she was just a member of the orchestra he had known for three or four years. He cannot remember when she joined. But now he has met her children and knows about her work and her ex-husband, her mother, her sister and brother. Even her daughter's boyfriend and her son's canaries.

She is coming back tomorrow. Would it be too soon to go round in the evening? Perhaps he should just phone. And her birthday is only a fortnight away, so that will be an opportunity.

An opportunity for what? He imagines himself taking her out to dinner, watching her opening a present (this will need thinking about), driving her home. And kissing her? Is that where this is all going?

He turns over and thinks about the thousands of times he has lain in bed with Estelle. He thinks of their decades of love-making, their little familiar codes of meaning, the way she stroked his neck, the way he reached round her waist, licked her soft earlobes.

What would it be like to make love with someone else?

When I wake I find Khadija sitting on the floor. Her eyes are shut but she's awake. I put my blanket over her and then she lies down and I hear her begin to breathe quietly and steadily. I unroll my prayer mat and pray because it is close to the middle of the day.

After that, I go out of this hut for a few minutes. There are many footprints outside the door and I think men must come here to shoot birds. That's why there are these narrow windows that open up. Over the last few miles we've seen more cartridges, and I expected to find some in the hut, but there aren't any. We have not heard one shot yet, either, but perhaps we will today. There is a cold wind, so I go back in, but I have fixed one of the windows open because I do not want to sit in the dark and I like seeing the small lake and the reedbeds outside. Further away is a long, dark patch that I think must be a line of trees. I sit looking out of the narrow window for a long time, moving my beads, telling the names of Allah.

Just in the last day, the landscape has changed. Before, there was the river, and the reeds and the fields. But today bushes and trees lined our path, and the path had many footprints. So although it is less wild there are more reedbeds. They stretch out on each side of the river. Even though we are getting closer to the city, where we are today is more like my own marshes.

We passed a sign on a post this morning. I could not read it of course, but any sign means people. For the first time since we started to walk, I find myself wanting to reach somewhere, not to go on getting away from somewhere. And the time has come to get help for Khadija.

So, I go outside again to see where I might go to find help, but within a few moments I see two of those big white birds on the water in a small ditch nearby. Although I approach, they hardly move. Khadija has described them to me, and I have seen many of them in flight or in the distance, but now I am close up to them. They turn slightly on the water to keep me in their sight as I pass. They are beautiful. Not like pelicans, or herons, nor like any bird in my marshes, but beautiful in their own way.

I walk back to the signpost where two paths meet. One continues along the river; the other turns away from it to the right and past the end of the track to the hut we are resting in. I shut my eyes, listen to the trees swaying.

This path of Mine is straight.
Follow it and do not follow other paths,
for they will lead you away from Me.

I choose the river path again, but I do not want to take it yet and say to myself that I cannot leave Khadija without telling her what I am going to do. But the truth is that I do not want to bring this journey to its end, and I go back to the hut. And so today passes. I sleep for a while and am then awake for a while, but Khadija hardly stirs. Just once she goes outside but even that is difficult for her, and she begins coughing again.

I watch the wind move across this little lake, and I see coot and ducks. Three geese land on the water and stay for a short time, but my eyesight fails me and I wish Khadija could describe them to me in detail. Khadija is with me but she is not with me. It is not just that she is asleep. It seems that now she is more than asleep, in some state where I cannot reach her. At sunset I pray, and at night I can see lights far across the reedbeds. We are getting near the city.

I must go there tomorrow. I cannot just wait here, avoiding the future. Sometimes in life it is better to wait, but I do not feel that now. Tomorrow I shall say my prayers and then set off for the city on my own. Allah will watch over Khadija. She will be safe until I return.

Richard decides to leave the clearing up from the previous evening until later. He creates a space on the kitchen table and spreads the Explorer map across it, then folds it back so he can see the part he needs. He examines it carefully. Where will they have got to by now? They must be somewhere around the empty bit in the middle here – between Strumpshaw and Cantley and Claxton. The blue Yare wanders across the white background of the map which is divided up here by tiny straight blue lines. The effect is of a sinuous curve set amongst unevenly sized rectangular fields. It reminds him of some modern patchwork quilts he and Estelle once saw at an exhibition at Blickling Hall.

He finds the railway crossing he saw at Cantley, and follows the railway line with his finger in the direction of Norwich. It lies much closer to the river than any road does. And what is this yellow shading? He opens out the unwieldy map again – no one would want to do this in the open on a windy day – and finds it marks the boundary of the Broads Authority. That's interesting. He has not really thought about this area as being part of the Broads.

He moves his finger upriver from Cantley, and stops when he reaches the words River Yare, printed in blue. Surely they can't have got further than here? But he doesn't want to miss them, and anyway, there seems to be no path from the nearest road which he can see is Station Road at Buckenham. He moves his finger further upstream. There is a big P and the image of a footprint indicating walks and trails. There is a bird too, showing that the area here, Strumpshaw Marsh, is a nature reserve. He has heard of Strumpshaw Fen. This must be it, and it seems the best bet as a starting place. He will go to the car park, walk to the river and then go downstream. He's likely to meet them along there, and if he doesn't he can always go further on, even as far Brundall, and then work his way backwards.

Within half an hour he is driving through Thorpe St Andrew and en route for Strumpshaw. It is windy and he has wrapped up well and made sure he has his mobile with him, bearing in mind Mary and Eric's concern about risk.

The car park is virtually empty apart from the vehicles of contractors working there restoring an old cottage. He crosses the railway line and goes into the reception area – a welcoming place full of posters of dragonflies and ducks, and a whiteboard covered with lists of recent sightings: marsh harrier, lapwing, an otter, a bittern, pinkfooted geese, widgeon, a fox, teal, godwits, plovers, barn owls, bean geese, greylag geese, Chinese water deer.

No one is there. He puts some money for entry to the reserve in the box, and checks the map on the wall. He can walk through the wood, down to the river by a hide, along the river to a pumphouse and back. He can see now that most of the area is marshland, and cannot just be walked across. That means that the man and the girl will have to stick to the river path too.

He sets off through the woods past big clumps of snowdrops. His mind is running away in different directions, and he finds himself hurrying. He makes himself slow down, then comes out of the wood and turns right onto the path that leads to the river. Ahead, he sees the pumphouse.

But this isn't right. He meant to come out by the hide. Damn. He must have gone wrong somewhere. Then he hears a noise which at first he thinks is a chainsaw but suddenly realises is a train pounding along the line behind him, alarmingly close.

Anyway, here he is, and he is not going back. He approaches the pumphouse cautiously so as not to disturb the dozens of geese feeding in the field next to it. It's locked. He searches for signs and finds remnants of a fire by the building. The ash is cold but dry. He waits a little and looks back downstream, but the path is deserted so he sets off upstream. Sooner than expected he comes to a signpost indicating Fen Hide (to his right), and Tower Hide (straight on). Which way might they have gone, assuming they have reached this far by now?

He decides to go towards Fen Hide. It is an easy walk along a grassy track, not like some of the river paths he has been on recently. And there is the hide, down to his left. They could be in there. He walks towards it conscious of his heart beating. He is unsure what to do. Should he just go in? Or might that be dangerous? Should he stand outside and push the door open so he can see inside? Why hasn't he thought about this before? And they might not even be here. He feels uneasy. As he stands there he hears a coot clucking at the edge of a channel beside him, dipping in and out of the reeds on the far side. Then a straggling flock of gulls flies overhead, and just a little further on a pair of swans in a ditch have their heads down under the water. When they come up for air they hardly acknowledge him but just bend their long necks over again so only their white, solid bodies are visible.

And then someone coughs.

Someone *is* in the hide.

He walks the last few yards and up onto the platform outside the door. He opens the door. Inside, on the floor, is a bundle of clothes but it moves and a person sits up. It is the girl. She immediately tries to move further into the corner. When he steps through the doorway, she says something he cannot understand. It is immediately clear that she is alone and terrified. When he sees this he stands still and looks around the hut. There is nothing else there except a stick and a bag lying on the ground. The girl stays frozen.

"Don't worry. I'm not going to hurt you. It's all right." Richard tries to speak quietly and slowly, despite his fear that the man might appear at any minute. The girl gives no sign of relaxing. Perhaps she is mentally ill?

"It's all right. There's no need to worry. I'll help you. Where's the man who was with you? Please talk to me, and then I can help you." His eyes are adjusting to the light in the hut now, and he can see the girl is in a bad way. He thinks of her foot, but it is covered over with the blanket. "You're ill. And I know you've hurt your foot. When I saw you before, I could see that something was wrong. How is your foot now? Will you show me?"

She shows no sign of understanding him, so he points to his own foot, and then to hers. The second time he does this, pulling his own trouser leg up from where it is tucked into his sock and pointing to his ankle, her face registers something different. He goes on talking to her quietly and calmly. "You need help, don't you? I want to see how your foot is. Go on, show me what the matter is. I promise I won't hurt you."

Slowly, she pulls the blanket from off her leg. And there it is. At first his eye goes to her red, swollen calf, but then he sees the bloody and dirty mess at her heel. An area about the size of his hand is covered with blisters, scabs, pus and dirt.

He stands up at once, trying not to move too fast and making it clear to the girl that he is not going to touch her. He goes outside the hut and phones 999. It's an ambulance that is needed, not the Police. He tells them about the girl's condition and describes where he is, and then goes back inside.

"Someone's coming to help. We'll have to wait a bit, but they won't be long."

How long might they be? Even though this place feels a long way from Norwich, it is only about eight miles. Thank God. But it will take time for them to get from the ambulance to here. How on earth can he have failed to bring any food? He leaves the door open and sits down on a bench, keeping a good distance from the girl. He looks again at the stick and wonders if the man has hit her with it.

Rather than sit in silence, he keeps talking. It seems less threatening, somehow. He speaks slowly. At first he talks about Estelle's interest in birdwatching, which was what brought him to the river. He tells her about going through Estelle's books and about seeing the cormorant. He says that he left his thermos behind, and went back to find it, but saw her and the man. He tells her what he had thought about them, and how he wondered what he should do about them. Nothing he says makes any difference to the girl. She keeps her eyes on his face and her expression hardly changes.

Her lack of response makes him say more. He finds himself talking about Estelle. "I loved her so much, you know. We did almost everything together. And it's hard now. It's hard on my own. It's not that I want someone else. I want her, and I can't have her. I've met Harriet, and I don't know what might happen between us, but she'll never be Estelle."

He can hear his own voice and knows it is neither steady nor reassuring. He knows it is he who needs steadiness and reassurance. He has never said these things aloud before, and now he is saying them to this girl, a stranger.

At last it is all said and he leans forward and puts his head in his hands. He sits there listening to the wind, listening to the calls of gulls outside and to some coot. He opens his eyes when he hears the girl moving, but she is only adjusting her position and turning to look out through the open door. He leans back against the wall. He is thinking about being alone. About his aloneness and the girl's aloneness. He wonders about the nature of her aloneness. It must be different to his.

After a while he hears voices, and he gets up. Coming along

the path are two men and one woman, all in green uniforms. And behind them, unnoticed, is the man he is expecting. He is still some distance away, shuffling along, but alert and trying to walk faster.

Richard stands back to let them into the hut. He will be in the way if he stays where he is. As the man passes him, he sees he is eager to reach the girl, and as soon as he speaks to her it becomes obvious both that he and she are not English and that he cares about her. The two of them talk while the girl's leg is examined. It has not occurred to Richard that they might not be English or that the man could be looking after her.

The woman gives the girl an injection, and says, "It's a very nasty burn. And they're both suffering from exposure. We'll take them to the Norfolk and Norwich University Hospital, and we'll inform the Police."

"Do I need to do anything else?"

"No. We'll take care of everything. It'll be interesting to find out what all this is about. Doesn't look like your ordinary Sunday morning walk, does it?"

The two men help Khadija onto the stretcher, and a little procession sets off from the hide. First go the stretcher bearers, with the woman walking at Khadija's side. The foreign man follows slowly behind them. Richard goes last, noting how the man is walking in a rather awkward way. When he reaches the car park he sees the man's laces are undone. Why on earth doesn't he do them up?

He watches the girl and the man being taken into the ambulance, and before the doors are closed he looks in at them. The girl is lying flat, but the man looks back at him, and then holds his hand up in a half wave. Richard returns the gesture.

As they drive off he suddenly feels hungry. He drives home with his mind racing through all that has happened. He expected to have answers by now, but there are even more questions.

The following evening Richard drives to the Norfolk and Norwich Hospital. Harriet has agreed to meet him in the East atrium, near the amazing glass and metal sculpture. It was to this place, rather than to the low ceilinged white chapel, that he came when things were bad with Estelle. He looks up at the huge silvery branches, the red, green and yellow leaves. He has stood here many, many times. Driving in, parking and walking in here this evening brings it all back.

It will be so good to see Harriet again. He tries to picture her, but it's hard. He has an idea of her shape and of the way she moves, but strangely he can't quite get her face.

As well as thinking about her and Estelle, he is energised by what has happened. Are the foreign man and the girl Serbs or Bosnians? Or Roma? Perhaps they are gypsies after all. Now he has seen them and realised their condition he wants to know more about them. All he knows is that they appear to have embarked on a twenty-five mile hike in difficult conditions in winter without food, decent clothes or proper shoes. And to make things worse, the girl is injured. She especially must have been through an ordeal. In addition, they are in a strange place where they do not know the language and have no money. He wants to help them. There must be something he can do for them.

And here is Harriet, smiling broadly, her hair longer than he remembers.

"Hallo. Are you OK?"

He kisses her cheek. "I was miles away. It's good to see you."

"And you. Do you know where they are?"

"I'll take you to the ward the man's in, but first just tell me what you think of this sculpture."

Harriet stands back to look at it properly. "It's stunning."

"It's by a Nigerian artist. Look, here's a plaque about it."

While she is reading it a doctor walking along the corridor suddenly catches sight of Richard and comes over to him. He shakes hands and greets him warmly before he goes on along the walkway.

"Someone you know?" asks Harriet.

"Yes. This is where Estelle died. That was Lorenzo, one of the doctors we had most to do with."

"Oh, Richard. I'm so sorry." Harriet reaches out to take his hand for a moment. "I didn't think."

"It's OK."

But it is not. Seeing Lorenzo brings it all back. Nothing has changed. It hurts in the pit of his stomach.

"It's just that I can't seem to forget her. Not that I want to forget her. Of course I don't want to forget her but I don't want to go on feeling like this either."

They move to the side of the walkway to let a family pass, and stand facing the window.

After a few moments Richard says, "Come on. It's this way." He leads the way to the Emergency Assessment Unit where he has been told they will find the foreign man whose name he now knows, but his bed is empty.

One of the staff says, "Abbas? Oh yes. He's up and about. He's gone to see his granddaughter."

His granddaughter?

"Sounds like good news," says Harriet.

They find them sitting by a window. There is a group of three men in a circle with the girl who has a bandaged leg and is in a wheelchair. Two conversations are going on, one between the two younger men of the group, and one between the older man and the girl.

"That's them."

Richard approaches rather cautiously, not sure how to introduce himself, and knowing that another language is being spoken. When he is very close the young man facing him looks up and sees him.

"Excuse me," says Richard, "I'm the person who called the ambulance for these people" – he indicates towards the girl and the old man – "and I wanted to see if they were all right."

The young men stand up at once and each holds out his hand to Richard. Then one of them fetches two more chairs.

At eight o'clock Visiting Time ends. Amir goes back with Abbas to his ward. He tells Richard, "He can find his way almost to Norwich, but he'll get lost in here!" Sarwat starts to push Khadija in her wheelchair to the lift. Richard and Harriet say goodbye, and Richard promises to return the next day. As he and Harriet make their way to the exit he says, "It's too late to get coffee here, but I daresay alcohol would do. Would you like a drink?"

"I can't. I told Polly and Adam I'd be back by eight thirty. Why don't you come to our house?"

"I'd love to. Shall I stop off and buy a bottle of wine? See you there in a bit."

For once he does not put on any music in the car. What a roller coaster of an evening. He was so sure after seeing the girl and Abbas in the hide that they were destitute for they were both so beaten down. But now he knows they have an English speaking relative and at least one good friend, and a home. He did not expect this and is surprised to find himself slightly disappointed. He makes himself ask why that is so. It is because it seems as if they do not need his help. After all that has happened, even though they were in such a state, he is not needed, and he recognises that he wants to be needed.

At times the conversation in the ward was in English, or in a mixture of English and Arabic, but mostly it was in Arabic. During those times he had tried to work out what was happening between the four people.

The girl, Khadija, was happy. There was no question about that. Her leg seemed forgotten as she talked easily with her grandfather and her cousin. She was clearly attracted to Amir – Harriet particularly commented on this – even though he treated her like a younger sister. She was a pretty girl, and very young. How on earth had she survived this journey, let alone the terrible journey from Iran? How had they all done it?

What must she have made of him pouring his heart out in the hide? Of course she could not have understood his words, and she must have been too ill to understand what was happening. She was only very young, so why should he think that she had understood something? Yet he was hoping that she had understood.

Sarwat was difficult to make out, even though he spoke good English. He said he had a job and was looking after his uncle and cousin. But his relationship with his uncle, Abbas, was complex, for there were times when their conversation seemed sharp.

Amir always got an answer from Abbas, and from everyone. His natural warmth and good humour were apparent, and his English was excellent too. He was obviously a survivor and had sorted himself out with a job in a hotel.

The old man smiled a lot and Amir told Richard that he kept on saying that he would not have missed the walk up the river for anything, because it reminded him of his youth in the marshes in Iraq. He appeared really old, but Richard worked out that he was considerably younger than he looked and certainly younger than he was himself.

But why did they do it? Richard still could not make out exactly the reasons behind their decision to walk from Yarmouth to Norwich, and nor, he suspects, could Sarwat and Amir.

And now he is drawing up outside Harriet's. He has completely forgotten to buy wine. Polly opens the door and he suddenly remembers about her exam.

"Hallo, Polly. Do you know yet if you passed?"

"Yes thanks, I did."

"Well done you. Congratulations."

"Mum's in the kitchen." She disappears upstairs fast.

He puts his head round the living room door and Adam looks up briefly from where he is lying on the rug in front of the fire watching television. "Hi, Richard. Thanks for feeding Darren and Delia."

He sits down with Harriet at the kitchen table. She's wearing a stripey blue jumper.

"I'm shattered," says Richard. "I hadn't realised how involved I'd got."

"I did. You talked about it quite a lot, you know."

"I'm interested by it all. Especially after this evening. It's hard to know how they'll settle in England."

"It'll be difficult, even without whatever it was that made Khadija and Abbas run away from Yarmouth. I'm certain we don't know the full story, and we probably never will. But something must have been going badly wrong."

"I'm wondering if there's anything I can do to make things better for them."

"I'm sure there is. There's probably something as simple as taking Abbas out or playing cards with him. Volunteers are always needed and you'd be excellent. It's clear they like you. Almost everything must be hard for them, at least until they learn English. They need friends. They'll feel as if they're only on the edge."

Richard pours Harriet a glass of the sweet wine she won at a raffle. "How do you know?"

"Because that's what happens when people are in a minority, doesn't it? They feel they don't count as much as everyone else. And often they're right."

He thinks about this. Since Estelle's illness and death, he has noticed he belongs to a minority he had not thought much about before. As a widower he feels outside the millions of couples that seem to surround him. Does this make him feel 'on the edge'? Yes, it sometimes does. But surely this is because he does not have any family at all – no children, no siblings. All right, there's his brother Ian, but he doesn't count.

Harriet says, "And it's uncomfortable to be on the edge. People want to belong. You could help these Iraqis – all four of them – to belong."

He thinks about this too, and says, "But it's not only they who want to belong. I do too."

"We all do. We're all alone, deep down." Harriet is looking at her right hand and the glass it is holding.

"But you've got Polly and Adam, and your sister and brother, and mother. They all matter to you and you matter to them."

"Yes, I know. That's true. But right inside me, I'm alone. Aren't you?"

He runs his finger round the rim of his glass. How can she feel alone? Harriet seems in the centre of things compared to himself. But perhaps she isn't.

He considers the question carefully. "The only time when I'm not alone is when I play the oboe. Although it's only me who's playing the oboe, I feel connected to everyone else in the orchestra and, if things go well, to the audience."

"Are you feeling alone now?" asks Harriet.

He looks up at her. "No. I'm not."

"Good. Nor am I." She reaches across the table for his hand.

"I'd like to take you out on your birthday. To this pub I found by the river, the Reedcutter. Will you come?"

"Of course I will."

"Will Polly mind?"

"She may do, but I can't hold my life back because of that."

When it is late Harriet goes out into the street with him. She catches his arm, "Look at the moon!" It is a tiny white shred of a curve.

He drives home slowly. There are things in his life now that were not there even a month ago. It is the same life, but things are changing. Is it that things just happen, or has he made things happen? He thinks about the Iraqis and their decision to come to the west. This evening all four of them said that, once on the journey, they had no control over what happened. Abbas said that everything was in Allah's hands. Richard had never heard anyone say 'Allah' before, except in a film or on television.

Richard thinks about the decisions he makes and the actions he takes to maintain control of his life. Life without making decisions would be impossible. No one can just go through life putting up with whatever presents itself. Of course not. It is human nature to try to improve things. Harriet would not be going out to dinner with him if he had not asked her. Unless, of course, she had asked him. Might she have asked him? He isn't sure.

Sarwat pushes me back to my ward. Good, Donna is there although her family have already gone. As soon as she sees me she waves at me with her good arm and calls out my name in a sort of singing voice which makes everyone turn round. This makes me laugh, and Sarwat smiles too. He says hallo to her and then goodbye to me.

When I first came in here I was very ill and very worried. But then Donna started talking to me. Of course I hardly knew any of the words, but soon we began to understand each other. She's twenty and she works in a bank. She told me, in her actions and her face, how she fell downstairs. She was carrying a big pile of clothes, and she had loose shoes on, and there was a cat somewhere she thought she might tread on. Anyway, she tripped over and fell down eleven stairs, hitting her head on the corner of a cupboard at the bottom and breaking her right arm.

It wasn't easy telling her why I'm here. I could explain about the river, and the walk, and the cold and the fire, and I could explain about not liking school, but I couldn't tell her about Sarwat's appeal, and about Amir and about Grandfather being ill. It's all too complicated.

But she didn't mind. She showed me photos of her family. She showed me her mother, and her two younger brothers, and I've met all of them. I don't know about her father because she hasn't said anything about him, so perhaps he's dead. Then there's her grandmother who came to see her this morning. She's the youngest grandmother I've ever seen. And Donna has a boyfriend, Mike. She has a photo of him on his motorbike, but I couldn't see what he was like because he had a helmet on. When he came to see her yesterday he was carrying his helmet and he had black leather clothes on and a green and yellow scarf. It is hot in here so gradually he took off his top clothes, and then I could see that of course he was just an ordinary person underneath.

Donna tells the nurses everything about me, and as soon as I was allowed out of bed she took me down to the café with her and now we've been twice and I like it. She cannot steer the wheelchair properly with one hand and so she sometimes pushes me into the wall, and once she pretended she could not work the lift properly and took me up and down three times!

Here in the ward we can choose what food we eat from a list, and it's so funny when she tries to explain what some of the words mean. Grandfather told me to take the halal diet, and I do, but Donna gives me things to taste from her meals. I have not told Grandfather that I like sausages. When the meals come I cut some things up for her because she can't do that with one hand.

She is very kind too. She saw that I had no cards so this afternoon her mother gave me one, and her brothers have taught me how to play two games. For one, you need pencil and paper. You have to draw 0s or Xs in gaps in boxes drawn with crossed lines, and the idea is to get three of your signs in a row and to stop the other person from getting three of their signs in a row. Actually, it is boring once you have learned how to do it, but Donna's little brother loves it. He's seven, so I usually let him win. The other game is called snap. You play it with a pack of cards, and it's very noisy.

Donna pushes her bowl of fruit towards me before going off to make a phone call to Mike who's not coming this evening because a long time ago he promised to look after his sister's little girl. I think it's strange that a man should look after a child but she says he often does it.

I take a few grapes and think about all that's been happening over these last few days. I knew I was ill, out in that hut. There had been times on my long journey when my mind had felt worse than that, but my body had never been so ill. It was partly being out in the cold for days, but mostly because of my burn. The doctor told Amir and Sarwat that my ankle had become infected and that poison was spreading through my whole body. They have given me medication to stop the infection, and it is already much better. And I'm warm now, and there is plenty to eat.

I was very frightened when that man came into the hut because I remembered all the things that Sarwat had told me about English men. I wanted him to get out and I didn't know where Grandfather was. But now I know the English man is a kind man. When he and his wife came today to see us and I heard his voice again, I remembered how he talked to me in the hut. It was as if he knew me for he spoke for a long time and it seemed that what he was saying was important, and he was speaking directly to me. He trusted me, and that made me begin to feel safe. Sarwat and Amir like him too. He said he will come back tomorrow, and I hope he does.

Sarwat told me he has no idea about how his appeal went, but the fact is that the more people are killed in Iraq, the more likely he is to be allowed to stay here. He said he feels bad about thinking like this, but he's right. Amir told me it is not as simple as that.

When I was told Sarwat and Amir were coming to see us in hospital I was nervous. I thought both of them – even Amir – might be angry. But they weren't. They were both very concerned, though an hour ago I could see Sarwat getting impatient with Grandfather again, like he did before. Also, I think he's surprised by what I did. He thought I was a girl who always does what she's told, and now he knows he's wrong.

They kept on asking why we went, and I told them about being worried about the appeal and perhaps being taken away and about not liking school. But I didn't say anything about wanting to be close to Amir, or thinking Grandfather might die soon, so I don't think they really understand. It was so many things, all at once.

When Sarwat was outside making a phone call on his mobile, Amir said something special to me. He said, "I don't quite know why you wanted to leave and go to Norwich, but it must have been because you were unhappy. So, when things aren't good, why don't you tell me? Then I can try to help you."

When Sarwat came back he leaned over to Amir and said quietly, "Carl's been arrested."

"Has he? Why?"

"Something to do with a stolen car."

"It'll be for more than that."

Sarwat shrugged.

"I told you before. You should keep away from him."

"I do. I haven't spoken to him for weeks, not for months."

I didn't look at Sarwat and he didn't look at me. But at once I decided not to tell him about the package, unless he asks, and if he asks I'll tell him the truth – that Carl was trying to trick him with a bag of powder. I'm not surprised that Carl has been arrested.

Grandfather is looking better than I have ever seen him look. When he came into the hospital they shaved him and cut his hair, and Sarwat and Amir bought him a new shirt and trousers and shoes that he doesn't have to tie up. He can just pull across a flap of material that sticks. He told the doctors about his stomach and they gave him some more medicine. He's so cheerful!

I don't know what will happen. Here in the hospital everything feels better, but I don't know if it will stay better when we leave. Has anything changed? If we go back to Great Yarmouth, which is what I think will happen, will it be just the same again? Sarwat said today, "Well, what do you want?" and that was hard to answer. I want to feel different. I want Sarwat and Grandfather and me all to live comfortably together. And I don't want to be far from Amir. If all those things happened, then I would try my best at school, even at the same school I went to before.

I make myself think of the good things. I have crossed the world without being shot or hurt in an accident or raped. Grandfather and I have found each other again. I can see that although some people don't like me, like Kerry Ann and Debbie, the people I like most do like me: Grace and the other woman in the place with the wire, Sarwat (most of the time, anyway), Donna, the nurses, and the man who found us and his wife. And Amir and Grandfather of course. If all those people like me I must be quite a nice person. Donna has already said she wants me to come to her house. And another good thing is I have already learned lots of English words and since being in the hospital I have learned even more, like wheelchair, trolley, getwellsoon, sausages, identity bracelet, snap, marmalade.

Even though I can't say it was a good idea to walk along the river, I'm not sorry I did it. It was certainly a good thing for Grandfather. And that's strange, because if I am really honest, I decided to go to Norwich for *me*, and although I knew Grandfather was ill and might die, I told myself I was helping him.

So I was selfish. I thought things would improve for me, but what happened was that I became very ill and he became better. Perhaps Allah has punished me for being selfish and rewarded him for being good.

Donna's coming back now. She's singing and pretending to dance. Now she's picked up a toy bear and is pretending it's a man. She's dancing with it and now she's kissing it! Everybody is laughing.

And that's another thing, today I have laughed more than I have done since I was with Grace. Even more, probably, than at any time since being at home with my sisters, which was nearly two years ago.

So there are lots of good things.

I don't know what will happen next, but somehow I feel my life will be better.

After breakfast I dress, put on my new shoes without laces and go down to the place outside the building where smoking is allowed. A little snow has fallen in the night. Although it is cold out here I decide to have a second cigarette, but I shall not stay outside for long. When I go back in I shall go to Khadija's ward. I feel better now that she is safe again, and I can see she enjoys being with the women there.

It is good to see Amir again as well as Sarwat. When I was in the ambulance I managed to get the woman to understand that I thought Khadija could have Sarwat's phone number somewhere in her bag, and she found it and phoned him. Sarwat contacted Amir and they both came as soon as they could. Sarwat was happy and angry to see me – both at the same time – but Amir was curious. Most of all, he wanted to know why we had done it. They asked to see Khadija but by then she had been checked and treated and cleaned up and put to bed. She slept for many hours. I am thankful that Sarwat did not see how ill she was when she first came in, because he would have blamed me even more than he does now.

Was it my fault? I am not sure. It was not Khadija's, for even if she is growing up now, she is very young. Yes, it was her idea, but I agreed. It was only a week ago, but all I can remember is Khadija telling me we were going to walk to the city and we needed to leave there and then. I do not know exactly why I agreed. It was like the long journey here, in that no traveller can ever know what such a journey will be like, and if they did know, perhaps they would not have set off. But at that time I was sure that life in the west would be better, and this time Khadija thought that life in Norwich would be better. In the end, the journeys themselves became as important as where we were trying to get to, and turning back became more and more difficult.

We will leave here soon but I am not sure what will happen to us all. It is true that life is better in some places than in others, but if a man is in a bad place, it is hard to know whether he should move or stay. That is why I ask Allah.

I would not have missed that walk along the river for all the world. It brought back to me the place of my birth, of my family, of my tribe. Now that Allah has reminded me of these things I shall not forget them again. And so, although before I went I could not have answered the question 'Why are you going?' I now know.

Today they are arranging for a man from a mosque here in Norwich to visit me. I am looking forward to praying with someone else, especially as it will soon be Ashura – the time of mourning. I am saddened by the thought that I will never go to Karbala now, or to Najaf. But perhaps I have made a different sort of pilgrimage.

I am grateful to the man who found us. Without him it is possible that Khadija would have lost her leg or died. He is a generous man. When I am completely recovered I shall help him in some way to show my gratitude. I hope he keeps his word and comes again today with his daughter.

I walk away from the building and look out across the fields to where the grass is already showing through the snow. I take my beads out and begin to tell them as I look up to the crescent moon, low in the blue sky.

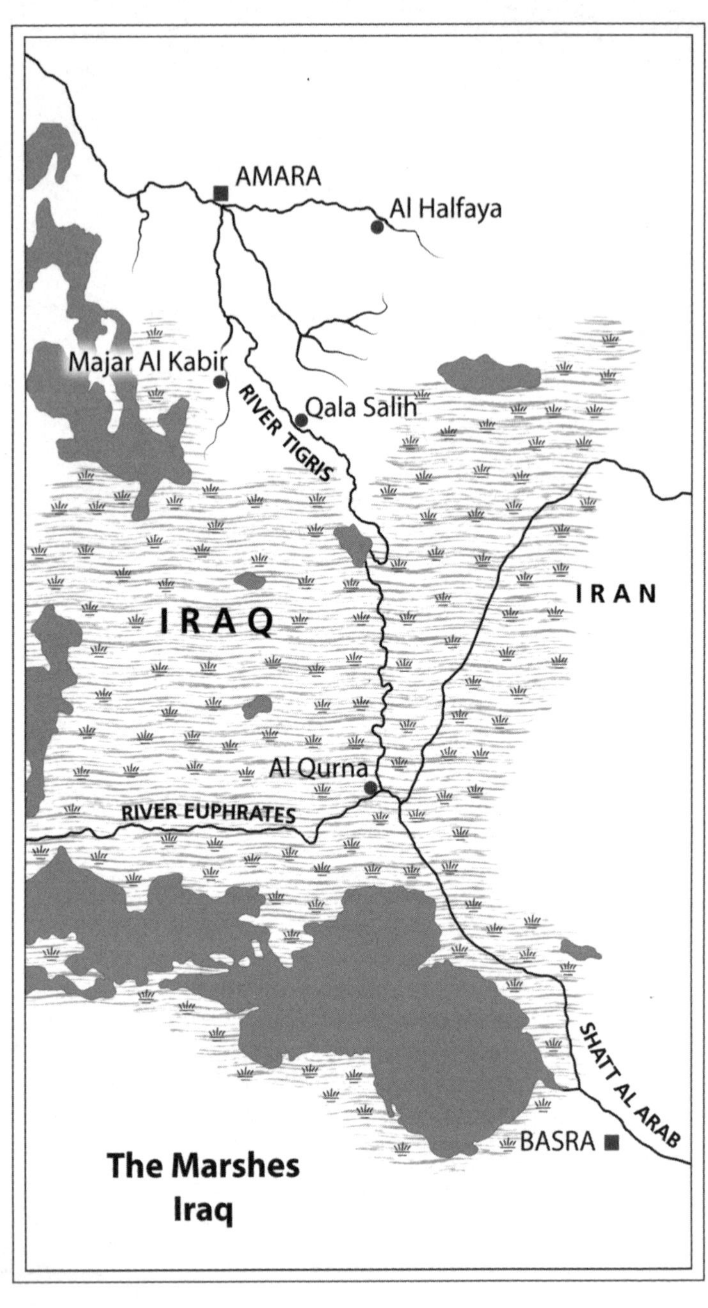
AMARA
Al Halfaya
Majar Al Kabir
RIVER TIGRIS
Qala Salih
IRAN
IRAQ
Al Qurna
RIVER EUPHRATES
SHATT AL ARAB
BASRA
The Marshes
Iraq